WALKER PRAIRIE

JENN HERRINGTON
BOOK 2

PAMELA FAGAN HUTCHINS

SKIPJACK PUBLISHING

FREE PFH EBOOKS

PROLOGUE

Walker Prairie, Bighorn Mountains, Wyoming
Mid-February

The dog sled cut through an opening in a stand of spruce so narrow that Jennifer Herrington sucked in her breath. *Like that will do any good.* If it got stuck it wouldn't be because of her slight frame, or that of her enormous husband Aaron standing on the runners behind her. It would be the basket, which protruded several inches on either side of him.

Getting stuck wasn't even her biggest worry. It was the eleven half-crazed dogs pulling against the harness. She'd quickly learned that dog sledding was roughly one-tenth control and four-tenths influence. She wasn't a math genius, but she could do that addition. That left half, which was determined by their instinctual love for running, pulling, and chasing. Combined with the dogs' physical abilities, it summed to an exciting experience.

The team was basically acting like she and Aaron didn't exist, no matter how many commands they shouted at them. The other sled team didn't respond much better for their owner, Tommy Campbell, who was mushing ahead of them. Only the foot brake and snow anchor had any effect on their speed. At least they were quiet now, all their energy focused on the joy of running. Their frantic howling when they'd been hooked to the bumper of Tommy's truck—the only way to keep that much dog power from a runaway start—had sounded like the inside of a primate house at a zoo, even if it had made her smile, too.

The lead dogs disappeared around a slight crook in the trail. The Herringtons' dogs attacked the curve, and their sled catapulted toward a rock outcropping. Tommy and his team had navigated the turn so effortlessly that Jennifer hadn't anticipated how terrifying it would be. Or how challenging. She and Aaron bent their knees and shifted their weight at the same time.

For a moment, the sled teetered. *No, please, no!* Tipping over would be a disaster. Sure, the dogs would stop because of the sudden drag, but if Aaron's weight didn't crush her or Jennifer didn't suffocate face first in the snow, she could die with her skull bashed in on a tree. But slamming into a giant slab of granite was no better. She eased herself back to center, hoping to correct the oversteer. Aaron's size and the muscle he still carried as a former tight end in the National Football League would provide enough counterweight.

Her pulse was so elevated that it felt like a continuous thrum instead of individual beats. The sled's right ski kissed the snow again, but the rock face loomed ever closer. Maybe the basket frame would provide some protection? But that was a ridiculous thought—it was little more than PVC pipe and wicker. The rock would pulverize it.

It was too late to brake. A strange squeaking noise came from somewhere. *Her,* she realized. It had come from her.

Jennifer held steady. What else could she do? The middle dogs disappeared into the turn. The sled fought toward the obstacle, pulled by centrifugal force away from the direction Aaron was leaning. Was it her imagination or was their new Alaskan malamute Willett pulling the wrong way against the others in mid-pack? This was the young female's first major training run. She was supposed to be learning from the more experienced dogs, not working against them.

Jennifer stepped on the brake, hoping to use it like a rudder to pull them to the left. The rear dogs—the strongest in the pack—dug into their turn.

Why did we say yes to this crazy sport, like some Call of the Wild *wannabes?* Her mind raced through regrets. That she hadn't tried her first official murder case in Wyoming yet. That she hadn't convinced the current administration to charge former prosecutor Pootie Carputin with the school shooting that haunted her from her childhood. Not seeing her first mystery novel published. The lost years of motherhood she'd squandered by putting off having a baby. Every minute she hadn't appreciated her husband enough. Shoot, if he survived and she didn't, other women would chase him even more aggressively than they already did, which he never seemed to notice.

I'm married to the best guy.

"I love you," she shouted to Aaron, then braced for impact, pulling her hands and arms tightly to her sides.

"I love you, too," he shouted back, his voice minus the terrified edge in hers.

There was a loud grating noise. The right ski scraped the granite and shuddered. The PVC supports bounced off the rock. Wicker splintered and peppered her face.

This is it. She closed her eyes, gritted her teeth. Sent up a prayer.

But then they were clear with the basket mostly intact. *It's a miracle!*

Adrenaline surged through her, and Jennifer whooped. She felt Aaron's body shaking with something.

"You're laughing!" she shouted.

"That was awesome," he yelled.

She leaned her head into his chest and laughed, too. "It was crazy!"

Sure, it had been a scary few moments but talk about a rush! Her whole body was electrified, except her weather-numbed toes. She'd fought to stay warm from the first freeze of the season. Maybe she didn't love everything about the Bighorn Mountains or living in Wyoming, but she'd never felt this alive back in Houston.

Aaron bent down and pressed his lips against her ear. "These dogs are amazing athletes. And Willett and Sibley are doing great!" Aaron appreciated physical prowess, in humans and animals. As a veterinarian, he'd long been fascinated by the cold weather adaptations and special skills of snow dogs. Now that they had the two young Alaskan malamute rescues, he was borderline obsessed.

Their sled glided across an open expanse of white. Tommy and his team vanished into the forest ahead of them. They should be getting close to Walker Prairie now. She recognized She Bear mountain to the southwest from Tommy's description.

It felt strange to be off road in the dead of winter, in national forest backcountry. Jennifer wondered where the closest human was and how far away help would be if something went wrong. And things did go wrong in the mountains, even without deep snow, subzero temperatures, and over-stimulated dogs. That was why she and Aaron were with Tommy and had emergency supplies, snowshoes, and equipment on both sleds as well as her associate Wesley "Kid" James behind them on a snowmobile.

She sucked cold air through her teeth. The slight whistling noise and the schuss of the runners were the only sounds except the wind in her ears. Icy air froze the inside of her nose. Drawing a breath was difficult and uncomfortable. She could still smell the dogs, though. Damp fur. Exertion. It was all strangely pleasant under the circumstances.

They entered the forest, dense except for their trail. The quiet from before gave way to utter silence. Jennifer's body tingled from the pure earth magic around her. It beat writing trial briefs or arguing motions in court, and it rivaled her highest highs during successful closing arguments in capital murder trials. It was far better than studying for the Wyoming bar exam, which she'd been doing for the last few weeks.

Never again. She'd said that the first time she'd taken the test in Texas, not dreaming she and Aaron would relocate to a ramshackle lodge with a tippling caretaker, feral cat, incontinent dog, and destunk skunk. The thought brought a smile that hurt her cold cheeks. But she needed that license. She was on her second Wyoming murder case as nothing more than a consultant. It was a waste of her skills. The courtroom was where she belonged.

The dogs burst out of the trees and into an open space that was probably technically a park but more like a good-sized meadow. *Like a scene from* Dr. Zhivago, *but more beautiful.* It was in this idyllic white wonderland against a backdrop of evergreens and an impossibly clear blue sky that all hell broke loose.

On the far side of the clearing, Tommy's lead dog let out a shrill yip, which was unusual. All she'd heard were howls and a-woos so far from the huskies. Whatever lay ahead was upsetting Tommy's dogs. She saw a tumble of fur then heard more dog noises and Tommy's shouts of "whoa" and "easy."

When Tommy's forward progress stopped, both dog teams started howling in chorus. It sent chills up her spine, all the way into her scalp and the tips of her ears.

"Whoa," she called. She stomped the brake, then released it. Stomped, released, stomped, released. "Whoa. Easy." Finally, she pressed and held the rubber cleat against the snow.

The dogs came to a noisy, agitated stop.

Aaron leapt off the sled and ran for Gizmo, a husky mix and their lead dog. Her husband's big feet kept post holing in the snow, so his progress was slow. Gizmo strained against the harness, panting, howling, and whining all at once. Finally, Aaron reached him. Bending over and holding onto the harness's hand strap, he spoke to the dog in low, soothing tones that Jennifer could hear but not understand. When the dog had calmed somewhat, Aaron straightened.

Behind them, the snowmobile engine turned off. Kid called, "Are we stopping?"

Aaron had a deep, carrying voice that didn't require shouting most of the time. "Tommy? What's up?"

"Son of a bitch." It was Tommy's voice, but his words weren't in response to Aaron's question.

Is one of Tommy's dogs hurt? Jennifer sank the anchor. Between it and Aaron holding onto Gizmo, the other dogs would stay put. Probably. Maybe. She hopped off the sled and fought her way forward through powder. Her feet planted on packed snow below it. She was half Aaron's weight, so she didn't break through the lower layer. Her progress was easier, which was not to be confused with actually *being* easy.

"What is it, Tommy?" Her breaths seared her lungs. The altitude here was over seventy-five hundred feet—about one thousand feet higher than their Big Horn Lodge.

A drift trapped her foot. She toppled like felled timber, and her body sank. Gaining high ground was a monumental struggle. Her muscles shook. How were the dogs able to stay on the surface of the snow? Their light weight, she guessed. The heaviest huskies in the rear of the team couldn't have been much more than fifty pounds, although their malamutes were twenty-five pounds heavier. A former competitive golfer and gymnast—and University of Tennessee cheerleader, a lifetime ago—Jennifer was small but muscular, which made her heavier than she looked.

She paused on all fours to catch her breath. Perspiration soaked her sweater, and snow had crept into her coat at the collar and cuffs. She was muttering words that would have irked her southern mama. She tried to stand but sunk again. She gave up and crawled, head toward the ground, spitting frozen hair out of her mouth.

"Jenn, stop." It was Aaron, his voice a whisper.

Gladly. The break allowed her to look up and around. She'd closed more ground between their basket and Tommy's than she'd expected. In fact, she was only ten feet away and slightly uphill from it, which gave her a good vantage point of him—in his red wool cap and black winter gear—as well as the sled, the dogs... and a giant bloody mass of dark brown fur. Her insides flipped over.

"What is that?" she asked.

Tommy answered without looking back at her. "Moose."

"Is it . . ."

"Dead. Yes."

"Do you think a bear got it?"

"No. A black bear won't take on a moose, and we don't have grizzlies in this part of Wyoming."

This grizzly-free claim had always struck Jennifer as wishful thinking. There were no bear-proof fences between western Wyoming, where grizzlies were commonplace, and the Bighorns, where they weren't. Yet. "It doesn't look like it died of natural causes."

"I don't believe it did. Someone gutted it."

"Gutted but didn't harvest it?"

"Correct."

It was well past hunting season. Killing a game animal out of season—or without a license during season—was poaching. But poachers usually harvested at least some part of the animal. Not many people gutted the carcasses of animals they found already dead either. A queasy unease settled over her. Poachers got high fines and jail time, and criminals didn't like to be caught, something she knew well from her years prosecuting them as an assistant district attorney in Harris County, Texas.

"A little information back here, please," Kid shouted.

She licked her dry lips. "Who do you think would do something like this?"

Tommy pointed. "I don't think, I know. Him."

Jennifer couldn't see anyone. But then a figure moved closer, coming toward Tommy, his lead dog, and Jennifer. Effortlessly. Like walking on water. *Snowshoes. Dang it—I should have taken the time to get mine.*

Cradling a rifle.

Jennifer wished she'd stayed with Aaron back at their sled.

"That's close enough," Aaron shouted.

The figure stopped a few feet away from Tommy's lead dog, with Sibley—Jennifer's favorite of their two malamutes—only a few spots behind her. The lead dog went into a frenzy. Snapping, growling, and lunging. The person raised the rifle and pointed it at the dog's head.

"No!" Jennifer screamed.

CHAPTER ONE

Big Horn, Wyoming
Two Weeks Earlier

Demarcus Ware—a vintage Jeepster Commando, not the former linebacker who'd ended his career with the Denver Broncos—bucked its rusted, dented orange body over the cattle guard at the entrance to the WP Bar Ranch. Aaron Herrington accelerated gently to avoid sliding on the packed snow. He was glad he'd put chains on the tires. Ahead lay the stables, home, and horse of his client, Glen Trusk.

"I wish I liked this guy." Aaron cut his eyes over to the passenger seat.

The tip of his wife's impossibly cute nose was pink from the cold. It matched her cap, scarf, and parka. The heater was cranked to full blast, but in February, Demarcus took about twenty minutes to reach an interior temperature Jenn deemed survivable. She had fully embraced the safety-first Wyoming practice of staying dressed for the outdoors while inside vehicles.

"He must be the devil if you don't like him. How far is it from here?" She glanced at her phone. "I don't want to be late to the doctor."

"A mile." Aaron had only visited the ranch headquarters a few times, but it had always been in warmer weather with a clear road. A road that was treacherous year-round, dynamited through the side of a rock ridge, and not much more than a narrow goat path with a sheer drop-off on one side.

"So, an hour, and I should take a nap?" Her teasing was music to his ears after a recent rocky patch in their marriage. Did multiple hard years count as a "patch?" He supposed it did if things got better on the other side, which they had and then some.

"Definitely. Close your eyes." He squeezed her mittened hand.

If the road made him nervous, he knew it was going to be worse for Jenn. Bringing her with him might have been a mistake. But they had her appointment in town afterwards. He couldn't have responded to Trusk's summons to examine the new reining horse, gone back home to pick up his wife, and still made it to Sheridan on time. They could have taken separate vehicles, but that would have been a waste. Besides, she'd wanted to join him. She liked riding along for his ranch calls and had been wanting to see their neighboring property, the WP Bar.

"Is that the road we're taking?" Jenn was staring ahead of them, where the cut across the rock face was now in view.

"Um, yes."

"Is a helicopter coming to get us?"

He smiled. "No."

"You're driving me across there?"

"I did tell you to close your eyes."

"No. Just . . . no."

"The horse is on the other side."

"Then park here, and we'll walk."

"We won't make your appointment if we do that."

Jenn bit her lip.

Aaron wanted to do it for her. His blonde wife was a beautiful woman, and he was just as mesmerized by her now as he'd been when he met her at the University of Tennessee.

She shut her eyes. "Just go. If we die, at least we'll be together."

"It looks well plowed. We'll be fine."

She put her fingers in her ears. "Talk to you on the other side." Then she began chanting. "La la la la la la."

Aaron eased Demarcus across the face of the cliff. The traction was fine, thanks to his chains, and all was well, as long as he kept his eyes on the road. Besides, they had a good five or six inches of extra room on either side of the tires. It reminded him of the tight ends coach at the Detroit Lions who'd chewed him out if he strayed at all from a route. "Precision, Herrington. Precision wins football games." *Precision keeps us safely on top of this cliff.*

A snowball rolled down the cliff from above and landed with a plop followed by smaller balls and a puff of white stuff. He tried not to think about avalanches. Rockslides. Earthquakes. Sudden gusts of wind.

Sweat dripped from his temple to his cheek.

The putt-putt of an engine drew his attention. An orange tractor was a few hundred yards away, just approaching the narrow section. One of them would need to stop or back up.

Aaron coasted to a halt and pressed his horn. Two short blasts. The tractor kept chugging forward. Aaron held the horn down. A long, steady warning.

The tractor stopped. No one got out of it. It didn't back up or pull over.

"Come on, come on," he said.

"Why aren't we moving?" Jenn pulled her fingers out of her ears but kept her eyes closed.

"Standoff with a tractor."

"Nope." She jammed her fingers in her ears again.

Finally, the tractor started backing up a side road. It parked near a four-wheeler, leaving the entrance road clear. Aaron resumed the creep across the cliff face. He could feel the snow compacting under the tires and sense the slight differences in depth by the way Demarcus shifted from side to side, even though the fresh plow marks in the snow showed the road had been cleared earlier that day.

The sweat trickled from his cheek to his chin and dropped onto his coat.

When the Jeepster's nose edged over the line between goat path and semi-normal dirt road, he relaxed a fraction. "We're good." He patted Jenn's knee.

She opened her eyes and lowered her hands cautiously, like she was expecting to encounter a goblin guarding the cliff crossing. "Is that Black Bear Betty?" She pointed up the side road.

A wool-capped head was barely visible over the tractor steering wheel in the enclosed cab. The bulldog face was unmistakable.

"Yep. She's been working for Mr. Trusk since the day he moved in."

"The ground is frozen."

His wife made a good point. Jobs requiring tractor work, other than plowing or carrying hay, slowed down to almost nothing in the winter.

The tractor door opened, and Betty hopped down from the cab in desert summer camo, Wyoming style—grease stains on tan Carhartt coveralls.

Jenn lowered her window. "Black Bear Betty! Hi!"

Aaron leaned over. "Hey, Triple B. How's it going?" He alternated between calling the woman Triple B and B-Cubed, neither of which she endorsed.

The woman put her elbows on Jenn's window almost without leaning over. A sweet and spicy smoke curled from the tip of the cigar she waved in one hand. "Don't start with the nicknames, Herrington. I'll empty a bag of hurt on you so fast, you'll beg for mercy." To Aaron's ears, bag and beg sounded exactly the same out of Betty's mouth. Both came out as beg. *The Wyoming accent, as slight as it is.*

He touched his forehead with two fingers. "Yes, ma'am." The tiny woman regularly threatened him with grave bodily harm. She was tough, no doubt. Wyoming born and raised and the self-proclaimed sole female septic tank installer in the state, as well as a jack of all trades. Or Jill. She pitched in at their Big Horn Lodge from time to time.

"Is something the matter?" Jenn asked.

Betty snorted. "I'll say. That son-of-a-buck Glen Trusk is what's the matter."

"What's he done now?" Aaron asked.

"He's making me rip out a perfectly good install because he changed his mind about where he wants it to run."

"Install of what?" Jenn said.

"Oh, we laid some new pipe for him, acrosst his back yard out to where he plans to put his pool."

"A hot tub?" Jenn asked.

No one in Wyoming put in a pool at this elevation, especially not on a ranch where every precious drop of water is spoken for, between the people, the livestock, and the hay fields.

"Oh, no. A swimming pool deep enough for a diving board and long enough that his new wife can swim laps. For exercise. I guess she don't get enough of that since she don't work for a living." Betty's expression was pure bafflement.

"Above ground? Like one of those Michael Phelps Swimspa things?" Aaron said. A large hole in the ground for a real pool took up growing space in the summer and was a waste of good hay stacking space in the half of the year it was winterized, if there was even a level spot to put one. If not, loads of fill dirt would have to be hauled in to make a suitable pad. At least above ground units had a smaller footprint, and some could be stored out of season.

Betty puffed on her cigar, then spat and wiped tobacco leaves from her lips. "That would have been bad enough. But no. He's gonna have me break a coupla few tractor blades for him digging to China this winter. So, it will be ready for Charity to use by March fifteenth. For 'spring'." She used air quotes on the last word.

Aaron chuckled. "I hope he's putting in one heckuva heater,

then." He hadn't spent a whole winter in Wyoming yet, but he knew to expect it to last through April or longer at this latitude and elevation.

"Right?" Betty winked, and her eyes sparkled. "But I won't be doing anything on it until we dig up this pipe and move it three feet over. It wouldn't be so bad if he weren't such an a-hole about everything. We put it where he told us to, then he changed his mind. He acted like I made him choose that durn spot in the first place. And that's not all. This morning, he forced me to fire Will Renwick for sleeping in his barn. I didn't like it either, but Will doesn't have a vehicle. If he misses his ride to town, it's not like Trusk can expect people to sleep out in the elements. I swear, I'ma kill the man one of these days. Just see if I don't."

"I'm sorry." Jenn glanced at the time on her phone. Discreetly, but Aaron knew she was worried about making it to the doctor.

He waved at Betty. "Hate to cut this short, but I've got a horse to examine."

"That fancy new stallion? One guess who it's for and the first'un don't count." She stalked back to the tractor.

Aaron and Jenn drove on to the stables and barns, which were now in sight. Huge wooden structures wearing new coats of bright red paint. Snow had slid from the white metal roofs to pile under the eaves. In some places, it reached the roofline. *Good insulation to keep the inside warm.*

"This Charity sounds spoiled," Jenn said.

Aaron parked next to a red Rivian electric truck, as close as he could get to the horse stable doors. He was surprised to see Will Renwick looking like a big Yeti loitering there, in his cold weather gear and a backpack. His brown hair hadn't gotten any shorter or cleaner. B-cubed had said Trusk had fired him, so it was surprising he was still there. *Probably waiting on a ride to town.* The former Army maintenance mechanic had worked at the Herringtons' lodge for the old owner George Nichols—who was now their operations manager—until the business had waned and George sold them the property.

The lodge was now closed to guests pending renovations. Will had tried to take up residence on their property when the Herringtons moved in, but Jenn had put her foot down. She didn't like flipping on the lights in one of the outbuildings only to find a defiant squatter squinting up at her. They had strongly suggested Will find somewhere in town after they'd looked up accommodations for people without homes and discovered some good options that they referred him to.

He had been less than happy about it.

"Hello, Will," Aaron said.

Jenn chimed in. "Hi, Will. How are you?"

Will didn't speak, but the answer to that question was obvious from the glare he shot them. Jenn raised her eyebrows at Aaron, but he just reached for her hand.

An enormous white dog charged from around the corner of the stable. A Great Pyrenees—a livestock guardian dog. They were common in the area. This one didn't look happy to see them. Aaron hadn't encountered a guardian dog at the ranch before.

Will screamed. "Get the hell out of here, dog!" He shrank back.

Jenn dropped Aaron's hand and stretched hers out, palm down, to the wooly animal. "Hey, big fella," she crooned.

The dog's affect changed completely. Tail wagging, it bounced over to Jenn and gave her a sniff. Aaron held his hand out, too. The dog growled. Aaron could respect that. He withdrew his hand and gave it space.

"Be careful," he said.

"See? He's mean. I'm outta here." Will backed away quickly and disappeared around the stable.

Aaron had thought Will already was, but he withheld comment. "He likes you."

Jenn stroked the dogs big head. The voice that came from her lips was close to baby talk. "Maybe some big man has just been mean to him."

"Maybe he thinks you smell good." He knew it was more than

that, though. Canines loved Jenn. He didn't think she was even aware of the extent she exuded dog magnetism. It was one of the reasons he had always wished they had a dog. But it had never fit into their lifestyle before. He hoped it would here in Wyoming.

She gave the dog one last rub and reclaimed Aaron's hand. The dog trotted away, roughly in the direction Will had gone. Aaron hoped Will had taken shelter.

They walked into the stables, following the sound of raised voices. The first person Aaron saw was a tall young woman with a long blonde French braid. She was standing in the alley between two rows of stalls. Her eyes were cast down and her posture slumped, but even from this angle, something about her gave Aaron a sense of deja vu.

Glen Trusk and his brand-new bride Charity Ellis were standing in front of the young woman. Trusk had his arms crossed over his concave chest. Gray hair stood up in a cowlick off the back of his skull, making him look a head shorter and a couple of decades older than Charity. Out of long habit, Aaron immediately sized Trusk up as if he was on an opposing football team. No question he'd be the owner who'd inherited the franchise from his grandparents and was running the organization into the ground. And had never played a single down of football in his life.

Glen's voice was a sneer. "I left you one thing to do. Take delivery of the new horse. How hard is a simple lameness check?"

Charity flipped long red hair over her shoulder. If levering into tight-fitting jeans was an Olympic sport, she'd be a gold medal winner. Between the jeans and the projectiles threatening to unsnap the front of her shirt, there was nowhere safe to look, so Aaron kept his eyes averted.

"This horse costs more than you make in a year," Charity said.

Glen snorted. "More than she'll make in her lifetime, I'll bet. He's a reining champion, Casey. That stud has sperm of gold. Unless he can't compete again because of you."

Aaron didn't love reining, a Western equestrian event where

riders guide the horses through a precise pattern of circles, spins, and stops at a lope or gallop. The sliding stops and amazing spins make it popular with riders and fans. But repetitive trauma on the joints from the athletic performance risked harm to the horses by causing degenerative changes to the cartilage and bones. Reining horses were known to break down at nearly as high a rate as with racehorses, with the same grim outcome—injuries that could result in horses being euthanized. In Aaron's experience, the odds grew worse with crappy owners. He suspected that would be the case here.

"I want to enter him in an event next month," Charity whined.

How can Glen and Charity stand each other? But probably no one else would put up with their abominable personalities and behavior.

"I didn't hurt him," Casey finally blurted out. "He was going crazy. He probably hurt himself kicking his stall." As if to emphasize her point, hooves pounded against wood. WHAM. WHAM. WHAM.

Glen sniffed. "Any idiot would have known to stop him."

A slight movement at the far end of the hallway between the stalls caught Aaron's attention. A smirking cowboy, hat tipped low, giving Charity some competition in the tight jeans category.

Aaron squeezed Jenn's hand. He wanted to ask the Trusks how important the horse really was if they couldn't be bothered to be present for delivery themselves, but it wouldn't help. Instead, he cleared his throat. "Mr. Trusk, Ms. Ellis—I'm here to look at your horse."

The Trusks whirled to face him and Jenn.

"Mrs. Trusk," Charity said. "We're married now. I believe I'm entitled to that respect."

Aaron nodded, his cheeks hot. It had been an honest mistake. She'd been Ellis when he'd met her before. "Of course."

"Dr. Herrington. About time. And you are?" Glen rolled his hand at Jenn.

"Jennifer Herrington. I'm Aaron's wife. I came to assist," Jenn said, reading the room and modifying slightly the reason for her visit.

"Smokey's Spinning Devil is in there." He pointed toward the noisy stall. Then he turned back to the young woman. "We'll discuss whether or not to continue your employment later. You're dismissed, Casey."

"You don't want me to finish up my work today?"

"Go!"

She scurried out, her light blue eyes meeting Aaron's for a moment. The deja vu hit again. Had he seen her around here before? Maybe in town? But he didn't think so.

"Where were we?" Glen said to Aaron. Then, "Oh, you were standing there instead of taking care of my injured horse."

Aaron smiled. It was the only response he could think of to Glen's bullying behavior. Well, he could punch him in the nose. It would be satisfying, but it wasn't worth the lawsuit. "Would one of you accompany me, please?"

"Isn't that what your 'assistant' is for?" Charity said.

"With such an expensive animal, I'd like an owner present."

Glen's pocket emitted a shrill ringtone. "You go, Charity. I have to meet with Arnold." He turned his back on them. "Hello?"

Apparently he'd answered his phone on speaker, because a woman's deep voice boomed down the hallway as Aaron, Jenn, and Charity moved toward Smokey's stall. "This is Carolyn Barrett. Is this Glen Trusk?"

"I am but who the hell is Carolyn Barrett?"

Aaron unlatched the stall gate. Inside, the stallion snorted and kicked the wall.

"Your neighbor. And your dogs are on my property again. They're chasing my pregnant cows. Someone needs to come get them, or I'm going to shoot them."

"The hell you will! Sookie was best in breed at Westminster."

Aaron made soothing noises at the sorrel stud eying him from the back corner of the stall. Charity huddled behind him. He held out a hand, palm down. *They should have haltered him and had him ready for me.*

"You have half an hour." Carolyn rattled off her address and hung up.

Glen screamed and stomped his feet, not unlike his horse, except the horse was more rational. "That's... that's bullshit!" He charged after them into the stall.

Smokey reared and pawed the air.

Charity screamed.

Aaron stood his ground. "Whoa, boy. Mr. Glen, I think Smokey's spooked, which makes him dangerous. We need to give him complete calm, please."

"Well, excuse the hell out of me. I just came to tell you to leave a bill with Charity when you have him fixed up. Charity, I'm taking the Rivian."

Jennifer said, "Maybe you can give Will a ride then. I know you want him off the property, but he's stranded."

Aaron braced himself for Trusk's explosion. But it didn't come.

Instead, he shook his head. "I had high hopes for that kid. Treated him like a son."

Aaron didn't imagine that was all that good, really.

Then Trusk shook his head. "But no, I'm done with him. He'll figure it out. I've got to go deal with my asshole neighbor. Another one of them."

Aaron didn't bother chiming in about the prevalence of asshole neighbors on the mountain face—present company very much included—or what driving an electric truck at this elevation on these grades in the winter said about a person's common sense. He just kept his eyes on the horse as Glen made his dramatic exit.

An hour later, Aaron and Jenn climbed back into Demarcus Ware. He glanced at his watch. They still had time to make Jenn's appointment if they hustled.

"My God, that poor horse," Jenn said.

Aaron backed away from the stables and turned toward the exit. The sky was a brilliant cloudless blue. No new snow had fallen while he was treating Smokey, who appeared to have a moderate sprain to his right knee. He'd put the horse on box rest for a week, applied Bute for inflammation, wrapped the knee to immobilize it, and left Charity with instructions on rest and cold hosing three times a day followed by a kaolin poultice. When the roads cleared, he would have Smokey brought to the clinic for an ultrasound. In all likelihood, the stud was going to undergo a lengthy recuperation with light exercise and be off work for months. But they'd know more after the images.

Aaron said, "Most of my clients are great. But every now and then, I want to stage a middle-of-the-night rescue. This is one of those times."

The goat path was fast approaching. The tractor was parked in the road.

"What is the tractor doing so close to the drop-off? Is it blocking us?"

Aaron frowned. "I don't think so." He pulled to a stop and set the emergency brake. "Let me go take a look."

He stepped out onto the roadbed. The snow seemed more packed than earlier. Heavy vehicles passing could do that. The passenger door slammed. Jenn joined him in front of the Jeepster.

He said, "I think we can get by, but I don't see our short friend in the tractor."

Jenn was shoving her hands into gloves. "The engine's not running either,"

Aaron nodded. The world was eerily silent except for the crunch of their boots. As he passed the Kubota, he pulled off a glove and touched the engine housing. It was warm to the touch. "It hasn't been turned off for long."

"Black Bear Betty?" Jenn called. There was no answer. "You should check the cab. What if she's had a medical issue?"

Aaron pulled his glove back on and jumped onto the step, opened the door, and peered inside. Keys were in the ignition, but the cab was empty. "No sign of her. I guess I could move it back up that side road further out of the way."

Jenn was walking away from the tractor, walking toward the cliff it faced. She moved closer to the edge, which was a surprise given her deathly fear of heights. She shielded her eyes, then her hand flew up to her mouth and she sank to her knees.

"Aaron." Her voice was a shaky rasp.

Aaron was already on the ground and running to her. He pulled her back to her feet, but she struggled against him to the edge.

She pointed down.

Below them—far below—rust red metal contrasted with white. It was Glen's fancy new truck. But it wasn't shaped like a truck anymore, and there was no sign of life in or around it.

CHAPTER TWO

Big Horn, Wyoming

Jennifer paced the hallway between the stall rows in the WP Bar Ranch stables an hour later. Aaron was leaning against the door to Smokey's box, stroking the horse's nose. The animal seemed far less high-strung without the Trusks around. The cold hose, poultice, anti-inflammatory, and wrap Aaron had administered had probably taken a pain-stoked edge off the stud's behavior, too.

Jennifer wished she had something to take the edge off herself. Today had started out so well. Her agent was shopping her first mystery novel to publishers. The bar exam was only a few weeks away. She'd been harboring a secret and growing urge to vie for the county attorney position in Sheridan, to make up for her lost opportunity at district attorney in Houston. Her relationship with Aaron was back on track and sizzling. And she had the cutest little destunk *mephitis mephitis*—which literally meant 'bad odor' in Latin—in the history of skunkdom.

She'd even been scheduled for a fertility consult appointment with her new OB/GYN. Not that she'd made up her mind yet whether to have a baby. She was just gathering information about her options. Call it *informed decision-making.*

Until Glen Trusk had taken a long drive off a short cliff face. Sudden loss of human life was always tragic. She was still slightly in shock and felt horrible for him, his wife, and everyone involved —except for their animals and employees. It would be a lie to pretend he wasn't one of the most unpleasant people she'd ever met.

Now she was on hold to reschedule her doctor appointment while she and Aaron waited to talk to Deputy Travis of the Sheridan County Sheriff's Department. The deputy had promised to come interview them as soon as he and his colleagues preserved what they could of the scene. More snow was expected that evening, and the road was the only way in and out of the ranch. Vehicular traffic was unavoidable across the accident site.

"Ms. Herrington? Are you still there?" A man's voice said through the phone connection.

"Yes. Right here."

"The doctor has an eight-a.m. cancellation tomorrow. Will that work?"

Would it ever—she'd waited weeks for this appointment! "Yes. Thank you so much. I'll see you then."

Jennifer ended the call and pumped her fist. "Eight a.m. tomorrow."

Aaron glanced over at her, looking conflicted. "I have a seven-thirty appointment in the morning. Do you want me to reschedule?"

"No, it's okay. You get credit for today." Jennifer joined him at the stall door. She rose on her tiptoes, and he leaned down for her to kiss his cheek. "I appreciate the moral support. Although I suspect your motives."

"Who? Me?" He raised one eyebrow. It was his signature move, and it had a devastating effect on her. That irresistible charm was part of the reason she was considering a pregnancy at the age of forty.

"You're afraid I'm going to chicken out."

He smiled at her. "You don't have to do this for me. It's a hundred percent up to you."

Loud grumbling heralded the arrival of Black Bear Betty.

"There you are!" Jennifer said.

"Waddya mean there you are? Who's looking for me?" Betty said.

Jennifer could feel the furrows between her own brows. "Your tractor was in the road... you weren't in it... and..."

"I left it up on the hill before I took the four-wheeler back to the house. Not that it's any-a your never mind, but I had to visit the necessaries. Back door if you get my drift. My guts been gripin' ever since I ate some chili that got left out a few days."

Jennifer ignored the TMI. "You've been up at the house for the bathroom?"

"Ain't that what I just said? The facilities here at the stables are out of order. Froze up because that dumb sunuva buck left the heat off for two months and didn't discover the problem until he turned things on to get ready for the pretty pony."

"Got it. But I mean... for an hour?"

The older woman cackled. "Wait until you're my age. Things affect ya different. But I did take the opportunity to warm up my chow and eat."

"So, you didn't hear what happened?"

Aaron put his hand on Jenn's shoulder.

"All I know is I feel about ten pounds lighter. But spit it out. What happened?"

"Glen. Mr. Trusk. He's, uh—his truck went off the road. By your tractor. He's dead."

"That would make my life a heckuva lot easier." She laughed. "You almost had me there."

"I'm not kidding."

Betty's face scrunched in confusion.

The door to the stables slid open. A burly figure cut a black hole in the sunlit, snowy scene. The door shut behind Deputy Travis.

"Well, I'll be gol-durned," Betty said.

Jennifer stretched her legs out, toes pointed, ankles flexed, then relaxed them. The metal-legged couch was form over function and killing her lower back. Cushionless. Armless. A deep seat that forced her to perch forward although Aaron filled it up beside her perfectly. It was likely the first white couch in the history of ranch houses in the mountain foothills. And in the middle of chaos, no less. The house was undergoing a major remodel. Scaffolding and plastic tarps obscured the fireplace and windows. A strong paint odor permeated the air along with enough sawdust grit that she felt like she'd been licking sandpaper.

Deputy Travis stood scribbling in a little top-bound spiral notebook, one hip on a credenza that seemed like it had been moved out of its normal spot due to the construction.

"Did anything about Mr. Trusk seem 'off' to you?" Travis was projecting a new gravitas. He was the front-runner to take the Republican nomination for sheriff that year, which would make him a shoo-in in the general election.

Jennifer said, "I'd never met him before today. He seemed like a very unpleasant person, though."

Somewhere in the house a door slammed. Expensive art and construction equipment rattled against walls.

"He was his normal self," Aaron said.

"Impaired in any way?" Travis wrote quickly.

"Not that I could detect."

"And why were the two of you here?"

"His horse needed veterinary attention."

Jennifer shuddered. "I just tagged along so I could see the place. I got more than I bargained for."

Travis nodded. "When you drove up to the accident site, did you see anyone?"

"No. Not from the time we left the stables until—well, no one."

"You left the tractor where it was?"

"Yes."

"Any other vehicles visible?"

"No. Just the crashed truck."

"Did you know of anyone who might have wanted to hurt Mr. Trusk?"

Aaron said, "Hurt him? No."

"You sound like you're equivocating."

Jennifer smiled at the fifty-cent word. Big city transplants like herself sometimes forgot they weren't dealing with rubes here. Travis had a college degree and was a graduate of the FBI National Academy.

"Plenty of people disliked him."

Jennifer cut in. "He'd fired a contractor, berated an employee, and been extremely unpleasant with a neighbor just today."

"Names?"

"The contractor was Will Renwick. The employee was Casey something. The neighbor I think was Carolyn Barrett."

"He said he had a meeting with someone," Jennifer added. "Although I don't know if that was someone who disliked him, too."

"Did you get a name?"

Aaron shrugged. "I can't remember."

"Arnold," Jennifer said.

"Arnold who?"

"That I do not know." She heard footsteps approaching, then a shrill voice.

Charity descended upon them. "My husband was a very important man under enormous pressure. I don't expect the small-minded people in this backwater town living their little bitty lives will understand. He didn't have time for incompetence. And now he's dead because people around here don't know the first thing about plowing roads and ensuring public safety." She broke into awkward sobs.

The plowing had looked pretty good to Jennifer. She wondered what public safety on a private mountain road had to do with Glen's wreck. It was every man for himself up here. She figured he'd been on his phone or ill-equipped for the driving conditions. Aaron and Betty had driven the same road with no problem.

The cowboy Jennifer had seen holding up the wall at the stables earlier materialized at Charity's side and put a hand under her elbow. He looked like an actor playing a cowboy for a daytime soap. All white teeth, tan skin, and over-the-top wardrobe. "Mrs. Trusk, don't you want to rest? I can get you something to drink."

She sniffled, then brought her sobs under control in between breaths. "White wine. Bring the bottle. I need something to help me cope. I'm all alone here now, you know. With no one to take care of me."

Jennifer worked hard to keep her eyebrows from rising to her hairline. Then she realized that Glen's death could have left the woman destitute. A prenuptial agreement could limit her inheritance, if she wasn't covered by life insurance or already well-heeled. They were newlyweds, Aaron had said. Maybe Charity was emotionally devastated. Maybe she was scared. Maybe both. Or neither.

The pretty boy said, "Of course."

As the two of them left the living room the cowboy's hand drifted from Charity's elbow to her hip. Her lower hip bordering on her tush. Jennifer and Aaron shared a WTH look. *So much for emotional devastation.*

Travis scribbled a note then cleared his throat. "I guess I'll let the two of you go. If you think of anything helpful, please let me know."

Jennifer and Aaron bid him goodbye then walked out together.

"Who was the rhinestone cowboy with Charity?" she whispered to Aaron.

He opened the door for her. "I don't know. But he seemed like a real hands-on kind of guy."

Jennifer couldn't have said it better herself.

CHAPTER THREE

Sheridan, Wyoming

Dr. Lizbeth Ashton took a seat on a rolling stool. Because she was on an exam table, Jennifer was several feet higher than her. At five foot two, it wasn't Jennifer's usual vantage point. She admired the perfect part in the doctor's sleek gray hair and wondered if hers looked like a serrated knife edge in comparison. She'd been in a huge hurry that morning, giving extra time for her drive in case the roads were bad. Luckily the plows had been at work early and done a good job. Because she'd ended up with time to burn, she'd stopped in Walgreen's and bought them out of ovulation kits and pregnancy tests. She believed in being prepared for anything.

"How long have you and your husband been trying to conceive?" Dr. Ashton asked.

"We haven't yet. We're considering it. And with my age, I want to make sure everything is okay first."

Dr. Ashton glanced at her tablet through thick-lensed glasses that slid down her nose. "You're how old?"

"Forty."

"Do you use oral contraceptives?" She pushed the glasses back up.

"Since I was nineteen."

"Are you still taking them?"

"I stopped about a month ago."

Dr. Ashton talked Jennifer through the process of pregnancy after quitting birth control pills. In a nutshell, there were no guarantees, and even if it worked it could take a long time. That pregnancy was possible for women until menopause, which probably wouldn't happen until her fifties, but could start earlier. *She "equivocates" like an attorney,* Jennifer thought, remembering the Sheriff's words the day before.

"But is it *safe* for me to get pregnant?"

"Maternal and fetal risk increases with advanced maternal age, although pregnancy is never without it."

"When will I reach advanced maternal age?"

"Five years ago."

"Oh." That hurt.

They talked through the risks. High blood pressure, which can lead to preeclampsia and cause even higher blood pressure and organ damage. Gestational diabetes. Miscarriage or stillbirth. Labor problems that could necessitate a cesarean section. Premature birth. Low birthweight. Chromosome disorders. Jennifer felt a heaviness in her chest, like Aaron was sitting on it.

Dr. Ashton tucked her silver bob behind her ears. "When you're born, you have a certain number of eggs. You release one or more with each menstrual cycle. As you age, the number of eggs left decreases, and those are more likely to have chromosome disorders. That's why the risk of birth defects goes up. The age of your husband contributes to the risk as well. You also have a higher chance of chronic conditions yourself as you get older. Pregnant or not, you're more likely to have high blood pressure at thirty-five than twenty-five, for instance."

"I don't."

"That's something in your favor then. But having a baby later in life increases the chances of twins or other multiples, and that also raises the risk of complications."

"But that's just if I do IVF or take fertility drugs right?"

The doctor shook her head. The hair slid back from behind her ears. Jennifer was beginning to feel the need to help her keep just one thing in place, the poor woman. "Hormonal changes as you age increase the chance that your body will release more than one egg per cycle."

Jennifer looked down, thinking. Multiples? She'd never be able to balance a pack of children with her career and Aaron's. The weight on her chest intensified. "Well, I don't think I even have time left for IVF."

Dr. Ashton smiled. "Don't get in a rush. Let's just see what the next few months have in store for you. Since you've been off birth control for a month, would you like to take a pregnancy test today just to check?"

Jennifer considered, but everything had been normal and on schedule so far. "I don't have any reason to believe I'm pregnant yet, but I have at-home tests on hand if that changes."

"Very well," said Dr. Ashton. "We'll start you on prenatal vita-mins immediately, of course. You need to exercise, eat well, and get good rest. Then just focus on all the benefits of pregnancy and babies at your age. You have resources to provide for a baby. You're mature and can raise a healthier and more well-adjusted child. Women who wait to get pregnant live longer, which will be great for a child. How is your stress level? Because keeping that under control is very important."

Jennifer raked her teeth over her top lip. Should she be honest? She didn't want to tell this woman how badly she needed Pootie Carputin held accountable for the kids who had died in the school shooting that haunted her dreams every night. The County Attor-ney's reluctance to bring charges against him based on her testimony wreaked havoc on her emotions. But no one could deny Pootie had a distinctive tattoo of a snake coiled in rocks with D-T-O-M inked below it. The problem was that Jennifer hadn't remembered the tattoo on the shooter until she'd reached adulthood. Literally, when she moved to Wyoming and started having flashbacks.

Jennifer said, "Not great. A move, a career change, studying for the bar exam. Thinking about having a child. I have trouble sleeping. Nightmares." She hurried the last word, shrugging and de-emphasizing it.

Dr. Ashton nodded, her eye contact direct. "And your marriage?"

Jennifer was relieved the doctor didn't probe about the nightmares and glad Aaron wasn't here for this part of the conversation. "We've been together since college. We've had our ups and downs. Lately it's up after a long down."

"How would you feel about talking to someone about the sleep problem? A friend? A pastor? A counselor?"

"I don't really have anyone here, except my husband." She was close to her friend and former colleague Alayah back in Houston. She missed their talks over coffee, drinks, shopping, and lunches. Maybe she could invite her to visit? "I really don't want to go to anyone in the medical community." *Because I might want to run for public office someday and those things have a way of getting out.* A face flashed in her mind. Trish Flint. The wildlife biologist with the National Forest Service was older than Jennifer, but they'd really clicked. She'd ask Trish to get a coffee.

Dr. Ashton smiled. "I know someone. He's excellent, discreet, and semi-retired—works part-time at the Veterans Affairs Hospital and occasionally sees patients privately. Chaplain Dean Abel." She clicked a pen and pulled out an old school prescription pad. She scribbled on it and tore off the sheet. As she handed the page to Jennifer, she said, "This keeps the referral out of our system," and winked.

A wave of relief flooded Jennifer. She'd spent so much energy lobbying to get Pootie charged for the murders. She tried to hide it, but she knew it had taken a toll on her mental health. Suddenly, talking to a discreet professional seemed high priority. Chaplain Abel sounded pretty perfect. "Thank you."

"You're welcome. Now, your general health seems great based on your vitals and the information in the system from your primary care physician. I see no reason at this point that you can't conceive. Get on those prenatal vitamins. Relax. Have fun. Make it romantic. It's a big deal creating a life together."

"I will."

"You'll be given a pamphlet on increasing your chances of conception when you check out."

They shook hands. Dr. Ashton left, and Jennifer decided to text Chaplain Abel before she got dressed. She opened her messages and saw one from her agent, Joe.

The first publisher passed, but I have high hopes for the next one. I love your book. Don't worry about it—I've got this. Best thing for you to do is be working on the next one.

A sharp disappointment stabbed her midsection. That was a stressor she hadn't even considered. Getting her first novel published. She sent him a quick thanks with a muscle arm emoji meant to buoy herself up as much as reassure him. But she avoided the topic of her next book. There was no next book yet. She'd tried but was in total writer's block.

She texted a message to Chaplain Abel explaining who she was and that she'd been referred by Dr. Ashton because of general stress, nightmares, and difficulty sleeping. Then she dressed, checked out, and hurried through the lobby.

"Jenny from the block, fancy seeing you here." The Texas drawl and the smoky voice stopped Jennifer just as she was opening the door to leave.

No. She drew in a breath and turned, a smile plastered on her face. "Maggie. Hello." Maggie Killian. Famously infamous musician and uber irritating partner of Jennifer's cousin Hank Sibley. The waiting room was packed and every eyeball in the place was ping-ponging between Maggie and Jennifer. Maggie had probably been the subject of covert scrutiny already.

Jennifer gave a little finger wave then felt stupid. Maggie was too cool for finger waves. The woman was a sexier, slinkier, younger version of Sandra Bullock.

"We still on for getting together at your place?"

Jennifer had forgotten it was hers and Aaron's turn to host their monthly couples night. Honestly, the dinners were fun. With enough iced tea laced with Maggie's favorite booze—Koltiska Distillery's KO 90—Jennifer could admit Maggie was hilarious. *Why does she rub me so wrong when I'm sober?* But should Jennifer even drink if she was off birth control? She did the mental math again. There was no way she could be pregnant. *Bring on Maggie's TKOs.*

"Absolutely," Jennifer said.

"Vegetarian or carnivore?"

Jennifer was holding on to her vegetarian lifestyle in cattle and wild game country with a death grip. "Both."

"What can we bring?"

Jenn's phone rang. She glanced at it, praying for an end to their public conversation. Her screen read SHERIDAN COUNTY JAIL. She frowned. "Sorry. I have to take this. I'll text you." And she did the finger wave again before she could stop herself.

Maggie did it back. Anyone could see it was ironic. "Toodle-oo."

Jennifer pushed out the door into the hallway, cheeks flaming. She answered the phone and hurried toward her Jeep Grand Cherokee. "Jennifer Herrington speaking."

"They said I get one phone call, so I figured I'd better make it a good'un." It was a woman's voice. Familiar. Irascible.

"Who is this?"

"Do you have cotton in your ears? Black Bear Betty, of course."

"One phone call? What's going on?"

"The durn fool deputies arrested me. I'm in the county jail."

"Oh, no." Jennifer knew Betty was a drinker, but she didn't think the woman drove while she was impaired. In fact, she'd stayed over at the lodge more than once when she'd had a few. It couldn't be a DUI. But what else could it be? "What happened?"

"Do you want me to start with the part where Glen Trusk went off a cliff in his fancy EV or skip to where I got arrested for his murder?"

"Murder?"

"Ain't that what I said? I seem to be in a big pickle, and I'm counting on you to get me out of it."

Jennifer slumped against the door to her SUV and banged her forehead against it. She wasn't licensed yet. She couldn't represent Betty in court. But she knew someone who could. "I'll be there as fast as I can."

Then she got in her shiny new vehicle and drove straight to the offices of Wesley James, III, esquire.

CHAPTER FOUR

Big Horn, Wyoming

Aaron snuck into the lodge after finishing up with his first few patients of the morning—a lethargic border collie and an obese Maine Coon cat plus the ongoing care of a red fox recovering from being hit by a car. The fox would be turned over to Fish & Game to release into the wild when it recovered, which would be soon. Aaron was dragging after a late night watching the Hallmark Mystery Channel with Jenn. Lately she'd been obsessed with crime-solving writers, a la *Murder, She Wrote* and *Castle*. Aaron needed a strong coffee. Maybe two. He had a breakroom in the clinic he'd established in the former stables onsite where he saw patients a few days a week, with surgeries and the rest of his practice held in the full-service clinic he'd bought in Sheridan. But he'd just gotten a bare bones text from Jennifer. Black Bear Betty had been arrested for the murder of Glen Trusk. Jenn was on her way to start on the defense with Kid James.

No use sugar coating it. Aaron was thrown. He wanted to digest the bad news a beat away from his vet tech Tron, who was basically Sheridan's answer to TMZ. Anything he overheard would be posted all over social media in real time. Betty was like family. She didn't deserve that. Aaron was also hoping that George would be hanging around. He might have news. Even though he was managing the lodge construction, he had coffee in town at Perkins with his cronies once a week, and they were bigger gossips than Tron minus the tech savvy.

The lodge kitchen didn't look unlike the main house at the WP Bar Ranch the day before, with tarps, construction tools, and materials everywhere. The lodge renovations were lagging since most of the construction energy in the first few months had gone into creating the clinic and bringing George's former abode up to snuff for Jenn to use as an office and writing cottage. Luckily, the main house had remained habitable throughout the process. The lodge projects completed to date had been infrastructure, with the cosmetic slated for late spring. Still, the place was starting to come together. So much so that Aaron and Jenn might be faced with deciding whether to open it for business in the warmer months.

Aaron batted aside a plastic wall and heard a chittering sound. He reached down and scooped up the little black and white creature circling his feet. "Jeremiah Johnson, did I interrupt your mid-morning nap?" He raised Jeremiah to face-level. The skunk's black eyes regarded Aaron seriously, then he chirped and swished his plumed tail. "You want a snack? Or were you hoping I was George or Jenn?" Jeremiah hopped onto Aaron's shoulder and cuddled into his neck. Aaron grinned. "You are a very spoiled animal."

Aaron and Jenn had inherited three pets with the lodge. The skunk, an incontinent old St. Bernard named Liam who was the unofficial clinic mascot, and a calico cat named Katya who hated everyone except Maggie Killian and George. Jenn had a thing for skunks since falling in love with Flower in *Bambi* as a child. The chance to pet-share Jeremiah with George had been a key part of convincing her that the Wyoming lodge was a good idea.

The front door opened as Aaron and Jeremiah were putting the finishing touches on a cup of coffee fresh from the Nespresso machine. "Is that you, George?"

"Hello, Doc Herriott." George knew Aaron was a huge fan of the British veterinarian and author of *All Creatures Great and Small*. "Or should we call you Dr. Pol now?"

"Have you been watching *The Incredible Dr. Pol*?"

"I have. He's good, but he's got nothing on you." George used his one arm to enter the kitchen. His other had been ripped off a few months before by his own log splitter, a conical drill bit powered by a tractor engine. It hadn't been George's fault. He'd been pushed by Pootie Carputin, who blamed George for the death of Pootie's daughter in a traffic accident.

Aaron had since gotten rid of the splitter at Jenn's behest. She believed it was a blood thirsty beast that wouldn't be satisfied until it had killed someone now that it had a taste of George's arm.

George said, "I wouldn't say no to a cup of that."

Jeremiah leapt onto the other man's shoulder. *Fickle little beast.*

"Didn't get enough with the boys?"

"There's never enough. I'll be supervising contractors all day. They're late, by the way."

"Take this one. I'll make another. Did you hear anything in town about Jenn's new case?" He refilled the water tank.

George took the mug and held it to his face. "Holy smokes, I didn't know how to break it to you since you and Black Bear Betty are a little sweet on each other. Some nonsense about the sheriff's office arresting her for murder. She hated Glen Trusk something fierce. I wouldn't put it past her. But she's not the kind to hide things. If she'd done it, we'd have all been sitting around drinking and listening to her brag about it last night."

Aaron put a pod in the machine and slid a coffee cup under the spigot. "Right? This has to just be a mistake. I didn't even think the cops suspected murder."

"If they think someone killed him, there's a line of people to look at. I'd start with Samson Dale."

"Who's that?"

"The guy Trusk screwed out of buying the WP Bar Ranch. Not that I'm a fan of Dale since he backed out of buying my place when WP Bar went on the market. "

"How did Trusk screw him?"

"Scuttlebutt from the boys is Trusk paid off the seller's real estate agent to tell him what Dale's offer was. Trusk then came in over it after Dale already had a contract. The seller backed out on Dale and sold it to Trusk. And by then I'd already sold to you. The music stopped and Dale didn't have a chair. Or a mountain property anyway."

A knock sounded at the front door. A loud hiss was a good clue that Katya was guarding from her usual perch on a roll top desk.

Aaron said, "I'll get it."

"Maybe it's my crew. Better late than never. Or so they say." George's brows lifted with skepticism.

Aaron pointed two fingers at his own eyes then at Katya. "I'm watching you." The cat had been known to attack him or Jenn when they went to the door. He opened it to a blast of cold air then ducked his head in surprise. "Um... Hello. Ms. ..."

The tall blonde woman's direct blue gaze was unnerving. "Casey Hurd."

"Ms. Hurd. Yes. From the WP Bar." She'd left in ignominy the day before after getting chewed out. He looked for a vehicle but didn't see any unfamiliar ones. "How did you get here? I mean, I'm sorry, what can I do for you?"

"I walked out from the ranch. Hitchhiked up Red Grade with some snowmobilers, then walked from there. I'm looking for work. I've got a lot of experience with animals."

"Don't you work at the WP Bar?"

"I did until I walked in on Charity and Boot barebacking in the stables. She fired me on the spot. Like I had invaded her privacy when it's my workplace."

For a moment, Aaron didn't follow her meaning, until he did. Barebacking as in... "Oooooh."

"Besides, she's already said she's selling the place and everything on it."

George shouted, "Ask the girl if she's a certified electrician."

Casey's eyebrows lifted. "Tell him I'm not," she shouted.

Aaron liked her style. "I'm afraid we don't have anything at the moment."

"Maybe with your wife? She's a lawyer, right?"

"Um, yeah, you could try." He didn't want to crush her hopes completely, but Jenn was still a bar license away from establishing her own practice. One that didn't involve animals. "Could I give you a ride somewhere?" They were eight miles from the tiny town of Big Horn and nearly thirty from Sheridan.

"I guess I could go put in some applications in town, if you don't mind giving me a lift."

Aaron glanced at his phone. He had an hour and a half until his next appointment. Tron was handling some routine work and caring for the animals that were boarding. There were always things Aaron *should* be doing at the clinic or lodge—or even for his job as the offensive coordinator for the Big Horn Rams high school football team. Head coach Perry Flint had sent him a critique on a few new plays Aaron wanted to work into their offensive scheme next season. But with Betty's arrest, Aaron wanted to hear what Casey had to say about it as a WP Bar insider.

"No problem. Come on in. I need to grab my keys and a jacket."

She gestured to the porch. "Are you just going to leave these dogs tied up out here?"

"What dogs?" He stepped outside, into the wind. According to the weather, another storm was bearing down. There seemed to be an unlimited supply of them, one lining up after another. He turned in the direction Casey had pointed and took in the sight, shaking his head.

Two large, floofy, black and white dogs were tied to his porch railing. Two dogs he'd never seen before. One eyed him with suspicious wolflike golden-brown eyes, like he was responsible for their predicament. The other let out a tremendous A-WOO and wagged a tail that would make Jeremiah Johnson weak with jealousy. Then the dogs harmonized at length. They hadn't been dropped off because of anything wrong with their lungs.

"What the heck?" he said. "How did you guys get here?"

Dog number two answered him in fifteen seconds of multisyllabic explanation, but it didn't shed any light. He hadn't gotten a call or text. There was no note, although one could have blown away. But if someone had brought them all the way out here, why hadn't they followed the signs to the clinic out back? Aaron called Tron to see if he knew anything about them, but the answer was a negative. Aaron checked their collars. No tags. Maybe they were microchipped? He could check for chips at the clinic in town.

"Do you mind riding with a couple of dogs?" he said to Casey.

She grinned. "I like dogs better than people."

Casey might just be all right, since Aaron didn't trust anyone who didn't.

CHAPTER FIVE

Sheridan, Wyoming

Jennifer and Kid James took seats in the Sheridan County jail interview room. To call it sparse was an undersell. It was the poster child for desolation. *Face your ruin, all ye who enter here.*

Kid pulled at his signature yellow bow tie. He looked dapper and —with his baby face and skinny frame—all of seventeen years old. Jennifer had never seen his birth certificate to confirm his claim that he was twenty-three. As a recent law school graduate, that still put him on the young side, but he'd finished high school early and under-graduate in three years.

Jennifer said, "Good to be working with you again. Although I can't imagine this case will last long. Probably be tossed in a week if she's even charged."

Kid nodded eagerly. "Yes. So great of you to call me. Thanks."

She smiled at his familiar speech pattern. Agree, amplify, appre-ciate. "Have you been staying busy?"

"Busier, thanks to you bringing me along with George Nichols' case. I've had some court appointed cases. Here and in Kearny County. I'm looking at a place of my own."

Kid lived with his mom in a gorgeous old house west of downtown. His offices were above the detached garage. "To live or to work?"

"Live. I like the office. It's close to the courts."

"You can't beat the price either."

He grinned.

Jennifer checked her phone. Aaron had responded to her text about representing Betty. *WTH? Give her a hug for me.*

She responded. *I will. Oh, and FYI publisher #1 shot the book down.* She thought about telling him she'd been referred to a counselor and that she'd been given the green light to make babies. Kid was watching her with interest, so she stopped there and hit send. "Are you reading my texts?"

"Not on purpose. I just sort of accidentally saw it. Sorry about the book. I'm sure you'll find a publisher."

"You are, huh? You haven't even read it." Or anything she'd written. It was a fictionalized version of George's case. Which mostly meant real life with more violence and less boring parts. She'd called the Kid James character Young Gun. It was possible he'd recognize himself in it. *Okay—it's one hundred percent certain he will.*

Aaron's reply came in quickly. *You're the best. And maybe this case will be fodder for your next book.*

She'd been struggling to come up with a new story to write. Something she hadn't admitted to her agent yet, citing instead her busy schedule studying for the bar. She'd omitted telling Joe she'd taken up snow golf, too. She loved playing in the thin air at this altitude. At first she'd been worried about losing balls against the whiteness of the snow, but that was easily solved with colored balls. The next hurdle had been balls sinking into the snow, but that was more of a problem for Aaron than her. She kept hers in the fairway or on the green. A notorious slicer, Aaron had to take a lot of one-stroke penalties when his balls went into the rough and buried themselves in drifts.

Another text from him came in. *Casey Hurd, the hand at WP Bar, wants to come by to interview with you and Kid. Can I drop her at his office?*

Jennifer frowned. She and Kid didn't have a practice, but she could ask him whether he needed someone.

The door opened. Jennifer flipped her phone facedown without answering Aaron. A guard shuffled Betty in. Not that anything was binding her feet. She always shuffled. The guard was tall and young —of the Kid James body type—and nearly twice her height.

"Hello, Jenn. Kid," she said, with no sign of embarrassment or consternation.

They greeted her in return.

The guard escorted her to her chair and started to leave.

"Can you uncuff her, please?" Jennifer said.

"Ma'am, she's a suspected murderer," the young man said, eyes wide and serious.

"Kid will protect me."

"What?" The guard's expression was skeptical.

Kid's was horrified.

"It's fine. She and I go way back. Just free her hands, please."

He complied with a look that said *It's your funeral.*

Betty rubbed her wrists and nodded briskly. "Okay now, my crack legal team. Tell me how fast you can get me out of here. Even though one of my main clients croaked, I've still got a load of work piled up."

Jennifer held up her hand. "You'll be arraigned quickly. They'll set bail then."

"How much you think it'll be?"

"For a murder charge? A few hundred thousand or more."

Betty's voice squeaked. "Pennies? Pesos?"

"Dollars."

"I ain't got that."

Jennifer had suspected as much. "You only need ten percent of it to get a bond."

"I don't have a ten percent of big bucks, either. No rich relatives or lovers."

Jennifer was intrigued by the lovers comment. Betty had always seemed asexual to her. "Think about it. Anyone you can borrow from, for instance. We can talk about it later. Right now, we need to hear your story about what happened."

"It's a short story. They arrested me and threw me in the pokey."

"Let's start with everything you can remember about where you were and what you were doing when Glen died. Then the same for your arrest."

"I already told you. You saw me at the stables after I'd been up using the facilities at the house. You were the one who told me he was dead."

"Did anyone see you at the house?" Jennifer asked.

"Will Renwick rode double with me on the four-wheeler. He was waiting on me to finish up and give him a ride to town."

"So, the two of you were together?"

"For a minute. Then that hand Casey showed up. She was in a state. Will went off jabbering with her."

"When was the next time you saw him?"

"I didn't. I assumed he musta been talking to the fuzz and then hitched a ride home with someone else. Was it you?"

"Me, his ride?"

"Yeah."

"No. I didn't see him after we found Glen's... truck." Jennifer hadn't lived in Wyoming long, but even she found it hard to call a Rivian a truck.

"Well, anyway. He knew when I went up to the house, and you knew when I came back. But I didn't take anyone in the can with me. And I ate my lunch by myself."

"You don't happen to know if they have security cameras, do you?"

"I don't think so. Mr. Trusk wanted to put some in after he was missing some materials, but something about needing connectivity in places he didn't have it. I told him to put up some wildlife cameras. He gave me one of those *were you born this stupid or did you get hit in the head by a rock* kind of looks."

Jennifer nodded at Kid significantly. He jumped in his seat then started taking notes. He might be a grown-up lawyer when he was working on his own, but they'd gotten into a routine on George's case. Even without her license in Wyoming, she was the senior attorney and he the junior. And it amused her to no end how seriously he took her instructions.

To Betty, she said, "Did the deputies tell you why they arrested you?"

"They mentioned orange paint flecks on that stupid EV truck he drove."

The Kubota tractor was orange. "And you do lack a confirmed alibi."

"But that paint was from a few days ago. I hit his truck with the tractor. Ask Will—he can tell you. He was there. I fessed up, too. Bossman was going to take the cost of repair out of what he paid me."

Jennifer glanced at Kid. He was already on it, pen waggling. "Did you tell the officers that?"

"I did. Plus, I told them I hated the sunuva buck. Deputy Travis said, 'So we've heard,' when I said it."

Jennifer winced. *Great.* "Motive, means, opportunity. You gave them the motive with a red bow on it."

"Doesn't mean I did it."

"But it does mean they'll stop looking for someone else who did."

"Who will hunt down the truth, then?"

Jennifer raised her brows and gestured at Kid. "I guess you're looking at them."

CHAPTER SIX

Sheridan, Wyoming

It was hard for Aaron to concentrate on his conversation with Casey with the goofier of the two dogs snuffling in his ear all the way to town. Since he and Jenn had never had pets—her choice, not his—until they'd inherited them with the lodge, he wasn't set up with dog restraints in the Jeepster. He pushed the dog back, again.

"Where are you from?" he asked Casey.

"A little town in Tennessee," she said, her face turned away from him.

"Really? I'm from the Nashville area."

"Cool."

"But we lived in Houston before we moved here."

"Yeah, everybody kinda knows all about you in town. Weren't you like some famous football player?"

Aaron had played less than a full season for the Detroit Lions. But he'd been an All American at the University of Tennessee in Knoxville many years ago. "I played. But as you know I'm a veterinarian now. What brought you to Wyoming?"

"My dad."

"He lives here?"

"Yeah. Do you have kids?"

A long-repressed memory arose at her question. The secret he'd kept from Jenn when they first met had grown bigger and more impossible to share with each passing year. Did it even matter anymore? He still felt guilty for not telling her. "Maybe someday. How do you like it so far?"

"It's cold but pretty. I just need a job."

"Unfortunately, we just filled our open positions at the clinic. But there are other vet practices in town."

"I'm good with office work, too."

Aaron pulled into a parking space at his clinic on the eastern edge of Sheridan. "Might as well come in with me and meet the staff while I check these ladies for chips. Want to help me with them?"

"Sure. What kind of dogs are they? Huskies?"

"I think they're Alaskan malamutes." He felt a little thrill as he said it. It was his dream breed. They weren't just strong and cold-adapted. They were notoriously stubborn and independent thinking. He admired that in creatures. They had centuries less domestication than most other types of dogs. A lot of their storied behaviors were instinctual. "The markings and the coat is similar to a husky. But malamutes have brown, wide-spaced eyes. They're bigger than huskies. Their ears are more rounded. And those curled, plume tails are pretty distinctive."

They both got out. He opened the back door and handed the end of the first leash to her. Seventy-five pounds of wary docility bounded out. He saved the hyper younger one for himself. It had a wolfish face and body. He was guessing eighteen months and the other maybe a year older. The older dog had the eyes of a wolf. And why wouldn't they both have wolf-like traits—they were the closest genetic relatives to wolves.

Aaron peeked inside to check for other dogs in the lobby. It was empty, so he motioned Casey in ahead of him. Two women and a man were behind the counter. He felt a moment of pride in his place. It was spartan, like when he'd bought it, save for posters of dogs by breeds and photos of winners from the annual county fair. Unlike the snooty Houston practice that had been stocked for pet owners who treated and often dressed their pets like their human children, the waiting room here offered essential items for working dogs and livestock. Not that they didn't get their fair share of be-ribboned Yorkies and such, usually belonging to the biggest, toughest ranchers who walked in with *I dare you to say a word about it* looks in their eyes.

One of the women at reception, her face slack and mouth down-turned, stood. His practice manager, Loretta. "Didn't expect to see you today, Doctor H. New pets?"

"Foundlings. Is there an empty exam room? I want to check them for chips. Oh, and this is Casey Hurd. She'd like to put in an application. Casey, this is Loretta."

"Hi, Loretta," Casey said.

"We're not hiring right now."

Casey's face fell.

Aaron smiled at the younger woman. "You can leave an application on file."

"Exam two," Loretta said.

Aaron led the way. Casey did have a calm, confident way with the dog, he noticed. Respectful but firm. Kind but ready. When they were behind a closed door, he handed the hyper dog's lead to Casey.

Loretta suddenly popped in with a chip reader. "I figure you'll need this."

"I do, thanks." Aaron scanned the first dog, checking all the most likely places. He found nothing, then repeated the same process on the second dog, with the same outcome.

"They look purebred malamute to me." Loretta took the scanner back from him. "Expensive dogs not to be marked. Nothing on their collars?"

"Nothing. Not even rabies tags. They're both spayed, though."

He ruffled the fur on one head, then the other. "I guess I can put something on Upcycle about them."

Loretta produced her phone. "Hold them still. I'll get pictures." She took shots of the dogs separately and together from several angles, then airdropped them to Aaron's phone. "I'm worried someone will claim them just to get dogs like these free."

"I'll make them show proof of ownership," Aaron said. "You seem to know a lot about them."

"My daughter raises them out near Cody. But they chip the puppies. So, I know they don't come from her."

"Thanks for your help."

Loretta petted both dogs. She looked up at Casey. "If you want to fill out an application, come with me."

Casey smiled and followed her. "Thanks."

Alone with the dogs, Aaron quickly went on Facebook to Upcycle. *Found. Two female Alaskan malamutes, spayed, aged approximately 18 months and 3 years. Will surrender with proof of ownership.* He added the pictures and clicked to post, feeling a twinge of sadness. He looked at the dogs, who were now curled up, side by side but watching him. "I wonder what kind of training you ladies have had?"

He tried out a few commands on them. Come, sit, lie down, stay. They eyed him suspiciously but complied with his requests. He rewarded them with treats from the exam room stash.

Maybe no one would claim them. "I wonder if you've pulled before?" The hyper young one was just about old enough. "You definitely need names, even if you'll be leaving me." *Although he hoped they wouldn't.*

He opened his string with Jenn and sent a picture of the two dogs. She hadn't answered his text earlier about dropping Casey by. *Left on our front porch with no note! Aren't they beautiful? I've posted, but we may have ourselves two sled dogs.* He added the Facebook post link.

He picked up the two leashes and took the dogs back to the lobby.

The malamutes were completely different in personality. The hyper one bounced with sociable energy. The older one eyed the lobby, radiating nerves along the leash back to him. He stroked her head and kneaded her neck. "It's okay, girl."

Casey was just returning from the staff hallway with Loretta.

"Ready?" he said.

She nodded. "Thanks, Loretta. Nice to meet you."

Loretta grunted, which was practically friendly for her.

"So, where can I drop you?" Aaron said, as he and Casey loaded the dogs.

"Um, maybe your wife's office to apply there?"

Aaron pursed his lips, thinking. He could drive by and see if Jenn's Grand Cherokee was at the office, then call her if so. "I haven't heard back from her. We'll swing by and see if she's available."

It was only a five-minute drive from his clinic to Kid's office, since it was Sheridan, Wyoming and not Houston, Texas. He cruised to a stop and peered at the upper story of the detached garage next to a gorgeous old house. "I don't think they're here. I've told her you want to apply though."

Casey had opened her door and gotten out. "Okay. Well, I can just walk downtown from here."

"Are you sure? I can drive you."

"You're pointed the wrong way."

It was true, but not a big problem.

Casey waved. "Thanks. Hope you don't have to give back the dogs."

He smiled. "Is it that obvious?"

She nodded and walked away down the sidewalk. Too late, Aaron realized he'd never asked her about the events at the ranch the day before. Whether she had seen anything or knew anything that might help Black Bear Betty.

He drove home to keep his next appointment, talking nonstop to the furry creatures behind him about his plans for them along the way.

CHAPTER SEVEN

Sheridan, Wyoming

Jenn's mind was so deeply wrapped up in the case as she and Kid walked from her Grand Cherokee up to his office that she didn't see the woman lurking beside the garage until they were already on the stairs.

"Jennifer Herrington?" the woman said.

Frowning, Jennifer turned, holding the rail. The old stairs were wooden and tended to sway. She didn't trust them. "Yes?"

The woman walked so quickly that one moment she was barely distinguishable in the trees and the next she was blocking the bottom of the staircase. Jennifer tried to place her. Tall. Blonde. Young. Dressed in jeans, a sweater, and a black puffy jacket. "We met yesterday. At the WP Bar Ranch. I'm Casey Hurd."

Jennifer relaxed a little. For a moment, she'd felt threatened. All joking with the guard at the jail aside, she suspected that in case of an altercation, she would be Kid's bodyguard, not the other way around. Aaron had texted her that Casey was job hunting so the visit wasn't totally unexpected. But then she remembered Casey had been at the ranch when Glen died. Now she was here the moment Jennifer and Kid took Betty's case. It was a little overly coincidental. But it was also a great opportunity to talk to the younger woman about what she had seen. *And my job is to find viable suspects. Maybe even the real killer, if it wasn't an accident.* She wasn't convinced about that last part yet.

"Oh, yes. Hello. Kid, this is Casey Hurd. She worked for Glen Trusk at WP Bar Ranch. Casey, this is my..."

"Colleague?" Kid suggested.

"Associate," Jennifer said, as much to tease him as anything, since in the law firm world senior lawyers often had partnerships in the firm and the junior attorneys who worked for them were called associates. "Wesley James. But everyone calls him Kid." She glanced at him. He looked weird. His face was pink. His eyes, glassy.

He stepped down and reached out his hand. "I'm Wesley. A pleasure to meet you, Casey."

Oh my gosh, he's smitten.

Casey didn't seem to notice. "Hello, Wesley. I was hoping I could apply for a job. I don't know many people in town."

Wesley stood up taller. Not that height was an issue for him. Body weight was his challenge. If anything, stretching out his frame made that more obvious. As did his recent hairstyle, which reminded her of Kramer from *Seinfeld*. "I'm born and raised here and would love to show you around town. I make a great ambassador and tour guide."

"You mean, like an interview?"

Kid's shoulders sagged.

Jennifer broke in. "How about an interview now, and you young people can decide about tours and such after. But it's a small office. Could you give us a moment, Casey? I'll come back out for you soon."

She crossed her arms. "Sure. I'm sorry. I just, like, showed up unannounced. I'm sure you're busy." Casey flashed a one hundred megawatt smile.

Something about her voice pinged Jennifer's brain. She was

pretty sure that accent was Tennessean. "No bother. In fact, I'm glad you're here."

Jennifer tugged on Kid's sleeve to break him free of the spell he'd fallen under. The two of them went into the office where Jennifer set her briefcase down on the desk. It had been a few months since she'd been in the office. It smelled like Kid needed to eat less macaroni and cheese and take the trash out more frequently.

He froze in the middle of the room in a daze.

She snapped her fingers in front of his nose. "Earth to Kid. Casey is one of our most important witnesses to talk to for Black Bear Betty's case. We need to nail this interview down with her before we tell her there is no chance in hell of her coming to work with us."

Kid blinked his eyes several times. "Who says that?"

"I don't have a law practice yet, Kid."

"But I do."

"Healthy enough to take on paid help?"

"I could crunch some numbers. Wait to move out of my mom's house for a little longer."

Oh, my God. How could he have it this bad this fast? "Fine. For now, follow my lead. We need to know what she knows. And then we need to get on the phone with Ollie Singletary and pick his brain apart." Ollie was the temporary County Attorney who Jennifer was considering running against, if she could just get her license. And convince Aaron that it wouldn't consume her and them like working as a Harris County ADA had. Who was she kidding? She hadn't ever practiced law in Wyoming. She needed to focus on whether to have a baby and try some cases here. Then, in four years, she could consider running.

"Okay."

"Do you need to splash some cold water on that flushed face of yours first?"

"What? No. I'm fine."

Jennifer laughed and went to the door. "Casey? Come on in whenever you're ready."

The statuesque blonde entered. *Wesley* dragged a chair over for her. He pulled it back for her like she was taking a seat at a fancy dinner. Casey looked confused, Kid look mortified, and Jennifer stifled a laugh as Casey sat.

The funniest part to Jennifer was that there were only three chairs in the one room office, which boasted a bathroom with an actual door that closed but no vent fan. Kid had given Casey the nicest chair—one Jennifer had purchased for herself, but she didn't mention it now. Kid took the rickety kitchen chair that usually held legal briefs, leaving his original "some assembly required" Walmart desk chair for Jennifer.

"Casey, before we talk about Kid's practice, we wanted to ask you some questions about yesterday," Jennifer said.

"Actually," Kid interrupted. "First I wanted to see if you'd like a beverage?" He flourished a hand at the mini fridge on top of which sat an electric tea kettle and a Keurig, both added in the gravy days since he and Jennifer had defended George.

Casey shook her head at him. "I'm fine. But why do you want to talk about that?"

Jennifer smiled. "We represent Black Bear Betty."

"Represent her? What do you mean?"

"She was arrested by the county regarding the death of Glen Trusk."

Casey jumped to her feet. "Do they think he was murdered?"

"We aren't sure. We'll find out more later."

Casey sank slowly back into her seat. Jennifer felt the metal of her own chair under the meager cushion and wished they could switch.

"You're surprised?"

"It's just the first I've heard of it."

"Tell me about your experience yesterday. Where were you after you left the stables?"

"I went up to the house to use the bathroom."

"Because the one in the stable is out of order."

"Yeah. Black Bear Betty and Will were up there. I was kinda upset. Venting. Will and I went off to talk. Because, um, he'd been fired that day."

"By Glen."

"Yeah. Although it was Charity who found him sleeping in a horse stall and went apeshit."

"You and Will are friends."

"Yeah. I guess sorta."

"Go on."

"We talked, then I told him I needed to go. You know. To the bathroom. After I went, he was gone. Then I had to figure out what to do. I've been bunking in the tack room in the stable on workdays. Then I just have to find a ride up there at the beginning and end of the week. I don't have a car. So, I couldn't go to my room, and I couldn't leave the ranch. I was afraid I'd be in trouble if I stayed up at the house."

"Was Black Bear Betty there?"

"I think so. I heard somebody in the kitchen. I'm not sure."

"What did you do?"

She covered her face with her hands. "I went into Glen and Charity's bedroom and stole a joint. Then I went on their back porch and smoked it."

"Anything else?"

"No. Not until I heard the cops come in talking to you and Aaron. Then I went down to the stables."

"Did the police talk to you?"

"Yeah."

"Did you tell them this?"

"Most of it."

Jennifer cut her eyes at Kid. He was rapt, like Casey was speaking in iambic pentameter wearing a long, lace dress with daisies entwined in a coronet of braids. "Do you know how to get hold of Will?"

"Um, he has a cell number." She pulled it up on her phone and gave it to them. "I think he was going to stay in town with a friend. But I don't know for sure. He needs a job, like me."

"Thanks, Casey. Anything else? Like someone you think might have hurt Glen?"

She snorted. "Charity's boyfriend, maybe."

Bingo. Jennifer had known the cowboy and Charity were too touchy-feely. "What's his name?"

"Boot Taylor. Come to think of it, he had his boots on when I walked in on them going at it in the stable. Maybe that's how he got his name."

Kid had been drinking a bottle of Diet Coke. He made a strangled noise and struggled not to spit it out.

"That's why I'm job hunting. She fired me for invading her privacy."

Jennifer bit her lip. "Is Boot from around here?"

"No. Charity brought him from LA. He's her reining coach." Casey rolled her eyes.

"You don't happen to know how to reach him, do you?"

"I'd check Charity's panties."

This time Kid couldn't hold it in. Diet Coke sprayed out on Jenifer and Casey. Casey squealed with laughter. Jennifer wiped it off her face.

"Oh, my God. I'm sorry. I'm so sorry." Kid grabbed a roll of paper towels from the kitchen corner. He started mopping at Casey's face, hair, and arms.

She held out her hand. "I've got it. It's fine."

Kid tore off half the roll and handed it to her.

Jennifer raised her hand. "Um, Kid? Over here?"

His eyes widened. "Sorry, boss." He handed her the rest of the roll.

Jenn tried not to be too irritated at Kid. If she was honest she had to admit she liked Casey's witty boldness. Her glib comment sounded like something Aaron would say. "All right. If everyone's dried out enough to talk, we can discuss jobs."

Kid blurted, "How many hours do you need?"

"I need to make $1500 a month or I have to move home with my mom."

"Out of Sheridan?"

"Out of state."

"No problem. When can you start?"

Jennifer held a hand in front of him, like she was protecting him from crashing into the dashboard in a car wreck. "Kid, what will you have her doing? Do you want to know her experience or background first?"

Casey was smiling ear to ear. "I worked in a lawyer's office in high school. My mom was a secretary there."

Kid shot Jennifer a smug smile. "Overqualified."

"And I can start right now!"

"Perfect." He nodded eagerly.

"What do you want me to do first?"

Jennifer gathered up paper towels and held them out to her. "How about clean up after *Wesley* while he and I work out a plan on our new case. It's a small office and you've got to be a self-starter here, so just figure out ways to stay useful until we have more for you."

Casey made wide, mocking eyes at Kid, that she possibly thought Jennifer couldn't see. Kid guffawed like a teenage boy. Jennifer squeezed her hands into fists. What had Kid just done hiring this girl?

A text came in on Jennifer's phone. It was a reply from Chaplain Abel. *I'd be happy to see how I can help. How about tomorrow at nine a.m.?* He included an address in town.

She responded quickly. After Betty's imprisonment and Kid's impulse hire, her stress load wasn't getting any lighter. *Thank you. See you then.*

Then she looked back up at the other attorney. "Kid? Can we call Ollie now?" For a brief moment, it occurred to her that two of the witnesses in chief were involved now in Betty's defense—herself and Casey—but she pushed the thought aside. It was a small town. Casey was part of Betty's alibi. It was going to be fine. And if a conflict arose, well, the best interests of the client would come first.

"Who's Ollie?" Casey asked.

Jennifer ignored her and pressed the phone number for the County Attorney's office, which she'd saved in her Favorites during George's case. She mimed taking notes to Kid, claimed her own chair, and pulled it up to his desk. He took a seat and grabbed his pen and notebook, lovestruck eyes darting every few seconds to Casey scurrying around the office.

"County Attorney's Office," a woman said, sounding like she'd been woken from a nap and wasn't happy about it.

"Jennifer Herrington and Kid, um, *Wesley* James for Ollie Singletary. We represent Black Bear Betty." Jennifer flinched as soon as the name left her mouth. She had no idea of her friend's real name.

The woman perked up. "Do you mean Elizabeth Jurgenson? That's the only name we have anything like Betty-whatever-you-said."

"Maybe? She was arrested in conjunction with the death of Glen Trusk."

A snort exploded through the speaker. "She's your client but you don't know her name?"

"I know the name she goes by, and I know she hired us. We met with her an hour ago. Now, can I speak to Ollie please?"

"One moment."

Jennifer rolled her eyes at Kid, but he was casting moony glances at his new employee.

"Jenn? Wesley? This is Ollie. How are you?" The baritone voice conveyed confidence. If Jennifer ran against him, it would be a tough race. He was someone she'd normally vote for. Smart, competent, and —as a newcomer from the southern part of the state—without discernible local bias. But he was too cautious. Too quick to push a plea for lesser charges. No eye of the tiger. Some cases needed to be tried, for legal precedent, and to keep the system calibrated and robust.

Jennifer put a smile into her voice. "Confused as to why our client is in jail. What's going on here? I thought Glen Trusk's death was an accident. I mean, have you driven that road in the last twenty-four hours?"

"I was up there earlier today. It's not for the faint of heart, but Ms. Jurgenson's tractor tire tracks lead to where Mr. Trusk's truck left the ledge, plus there was Kubota orange paint on the back of the truck."

"If you can really call it a truck. An $80,000 EV is mostly a status symbol, don't you think?"

"I don't know how to answer that."

"As a Wyomingite. But we have a statement that the paint on the truck came from an incident a few days previously. And we have a witness." Or they would, when they could locate Will.

"Do you have another question?"

Jennifer rolled her shoulders. "Do you have a witness that my client was operating the tractor at the time of Trusk's accident?"

"Not yet. But I have her fingerprints on the steering wheel—"

"That she could have left at any time."

"—and her beef with Trusk."

He had nothing but circumstantial evidence. Flimsy. If she'd been in his role, she'd be looking for something meatier before filing charges. "When will you know if you're moving forward against her?"

"I already do. We are. Arraignment will be tomorrow."

She made wide eyes at Kid. It was a waste of effort. His attention was fractured. "Come on, Ollie. You can't prove murder. You can't prove the tractor came into contact with the truck at the time of the accident. You can't prove my client was at the scene at all. You don't even know for sure whether Trusk simply had a heart attack or stroke or an episode of bad driving that sent him off that cliff."

"The State has every confidence in the case against Ms. Jurgenson."

"What can I do to slow this down while the evidence develops?"

"You can talk to your client about a plea bargain. I'm willing to go down to fifteen years and reduce this to second-degree—"

She just thought she'd been dumbfounded at the quick charges. First degree was a travesty. She managed not to shout, but her voice could have julienned a bushel of carrots. "From *what*? First degree requires premeditated malice—"

"I think we can prove that, given that she told you and your husband she was going to kill him."

"Excuse me? That is *not* what she told us. You won't be proving premeditated malice with my statement or Aaron's. And you'll never prove Black Bear Betty did anything to Trusk in the course of committing another serious felony like sexual assault or burglary. Arson. Escape. Kidnapping. You don't have first-degree."

"Like I said, we'll entertain a plea."

She slammed her hand down on the table. Kid jumped, and Casey gasped. "My hind foot will I advise a client to plead to second-degree in these circumstances, even if you otherwise have a slam dunk case I wouldn't do it. Which you don't. You've got to do better."

"Give me overnight to think about it."

"An innocent woman is sitting in jail. This is harming her business, her livelihood, and her reputation."

"Those are harms consistent with committing a murder."

"Inconsistent with speedy prosecution while you sleep on whether to strong arm my client into an inflated plea with a ridiculous charge."

His voice grew testy for the first time. "I said I'd think about it."

Kid's eyes were like saucers. Jennifer realized that Casey was only making it look like she was working. One hundred percent she was standing like a statue, hanging on every word.

"You shouldn't have to." Jennifer ended the call and dropped the phone on the desk like it was radioactive.

"Whoa," Casey said. "That was intense."

Kid beamed. "We take no prisoners. Especially when our clients are imprisoned."

Jennifer sat dazed for a moment. How had things gone so incredibly against Betty's interests that Ollie was trying to use Aaron and Jennifer to sock her with a first-degree murder charge? The County Attorney was a skilled adversary.

She'd just have to be an even better one to keep her friend from being railroaded.

CHAPTER EIGHT

Sheridan, Wyoming

Jennifer brushed the thighs of her jeans. The armchair in Chaplain Dean Abel's home office was comfortable, but her nerves were on fire. The case wasn't the source of her stress. Per an email that morning from Casey, they had a day's reprieve on Betty's case pending a preliminary hearing before Judge Peters the next day.

No, her tension was around what loomed next—opening up to Abel. In the first fifteen minutes, they'd danced around the edges of her recurrent nightmares. She knew he was going to press her harder, and she dreaded it.

Abel rolled a pen between knobby fingers. "You've told me about many challenges in your life. Studying for the bar exam. Moving to Wyoming. Adapting to the weather and culture here. The work being done on your home. Leaving your position as a high-profile prosecutor. The new case against your friend. Your worries about whether to get pregnant and whether you can. And suddenly, two dogs have entered your life." He was sitting in a rolling chair to the side of his desk. Jennifer had expected him to be older, but he looked mid-fifties to her.

Younger than her parents. He had a full head of brown hair woven with wiry gray. Wire glasses perched cattywampus on a crooked nose.

She laughed, remembering meeting the dogs the night before. They were beautiful. Sweet. Funny. Loud. "The dogs may not stick. But they're fun while we have them."

She and Aaron had decided they had to call them something other than Dog One and Dog Two. They'd dubbed the younger one Willett and the older Sibley, both after lakes in the Bighorns, although she knew her cousin Hank would insist they'd named one after him.

Jennifer and Sibley had hit it off especially well. Something about the dog's yellow-brown eyes had bored directly into Jennifer's soul. Like they had something secret and bone deep in common. Petting her thick, silky fur had been oddly calming.

Willett had taken a shine to Aaron. Since both animals were house trained, they'd let them sleep in the bedroom, but Aaron had promised to get crates for the next night. When his alarm had gone off that morning, Willett had hopped onto the bed and laid her head on Aaron's shoulder, eye-to-eye with Jennifer who had her head on the other one. It was endearing. And Aaron had been wanting a dog so badly. Especially a snow dog, now that they lived in a cold climate. Jennifer wouldn't object to keeping them, she realized.

She'd found a note from Aaron on the refrigerator that morning. *I love you more than Alaskan malamutes.* Funny that a note about snow dogs could flood her with heat.

Am I just wanting him to get two dogs to replace having a baby? She didn't think so, but she couldn't reject the thought outright. It was something to let germinate.

"I think it's time you tell me about your nightmares." Abel crossed his chino-clad legs. He smiled and nodded at her. A nice smile.

She took a deep breath. They were fresh in her mind from her sleepless night. "When I was four, my family was visiting my aunt and uncle and cousins here in Wyoming. My mom was picking up my cousin Hank from the elementary school in Story for my Aunt Vangie. He was out on the playground. She let me run out to meet him. Just as I got to him, a man opened fire on us kids."

He nodded, his face placid but eyes warm and empathetic. "That must have been terrifying. Were you and your cousin okay?"

"He shielded me with his body. He was shot but recovered. Two other kids died."

"I remember this. They never caught the shooter."

"Correct. And I repressed the memory, completely, until we moved here last fall. Then I started having these weird nightmares. Grass in my face, kids screaming, the sound of rapid gunfire. I didn't know it was real until my cousin mentioned the event casually, assuming I knew about it."

"That's not uncommon. Your mind was protecting you from the trauma. But the dreams continued."

Jennifer clasped her hands together to keep them from shaking. "They became worse. More vivid. More detailed. I kept seeing a snake coiled up in rocks with a D-T-O-M below it. Then I realized it was a tattoo. In a weird twist of fate, a man with that exact tattoo attacked George Nichols, who we bought our property from. I was there and saw him. Saw it. The tattoo. In the same place as on the man in my dreams. And I began to wonder if the dreams of the tattoo are actually a memory."

"Do you think it is?"

She nodded slowly. "Yes. I feel certain it is. That I saw the shooter and his tattoo."

"Do you think the shooter was this man who attacked your friend?"

"Pootie Carputin is his name. He's now a convicted murderer and in the state penitentiary in Rawlins. I do believe it was him. I researched his background pretty thoroughly, and, while I can't prove it, there's plenty of circumstantial evidence. Enough to warrant an investigation. Only I can't interest any law enforcement or the Sheridan or Johnson county attorneys to take it on."

He rolled the pen in his fingers again. It was a mesmerizing habit. "How would you describe your feelings about that?"

She focused her gaze on the rolling pen. "Frustrated. Tormented. Angry. A child killer was never caught. I'm a witness. I've given all the information I have to the police. Information I repressed in my childhood. I should have remembered then so they could solve the case. Now, I'm helpless, dead in the water." She tore at a cuticle then forced her hands into her lap. "I'm very justice driven, Chaplain Abel. It's why I became a prosecutor. Even now that I'm doing defense work, justice matters to me."

"You did your part as soon as you had information. You can't take responsibility for everyone else's jobs."

The pen kept rolling. "Logically, I know that. Emotionally, it's hard."

"And it keeps you up at night."

"Nearly every night." She splayed her hands on her knees then gripped them, finally looking up at him instead of the writing implement in his fingers.

He put the pen on his desk. "We should meet regularly to work through this. Try to banish it from the forefront of your consciousness. But I really recommend that in the meantime you try to optimize the possibility of quality sleep." Abel talked her through sleep strategies. Not eating or drinking alcohol in the two hours before bedtime. Establishing a wind-down routine in the evenings that included no screens. Soothing teas. Setting and adhering to a wake up and bedtime. Not drinking coffee except between nine am and one pm. "I have a good pamphlet and an article on the topic."

Most of his suggestions she'd already tried, but she would implement the rest. "Thank you."

"As for your memories, let's—"

Her phone rang. She'd silenced all notifications except from Kid. She'd told him she'd be indisposed that morning and to call only for emergencies. "I'm sorry. My murder case. It must be important for my co-counsel to interrupt me."

"I understand."

"Hello?" She answered in a quiet voice.

"Where are you?" Kid sounded like a man on a ledge contemplating jumping.

"Doctor's appointment. What's the matter?"

"The preliminary hearing starts in twenty minutes."

She leapt to her feet. "What? Casey told me they were holding off until tomorrow."

"I think you misread her email. It's today at eleven. And if Black Bear Betty is bound over, she'll be sent straight to Judge Ryan's court for arraignment."

Jennifer knew the procedure, but she was sure about the content of the email from Casey. She didn't have time to argue or prove her case, though. She had to get to court. "I'll be there. Stall the judge. Try not to start without me."

"Got it. You'll run the show. Thanks."

Jennifer stuffed her phone in her handbag and shook her head. "Scheduling mix-up. My client has a preliminary hearing in twenty minutes. I have to get to court."

"Texting works well. Reach out when you're ready to get together again."

She nodded, already at the door. "I will. And let me know what I owe you."

"First one's on the house."

"Thanks!" She bolted straight out the door and into the driveway.

Before she could back her SUV out, another call came in on silent. Assuming it was Casey for Kid, she accepted, only to see too late it was her friend Alayah in Houston. She activated the speaker. "Hey. I'm driving. Rushing to court."

"What? I thought you'd taken time off to study for the bar exam."

"I did, too. Long story."

"Which I'll enjoy hearing about later. One quick thing."

"I have five minutes, and they're all yours." She could do a preliminary hearing in her sleep, just as long as she made it there on time.

"Jace has asked me to move in with him."

"Whoa. Your Texas Ranger?" Alayah had a type. A bad type. Dating someone in law enforcement was totally out of character for her.

"Yes."

"And are you going to?"

"Maybe?"

Jennifer laughed. "He's a good guy, right?"

"The best. And so hot."

"Follow your heart."

"My heart is an idiot."

"It has made some poor choices before, I'll grant you that. I think you're fine to move in, but if you have doubts, well, don't wreck his heart."

"I can't break my lease."

"That will buy you some time."

"Yes. A little time will help."

The courthouse loomed. Jennifer whipped into the parking lot. "I've gotta go. Update me later. Love you."

"Love you, too. Give 'em hell."

Jennifer ended the call and ran across the icy parking lot and sidewalks with her arms outstretched for extra balance, teeth chattering. She was wearing rubber soled ankle-high fur-lined booties with a pantsuit. Not the footwear she would normally choose for a court appearance, but much better to run in than pumps. She made it into the warmth and dry floors of the county building without falling. She ran faster until she burst through the doors to the circuit court at ten fifty-nine, out of breath and with a wildly beating heart.

Every head in the room turned to look at her.

CHAPTER NINE

Sheridan, Wyoming

Jennifer slowed to a walk and smoothed her jacket as she strode to the defense table, trying to look like she hadn't just run further than she had in a year.

"Elizabeth Jurgenson?" Judge Peters' bailiff called out.

Black Bear Betty raised her hand and shouted. "Here!"

Jennifer stepped behind the table, shooting Betty a quick smile. To Kid, she made wide eyes. Then she faced the judge's stand and its occupant.

Judge Peters' intense black eyes were amused, her long curly gray hair framing her entire head. "I note your presence, Ms. Jurgenson. But it's customary for your attorney to speak on your behalf in court. Unless you're representing yourself?"

"I ain't."

Kid stood and executed a courtly bow at the waist. "Wesley James for Elizabeth Jurgenson, Your Honor."

"I see you've brought Big City back with you today. Although without her little friend this time, I hope."

Jennifer winced. Under dire circumstances, she'd brought Jeremiah Johnson to court in his carrier, whereupon he'd outed her with happy chirps. It hadn't been the best first impression with the judge. "Jennifer Herrington. Yes, your honor. No animals with me today."

"Ms. Herrington, are you testing in a few weeks?"

"Yes, Your Honor."

"I wish you the best of luck, then. I'll be pleased to hear you speak for yourself in here, although I expect Kid is worrying he'll be out of a job."

"Wesley is a fine young attorney. I'm happy to take a backseat to him anytime."

"High praise, young attorney James."

He blushed crimson, matching what looked to be a new bowtie.

"Is the State ready?"

Ollie Singletary was already standing. He was tall, good looking, and undeniably black. The first and only non-Caucasian attorney to practice on either side of the docket in Sheridan County, although with the influx of diverse out-of-staters to the area, that status of "only" would change soon. His first lieutenant Jana Stephens stood erect beside him. She took good posture up to the power of ten. "Ollie Singletary and Jana Stephens for the State, if it pleases the court."

"It does indeed. A lot of firepower this morning, Counsel."

"Thankfully, we don't prosecute many first-degree murder charges here."

"Well, we shall see if you'll be prosecuting this one, then. That's the charge then, first-degree murder?"

"Correct."

"Attorney James, I suspect you have something to say about that?"

Kid straightened the shiny new bowtie and cleared his throat. "Notwithstanding we will prove our client is innocent if this case goes to trial, of course—"

Judge Peters' voice was wry. "Of course."

"This is a case of gross overcharging."

She cocked one eyebrow. *Is she related to my husband?* The devastating one eyebrow lift was Aaron's signature move. It still did Jennifer in every time. "Attorney Singletary?"

"The State is confident in the charge. We'll be proving beyond a reasonable doubt that Elizabeth Jurgenson with malice and premeditation murdered Glen Trusk. The evidence will show that with means, motive, and opportunity she intentionally caused his vehicle to drive off a cliff with the intent of killing him, and that the fall did in fact result in his death."

"That sounds like something you practiced in front of a mirror before you came in today."

Ollie's mouth opened and closed like a guppy out of its bowl.

Before he could respond, she turned back to Kid. "Your grounds for disagreement?"

"The defense is reaching. They have no evidence of premeditation. Ms. Jurgenson was on the property at their invitation, performing work she'd been contracted to perform. If all the other so-called facts they'll present are taken as true—which they aren't—they still won't be able to show anything other than an opportunistic crime. Mr. Trusk had learned from a neighbor that his dogs were loose. He left without any prior planning or notice to go after them. Ms. Jurgenson would've had no way to know he'd be driving along the road at that time."

"Hmm. You make a good point. But I'm inclined to give our Prosecuting Attorney some latitude to make his case. It's early going. And, of course, if appropriate a jury could be given the opportunity to convict on lesser included offenses, such as second-degree murder or manslaughter. Plus, Mr. Singletary could always lower the charge."

Jennifer clenched her hands together, nails digging into palms. *That will never happen.*

Kid was prepared. "Not until after Ms. Jurgenson's good name is sullied in her community, a community in which she is trusted to come onto people's property and into their homes to perform work. This will do irreparable harm to her business reputation. It's our position that the State should only charge Ms. Jurgenson with one of the lesser included offenses now, if anything. They can always re-charge her later if they find direct evidence to support first-degree. Right now, they have nothing."

Judge Peters shook her head. "First, second, and manslaughter."

Kid held up a hand. "And criminally negligent homicide and vehicular homicide."

Ollie jumped to his feet. "Wait a second. We have witness testimony that Ms. Jurgenson wanted to kill Mr. Trusk."

Judge Peters said, "I'll allow all lesser included offenses. Prove your case, Mr. Singletary, or take the charge that fits the evidence proffered."

Ollie's polite mask was slipping to reveal a very angry face. He didn't like the bottom rung charges being included. Juries sometimes solved holdouts by choosing the lesser degrees. He looked down, swallowed, and lifted a face that was determined but pleasant again, like the other one had never revealed itself.

"Okay, based on the felony information, I have everything in order to bind this matter over for trial in district court." She nodded at Betty. "Now it's your turn to talk, Ms. Jurgenson."

Betty rose, which didn't change her height by much. "Well, I don't like any of this one durn bit."

"That's not the topic we are here to discuss. Actually, I just need to explain a few things to you now." Judge Peters laid out the charge and Betty's constitutional rights. "You have the right to the assistance of counsel. If you can't afford a lawyer, the state will appoint one for you." She turned to her bailiff. "How'd I do?"

"Word perfect as always, ma'am." He grinned.

To Betty she said, "Are you satisfied with your counsel, or do you need the court to appoint new counsel for you?"

Betty lifted her shoulders and rose slightly on her toes. "Got the best 'uns around. Don't want none other."

"Excellent to hear. You may be seated."

"We ain't gonna talk about this tragedy of justice being permeated against me?"

Jennifer would have laughed at the malapropisms if the topic wasn't so serious. Betty and big words weren't a great match.

"That's what trial is for and will be the job of your attorneys.. And, as you said, you have the best 'uns."

Sometimes Judge Peters enjoys her job just a little too much.

Grumbling, Betty sat down.

"In the matter of bond," Judge Peters said, with a burst of sudden energy. Even more energy. The woman must be taking awfully good vitamins. "The court hereby sets it at four hundred thousand dollars, cash only. Will you be posting it today, Ms. Jurgenson?"

"If I had four hunnerd thousand, I wouldn't'a been working for the likes of that basspole Glen Trusk."

The judge's eyebrows shot to her hairline. "Basspole. Well, I learn something new every day. I'll take that as a no. Is there anyone who might post on your behalf?"

Betty glowered. "Ain't no Mr. or Ms. Moneybags in my life."

"Sadly, there's none in mine either Ms. Jurgenson. All right, bond will not be posted. Your next stop will be District Court. Bailiff, please take Ms. Jurgenson into your custody and see that she is delivered there forthwith. Everyone give Judge Ryan my best." She banged her gavel, and Jennifer and Kid whispered their goodbyes to Betty.

"What the devil we gotta do in another court?" Betty said.

Jennifer kept her voice low. "Plead not guilty and get a trial date."

"Why couldn't we do that here?"

"Different functions for different courts under the state rules. Trust me, there's no real explanation."

The bailiff said, "Time to go, ma'am. Judge Ryan will be waiting on you all."

Betty's protests were voluble as he escorted her out.

Jennifer turned away from the judge's bench and walked with

Kid into the gallery. She hadn't taken two steps before Casey was blocking her path.

Casey's arms were crossed over her chest. "Wesley said you accused me of giving you bad information. But I copied him on the same email you got, and he didn't mess it up."

It was far from the reaction Jennifer would have expected. At worst, the same words in a nice tone, at best a well-deserved apology. "Excuse me?"

"I work for Wesley. I don't appreciate you running me down behind my back to him."

Kid stood between them, an extended arm keeping each woman at bay. "I didn't say she ran you down, Casey. I said she thought you told her the preliminary hearing was tomorrow."

Jennifer drilled her eyes into the younger woman. Then she turned to Kid. "That's not how we speak to each other. Please make sure it doesn't happen with your employee again."

For a second, she toyed with the idea of pulling up the email and shoving it in Casey's face. But she couldn't compromise her reputation with a public tantrum. So, she stalked out before she showed Casey just how deserved the reputation for toughness of former ADA Jennifer Herrington was, wondering why the young woman was so aggressively defensive... and downright rude.

CHAPTER TEN

Big Horn, Wyoming

Aaron and Jenn walked out of their kitchen, her carrying a large bowl of fettuccine alfredo with broccoli and mushrooms, and him holding a plate with three New York strip steaks aloft in one hand and balancing a salad bowl in his other. They set the food on the cozy kitchen table. A fire crackled merrily in the potbellied stove in one corner. Snow had been falling outside for the last half hour. A weather station panel on the sideboard reported a temperature of ten degrees below zero, wind chill twenty below. *Cozy.* Or, as Jenn's Danish mother sometimes said, *hygge.* The whole Tennessee Sibley clan had joined them for a white Christmas the previous month, including Jenn's twin brother Justin, his wife, and their six kids. The word *hygge* had been uttered frequently. The word that had never been uttered was *peaceful.* The lodge shook to its rafters with running feet, laughter, and slamming doors as kids went in and out every five minutes. *Who needs peace when you have joy and hygge?* To Aaron, it had been a perfect holiday.

"Time to eat," Jennifer said.

Her cousin Hank Sibley was on his knees in the living room, wrestling with the two malamutes. Liam the St. Bernard was snoring by the fire. "Gotta take a break, you crazy mutts."

Maggie was sipping KO 90 in hot spiced tea, watching from a few feet away. "I can't believe you haven't broken something. Those dogs are wrecking balls."

"Are you going to keep them?" Hank asked Aaron.

Aaron shot Jenn a questioning look and she smiled at him. Earlier he'd heard from several commenters on Facebook that a couple from Alabama had moved back south a few days before, after the unseasonably heavy start to winter. They had two female malamutes. A little sleuthing yielded pictures posted to the woman's Instagram account. Undoubtedly, these were the same two dogs. Aaron fought the urge to blister them in their DMs for leaving the dogs behind, but he didn't know if they'd been the ones to tie them up on his porch. He'd opted instead to ask them for permission to keep the dogs. It had been eagerly given.

Jenn said, "We are now the proud parents of a very small sled dog team."

Aaron put an arm around her and squeezed. "The boss has spoken."

"The sledding part has me in a conundrum. I'm worried about hungry bears in the mountains in the winter. Because I don't run faster than Aaron or dogs."

"You're snack-size," Maggie said in her drawl.

Jenn nodded. "I practiced using bear spray earlier with one of George's expired canisters. I plan to be carrying one on each hip."

"Hopefully they'll be hibernating." Hank untangled himself from the fluffy black and white dogs, who gave him looks that defined *hang dog*. Completely bereft.

Hank moved to stand beside Maggie, a hair taller than her—very tall for a champion bull rider. Those days were in his past, now, and he and his partner Gene raised bucking horses and bulls at the ranch he and his sister Laura had inherited after the passing of their parents. Recently, Maggie had bought Laura's half of the ranch. In cash. *Must be nice to be a successful musician.* Maggie's collaboration with pop star Ava Butler was playing everywhere, all the time, and had rejuvenated interest in and sales of her old music.

The four of them took a seat and passed around the food, talking about the dogs, the wild fox Aaron was nursing back to health, the rodeo rough stock business, and Maggie's reluctant cooperation on a documentary about her, in conjunction with her opening for Ava on her tour starting that spring.

Maggie changed the subject. "But what I want to hear about is Black Bear Betty, straight from her lawyer," she said to Jenn.

Jenn twirled fettuccine on her fork. "There's not much to tell. She pleaded not guilty. We're really just getting started."

Maggie took hers and Jenn's mugs into the kitchen, where she topped off their drinks. "I hate to say it, but I could see her offing someone who crossed her."

Hank stabbed the fat Maggie had sliced off her steak and put it on his plate. "Trusk may not have been here long, but he'd already built up quite a reputation. No one has a nice thing to say about him." He added a sliver of fat to a bite of steak.

"I only met him once. He was pretty disagreeable," Jenn said. "Who have you heard has a beef with him?"

Hank didn't hesitate. "Peanut Hassenfratz."

"Who?"

"A rancher who lives downstream on the same ditch as the WP Bar. Peanut said that last summer, right after the closing on the place, Trusk was diverting water from the ditch out of turn. Peanut was trying to irrigate for his second alfalfa cutting. It ruined his yield."

Aaron and Jenn had water rights on the ditch that ran alongside their property. Ditch rights determined the priority order in which landowners received water from the mountain streams and reservoirs. The Herringtons were pretty far down on the list, but it was enough for their place. They'd quickly come to understand the value of water rights in a land of water scarcity. Properties were normally conveyed with their existing rights, although rights holders could also transfer them separately. The ditches were key to people's livelihoods and to the survival of their livestock. A water laws violation constituted a misdemeanor punishable by over twelve hundred dollars a day after notice from the state. The bigger penalty was in the bad will of neighbors, though. In rural Wyoming, official help was a long time coming in emergencies, and neighbors relied on each other. Until they didn't.

Or until blood ran so bad that the neighbors became the emergency? Wyoming history was rife with violence over water rights.

"How did he know it was Trusk?" she asked.

"Everyone else upstream on the ditch was a long-time member of their ditch association. Peanut talked to each of them. No one pulled water out of turn. So, he went to Trusk about it. Trusk told him he bought water with his place and ordered him off his property."

"Maybe he didn't understand his rights."

"Peanut said he acted more like he didn't give a damn. When Peanut told him the penalty, Trusk supposedly said, 'I spend more than that every time my wife refreshes her Botox and Juvéderm.'"

Jenn pushed her hair off her face, sighing. "Sounds like him."

Aaron held the pasta bowl up. "Seconds anyone?" Hank nodded, so Aaron said, "Tell me when," and began spooning. When Hank held his hand up in the stop gesture, Aaron switched to filling his own plate, piling twice as much on it. "From a husband's point of view, it seems like the main difference—besides the philosophical ones—between prosecution and defense is that as a prosecutor, the cops are your investigators, and you have one suspect by the time you have the case. But with defense, you are one woman looking everywhere at everything and everybody.'

"That about sums it up. And everywhere is a very big place in Wyoming."

Maggie pushed her plate back a few inches. She'd eaten less than Jenn and had stopped after her second drink. It was unusual for her, but she'd mentioned earlier that she was nervous about appearing in front of crowds and cameras again. The woman was already willowy.

Aaron hoped her musical resurgence was a positive thing. "Don't you have Kid James on your team?" Maggie said.

"Yes. And he's great when he's not in puppy love."

"What's this?" Aaron paused with his fork in midair.

"You sent Casey over, looking for a job."

"Who's Casey?" Maggie asked.

"A young twenties, tall blonde with blue eyes and tight jeans."

"Ah."

"It was love at first sight. One-sided, anyway."

"He hired her?"

"Yes. And he's making work for her and giving her most of his take home pay."

Aaron laughed, picturing baby-faced Kid and the tough young woman. "She's gonna eat him alive."

"But she's extra help, too, right?" Hank said.

Jenn frowned. "Hard to say." She told them about what had happened earlier that day.

Hank tsked. "This next generation was raised differently than us."

Aaron swallowed the last bite of alfredo. "I hope it wasn't a mistake sending her to you."

Jenn pulled her phone out of the back pocket of her jeans. "I keep thinking about that email from her, too. I'm sure she said the preliminary hearing would be Friday." She scrolled, read, then shook her head. "Weird."

"What is it?"

"I have an email from her to Kid and me. It sounds completely different than what I remember. But it's the only one in my inbox." She shrugged and put her phone away. "Oh, well. I was distracted. I must be misremembering."

Hank grinned. "Or you accidentally deleted the first one. I'm told I do that with Maggie's messages all the time."

Maggie rolled her eyes. "And he always accuses me of nefarious technological trickery. Like I've got those skills." In an exaggerated drawl, she spoke directly to Hank. "Honey, it's just operator error."

Aaron looked at Jenn. Hank and he both struggled with the impact of too many head injuries from their former professions. It was the reason Aaron had to quit professional football after less than one full season in the NFL. Hank had stuck out bull riding. As a result, both were regulars with their neurologists and followed traumatic brain injury protocols. But not Jenn. She was the epitome of on the ball. If she said it happened, it usually did, even if he didn't want to admit it.

Jenn made a show of brushing her hands against each other. "Over and done with. Black Bear Betty has been arraigned. Time to look everywhere into everything and everybody, with my team. Such that it is."

CHAPTER ELEVEN

Big Horn, Wyoming

Jennifer woke with a pounding head, the inevitable result of nights with Maggie and Hank. Maggie poured with a heavy hand, and last night she'd kept everyone else's drinks topped off and skipped her own glass, claiming she was the designated driver. Jennifer groaned as she stood.

"Water," she croaked.

When there was no answer, she flopped over under the heavy duvet. Aaron wasn't there. She put her hand on the flannel sheets where he'd slept. Cold. She checked the time on her phone. Seven-thirty. Maybe he had an early appointment? She couldn't remember if he was seeing patients there or at his clinic in town.

A paper fluttered to the floor from her bedside table. She rubbed her eyes then picked it up and shone her phone light on it. *I love you on snowy mornings.*

Sweet Aaron. Jenn felt a little guilty. She'd crashed after their guests left. No conversation. No progress on baby making, and, if her female cycle was functioning as expected, last night was a missed opportunity. Or a dodged bullet? *Why am I still so all over the place?*

She slipped from the warm bed into the crisp air of the bedroom and walked to the window. She tied back the blackout curtains, letting in blinding light. The weather forecast had been correct about the storm, although the sky was clear now. It was a pristine snowscape. So white that she needed to wait for the plows to finish before leaving for town.

Movement and noise outside drew her attention. Two black and white bullets were doing zoomies behind the house. She had a vague memory of both of them leaping onto the bed for a snuggle in the night. Maybe they should rethink sleeping arrangements? Crates, possibly? Aaron was backing out of the barn on their big Kubota tractor with its hydraulic plow and industrial sized snow blower. Mystery of his whereabouts solved.

A squeak announced Jeremiah Johnson's presence. She cooed to the little skunk and scooped him into a quick cuddle. He was cold and wet. Liam was lying on his thick orthopedic bed in the corner, snow melting on his thumping tail. Aaron had already let them out, too.

Setting Jeremiah into bunched up covers, she flipped Aaron's note over and wrote on the back. *I love you on a tractor.* She anchored it on his bedside table with his water glass from the night before. Then she texted Kid. *Zoom at 8? Snow on the mountain. Need a plan.*

Immediately three dots showed Kid composing a reply. A loud engine joined the tractor noise. *George.* He commuted from a restored cabin that was at a higher elevation on their property, most mornings in an ORV or his truck, but she thought this noise sounded more like his snowmobile. Even with only one arm, he handled it far better than she could with two, thanks to a long history of snowmobile racing and backcountry riding.

Kid was still typing, so she took five minutes in the bathroom and returned with a fresh face and teeth.

A "hello" from the front of the house announced George's arrival.

She shouted "hello" and then read Kid's reply. *Emailed you a draft plan. I'll send Zoom link next. This is why living across the driveway from where you work is a good deal.*

Jennifer sent back a smiley face and thumbs up. The tractor rumbled in the distance, somewhere on their driveway in front of the lodge. She imagined the dogs were with Aaron, enjoying the snow blower. She dressed hurriedly, grabbed her laptop, and tromped across the snowy yard to the cottage behind their lodge. It doubled as her home office and writing studio. She took a moment to appreciate that Aaron had shoveled her porch, then went inside. The cottage was so cold she could see her breath. Most of her personal energy had gone into decorating, not insulating. Unlike the spartan office without much more than professional photos and degrees, here she'd imbued her personality, although she'd had to dig deep to resurrect it. She'd started with family photos and moved on to coordinating fabrics in hot pink, white, and black. Throw pillows. Candles. A zebra print blanket. Some inspirational quotes and sayings she loved. When it was done, she'd realized it matched the way she dressed. Aaron called it chaotic, but it made her buzzy with contentment.

She raised the thermostat and built a fire. By the time she had her space livable, it was ten until eight. That left time to make coffee. She wished she didn't hate energy drinks. They would have been quicker. When she had the coffee going, she pulled up Kid's draft plan and connected to the Zoom session, happy that the storm hadn't knocked out connectivity and scanning the plan as she waited on him. A list of possible witnesses, evidence to pursue, and potential defense theories. Remembering the conversation with Hank and Maggie last night, she added Peanut Hassenfratz. Otherwise, Kid had been pretty thorough. She continued absorbing it: Talk to Charity, her coach and *close* friend Boot, Will Renwick, Casey (which they'd already done, mostly), the angry neighbor Carolyn Barrett, Samson Dale—the buyer Trusk had thwarted who George had told Aaron about—and any other family, friends, enemies, past wives or lovers, and business associates or employees they could find. She bolded *find out who*

Arnold is and read on: Obtain the autopsy report, any past or pending litigation Trusk was involved in, his will and insurance information, business filings, and property holdings. Dig into the internet and social media for dirt. Explore Betty's background. Follow-up with the county attorney's office about providing their discovery.

Kid's proposed theories of defense were the crowd favorite "the other guy did it" and "accident." Jennifer winced. Accident was a last resort. She preferred, "insufficient evidence of guilt, tell the damn cops to do their jobs." He'd ended with a note. *Talk to BBB about plea deal.* Jennifer added another. *Pull Ollie's record in murder cases.* She wanted to know how often he took cases to trial, what the results were, and what kind of deals he'd cut in the past.

Kid's voice broke into her thoughts. "Morning, boss."

She navigated over to Zoom. "Nice work on the plan. I don't have much to add yet, but I'll email it back with my adds now."

"I'll hold—but later I'm setting us up a Google Drive."

She emailed him then returned. Before she could speak, the door to the cottage opened.

Aaron walked in and kissed her cheek. "There you are. I followed your tracks in the snow."

Two dogs darted on either side of her, wet, wild-eyed, and loud.

"I can't hear you over the dogs."

Aaron waited for the cacophony to die down. "I said there you are."

Cold noses pushed into her hands and were gone in a flash as they ran around sniffing. This was their first time in the cottage.

"And there you are. Good morning! Thanks for the note."

He smiled at her. "You're welcome."

Kid said, "Hello, Mr. Herrington, sir," in a mock serious tone.

"Hey, Kid."

In the background, Jennifer heard Casey's voice. "Is that Aaron?"

Aaron said, "Jenn, the plows have made it up Red Grade. You should be good to get to town. It's already forty degrees. Like a chinook. The last of the snow will melt off the road fast."

"Thanks, honey. Oh, and do you mind pouring me a coffee?"

"Not at all." He entered the kitchen in one long step, poured her a cup, and returned it to her, then waved and called for the dogs.

"Be careful. Thanks again." Jennifer took a sip. The brew was piping hot and oh-so-seductive. She wanted to dive into the mug. She'd become quite the stan of good coffee in Wyoming, where between her sleepless nights and the cold weather, coffee always sounded just right.

Aaron and the dogs were gone in a flash.

Casey's face appeared on the screen. "Aaron is keeping the malamutes?"

Jennifer's insides tensed. She hadn't warmed toward the young woman overnight. "Yes, we are."

"That will make him happy."

Jennifer didn't like her familiarity. "Let's talk about division of labor."

"Whatever you need, boss. We're ready to march," Kid said.

Casey still hovered behind him, seeming to be searching behind Jennifer.

"I like starting with Charity and Boot. I'll give her a call and set something up. I'd like you two to work on the research elements today. Kid, I've added a line item. Pulling Ollie's old cases. That one's definitely for you, but how you divide up and prioritize the others is up to you."

Casey said, "I've got mad computer skills."

Kid looked at her with besotted eyes. "That will be great."

Jennifer sighed. "I'll work my way down the witness list. See who I can catch. Sound good?" When Kid didn't look away from Casey or answer, she repeated, "*Sound good, Kid?*"

"Oh, yes. Listen, Casey needs to pick up a car. We'll be out for about an hour. I'm going to give her a ride."

Jennifer felt her cheeks bulge from her gritted teeth and willed her face to relax. "Got it. My only concern is that we haven't talked to Black Bear Betty yet about the pleas offer."

"Want me to go by and do it? You and I agree it's unlikely she'll take second degree. "

"That would be a huge help if you can do it today."

"Perfect. I will. Thanks."

Jennifer said goodbye and they signed off. She texted Aaron. *Do you have a number for Charity?*

He immediately sent back a contact card. *I got it so we could stay in touch about her stud. She texted that he's not improving. I'm heading over there now.*

Jennifer thought about contacting the new widow. If she did and Charity refused to talk to her, Jenifer was dead in the water. But if she just showed up...

She typed fast. *Wait for me. I'll hitch a ride. I want to surprise her.*

Jennifer's cheeks were pink and numb by the time Aaron pulled their two-seater snowmobile to a stop in front of the WP Bar Ranch stables. The ride over had been a total blast—far less scary than in Aaron's Jeepster. She dismounted after he did and pulled off her helmet.

"Let me get started on Smokey with her, first, okay?" Aaron said.

"Yes. If last time is any indication, she won't give much attention to the poor animal anyway." Jennifer set the helmet on the seat.

Aaron opened the stable door for her, then followed her in. Charity and Boot were waiting outside Smokey's stall.

"Dr. Herrington. You brought your assistant again, I see." Charity's face had all the mobility of a block of ice. "Although I've heard a rumor that she's an attorney."

A sly smile crept over Boot's face.

"Hello, Mrs. Trusk. Yes, I brought Jenn. Now, tell me about Smokey," Aaron said.

"He's just not improving. I rode him yesterday and he was still favoring it."

Aaron's eyebrows and forehead telegraphed his feelings. Jennifer wasn't even a vet or a horse person, and she was angry. "Wait. You *rode* him? He's supposed to be on complete rest. This type of injury may take months to heal."

"We don't have months."

"You may not want months, but that is what it will take. That and continuing the therapies we talked about. I assume you're still doing those?"

"I lost my stable hand. And with Glen's death, I've had a lot of things to take care of."

"There's no one that can care for this horse? What about you, Mr. ... "

The rhinestone cowboy said, "Boot."

"Boot."

"It's not part of my job. I'm a reining coach."

Aaron licked his lips. "Obviously, the roads aren't good enough to move him, but I'd be happy to take him to my place to be sure he gets the care he needs."

"How are we going to train him if he's not here?" Charity said.

Aaron's voice grew frustrated. "That's the point, Mrs. Trusk. You're not. Not until he's given time to heal."

She gave an exaggerated sigh. "I'll just sell him. If he can't train, he's worthless to me."

Boot crossed his arms. "You're going to get pennies on the dollar."

"His sperm has to still have value."

"He's unproven. All he has is a good bloodline and a propensity toward injury."

"I just want to get the hell out of Wyoming and back to California. I can't stay here with him. I could move him with me, I guess."

"It will cost more to transport him than you'll get for him."

Jennifer had had all she could stand. She elbowed Aaron.

He took the hint. "I can save you the transport cost. Leave him with me."

"Like *give* him to you?"

"You can either pay me for his board and my medical care or transfer him to me and I'll do it free."

Boot was nodding slowly.

Charity stared at her boyfriend. "Fine. But you need to come get him tomorrow so we can leave."

"If I can't get him because of the roads, I'll make sure he's cared for until they're clear," Aaron said.

"You don't understand, I've contracted with a realtor to sell the ranch. We need him gone."

Aaron smiled. "I understand completely. The horse will be moved as soon as it's safe to do so. He won't prevent a sale. He makes the place look like a real ranch. It's a positive."

"I don't want just anyone coming and going to take care of him." Jennifer bristled at the insinuation. "He needs to be moved, as soon as possible. Boot, go get his papers. Let's sign him over."

Boot strolled out, whistling.

Aaron said, "Can you bring me the things I left for you to take care of him?"

Boot waved a hand in acknowledgement without turning around.

Aaron let himself into the stall and began talking to Smokey in a soothing voice. Jennifer peered in after him. The horse was less distressed than when Jennifer had first seen him.

Jennifer turned to Charity. "I've been wanting to talk to you, Mrs. Trusk."

"Whatever for?" Charity said, her nose wrinkled.

"I represent Elizabeth Jurgenson."

"What does that have to do with me?"

"You know her as Black Bear Betty."

Charity's eyes widened. "You're the lawyer for the woman who murdered my husband?"

"She says she didn't do it. Even if she did, the law provides for her to defend herself and only be convicted if the prosecution proves guilt beyond a reasonable doubt. I should know. I was a prosecutor for fifteen years."

"Well, isn't that nice for all of you?" Sarcasm dripped from Charity's voice.

"I was hoping you could help me with your husband's history. Past wives or serious relationships, kids, business partners. I'd love to get a list of anyone you think I should talk to."

"None of them saw your client shove him off the road with the tractor."

"There is no proof he was pushed off the road at all at this point. Talking to people who know him is an integral part of figuring out what may or may not have happened to him."

"No kids. No past wives. No business partners. Glen is self-made. Was."

"He mentioned he was meeting with someone named Arnold. Do you know who that was?"

"Yeah. Barty Arnold. They were doing some deal together. Maybe."

"What kind of deal?"

"A housing development called Sheridan Hole. Glen said Bart was in over his head and looking for money."

Jennifer felt nauseous at the idea. Lately she'd heard people referring to their area that way because of the influx of moneyed newcomers, a reference to Jackson Hole. "How can I get hold of him?"

"Um, the yellow pages? Google?"

"You don't have his information?"

"I wasn't Glen's secretary. I was his wife."

"Okay. Did he leave a will or have any insurance?"

"Get a warrant."

Jennifer bristled. "A prenup perhaps."

"Same answer."

I'm pretty sure that's a yes to a restrictive prenup and that she's inheriting. A man like Glen will have insurance money, too. M for money means motive.

Boot returned with an armload of unopened vet supplies and a folder. He handed the supplies over the stall door to Aaron and the folder to Charity.

Charity bared her teeth at him. "Dr. Herrington's *assistant* represents that squatty troll of a contractor. The one the police arrested for killing Glen."

Boot made an O with his mouth. "She had it in for Glen worse than anyone."

Charity snorted. "Except maybe Casey." She explained to Jennifer, "Our former stable hand."

Jennifer said, "Hmm. She didn't mention that."

"What do you mean?"

"Casey works for my colleague now. She's helping us on Black Bear Betty's case."

"That's a conflict of interest!"

"How is that?"

"She hated Glen."

"Even if she did, that wouldn't preclude her from working on the case."

"She's... she's... biased."

"You mean because she walked in on you and Boot having sex and can testify about your extramarital affair?"

"That's unfounded. Slanderous. And Glen was already dead!"

Jennifer didn't waver. "Has to be provably untrue to be slander. Something tells me you aren't going to win that one."

"I want you to leave."

Aaron emerged from the stall. "What do I need to sign to take responsibility for this horse?"

"I don't want this woman to have him."

Jennifer smiled. "I don't know the back end from the front end of a horse. Honestly, he'd belong to Aaron until we find a better home for him."

Charity looked to Boot.

He sighed. "Let's just blow this joint." Boot took a pen from his shirt pocket and handed it to her.

"Fine." She scribbled something on the cover of the folder.

Jennifer read it and smiled. "You'll need to date it and include that the payment is going to be the cost of his vet care and board."

Charity narrowed her eyes and kept writing. "There." She held it out to Aaron.

He took it and handed it to Jennifer.

She read it, checked the folder for the stud's papers, then thought for a second. "This will do."

Charity pointed at the door. "Then get the hell off this ranch and don't come back until I'm gone."

Jennifer didn't need further invitation. She marched out without checking to see if Aaron was behind her. But when she got to their snowmachine, he had caught up with her.

"That was something," he said.

"Do we own a horse now?"

"I believe we do."

They mounted up, and Jennifer was grateful for the quiet time inside her helmet to calm down. She hated that woman almost as much as she'd disliked her husband. She was liking the "other gal did it" defense for Betty. The other gal being Trusk's devious wife and her slick boytoy..

As Aaron turned west on Red Grade Road, Jennifer glanced over at a snowmobile with an older but pretty blonde woman on it. She was holding her helmet in her hand and laughing at something a tall, handsome, dark-haired man said. Trish Flint, she realized, although she didn't recognize the man.

She tapped Aaron's arm. "Stop," she shouted.

He pulled over in front of the two snowmobiles Trish and her companion were on. Jennifer pulled off her own helmet and waved.

Trish waved back. Aaron turned off their machine, and they

dismounted and exchanged greetings. Trish introduced her companion as Ben.

"I'm so glad we ran into you. I've been meaning to call you and ask you to coffee. Or lunch. Or dinner at our place."

Trish laughed. "All of the above and ditto. I'll text you."

When they'd remounted and pointed their double snowmobile back toward their lodge, Trish was smiling. She'd made a friend. And then she remembered the despicable Charity.

Yeah, a friend, and an enemy. She'd have to watch her back until that one left town.

CHAPTER TWELVE

Big Horn, Wyoming

After he and Jenn got home from the WP Bar, Aaron worked side by side with George and the contractors over his lunch break. Who needed food anyway? Better to make more progress toward the lodge they hoped to rent rooms in by the warm months, which seemed light years away in the thick of winter but in reality would come quickly. Days and weeks and months flew by faster every year of his life.

He watched through the window as the two malamutes wrestled in the snow. They brought more joy than he'd ever imagined. Talk about days passing quickly—the shorter span of animal lives was warp speed. He'd always understood that about his patients, but it was hitting home in a new way now.

George was watching them, too. "Got to get a job for those two. Lotta energy."

Aaron grinned. "I'm excited to try them out dog sledding."

"Used to see teams on Walker Prairie when I was up there on the snow machine."

"Are there trails there?" Walker Prairie was a large mostly open expanse in the lower elevations of the Bighorn Mountains. Aaron hadn't visited it yet, because he thought it was only a summer trail area, and he and Jenn had moved here in the fall. No summers for them yet.

"Not per se. But if you take Soldier Creek Ridge trail up from outside Sheridan and cut across Walker Prairie you can connect with the groomed trails. It avoids trailering up the mountain. Once the snow machines pack a trail down a bit, it's great for the dogs."

"That's good to know."

"The groomed trails are even better. Seen a fair number of mushers and teams around the lodges. Arrowhead. Bear. Elk View."

"I can't wait." Aaron set his tool belt on the kitchen counter. "Well, I'm headed back to my day job," he told George.

George gave him a salute. "Always good to have a strong back on the crew. But don't be expecting overtime pay."

Aaron laughed and walked out back to his little clinic, joined immediately by Sibley and Willett who already acted like they'd been part of the family forever. A familiar figure was standing at the door waiting for him. Not his vet tech Tron, but Casey. *What is she doing back here instead of in town at Kid's office?*

"Your dogs look happy," she said.

He felt the smile crack his face like a proud parent. "We love them. I've got an appointment with a musher tomorrow."

"What's a musher?"

"Someone who drives sled dog teams. He's going to help me get started with these girls." He ruffled two heads at once, then they surged forward to greet Casey, Willett with more enthusiasm than Sibley.

"That sounds amazing. I'd love to see real sled dogs. Can I come with you?"

Aaron didn't know how to say no. "I don't see why not."

"What time? And where should I meet you? I have a car now."

"Um, at his place?" He gave her a time. "I'll text you the address."

"For sure. I can't wait."

In the awkward silence that followed, Aaron had time to second guess himself. Regret washed over him. Something about this felt inappropriate. "What brings you out here?"

"I don't suppose you've had a job open up for me yet?"

"Sorry, no. And you'd hear from my practice manager if we did, not me."

"Oh. Yeah, right. I should have... never mind. I just, well, things are not going well with your wife."

Aaron's hackles rose. He didn't appreciate people disparaging Jenn. It came with her former territory as a semi-public figure, working as an ADA in one of the largest counties in the nation. He'd had plenty of practice over the years, but it had never gotten any easier. He'd enjoyed the break these last few months. He liked her not working as a prosecutor, he realized, and he was glad she hadn't run for district attorney in Houston. He wasn't going to entertain any griping about her now. He'd heard from Jenn that things weren't peachy with Casey, of course, but he played dumb and showed no interest. "Sorry to hear that." His phone notified him of a text. It felt rude to check his phone while Casey was talking to him. "Well, I have to get to work."

Casey looked hurt, but she laughed. "Hint taken."

"Aaron?" Jenn's voice.

He looked up. His wife didn't look happy.

"Hi, honey."

"Hello, Casey." Jenn's voice was frosty.

"Hello, Jenn." Was that a sneer?

"I'm going to try to track down a witness. I wanted to let you know if I find him, I might be leaving." She shot a pointed look at Casey.

Aaron got the message. The younger woman needed to go. He agreed. "I'm off to work then. Casey. Have a good day."

Casey pouted at him. "Okay. See you soon." She nodded at Jenn then walked back toward the front of the lodge.

After she'd disappeared, Jenn said, "Why was she here?"

Aaron tried to remember why. Was job hunting the real reason? "I think she's still trying to get a job working with animals."

"I wouldn't mind her moving on, but I'm not in love with her working for you."

"Don't worry. We have no openings."

"Good."

He put his arms around her. "Good luck with your witness." He kissed the tip of her nose.

She seemed to relax in his embrace. "Thanks. I love you."

"I love you, too."

They parted, Aaron into the clinic, and Jenn tracing Casey's steps out toward the car park.

Aaron walked to the window and watched her go. Truth be told, he was uncomfortable with the thought of Casey coming to work for his clinic, too. Her surprise visit was disconcerting. And why was she intimating to him that she didn't get along with Jenn? He dealt with advances and inappropriate behavior from women more than he liked.

He'd have to shut this down. Then he remembered she was meeting him at the musher's. It wasn't ideal, but he could do it in person after the session. He just hoped she took it well, and he wasn't at all sure she would.

CHAPTER THIRTEEN

Big Horn, Wyoming

Jennifer tried to tamp down the irritation she still felt about Casey showing up at the lodge to talk to Aaron. The young woman's obsession with him was not okay. Her sabotage of Jennifer was not okay. She turned into the driveway of the far-too-modern-for-Wyoming house that matched the address that Samson had given her when she called. She was five minutes late, which she hated, and she'd spilled coffee on her pants on the drive over. The whole Casey thing had thrown her off her game.

At the door, she rang the bell and waited. After a minute she rang it again. Waited another minute. Rang it again. So much for worrying about being on time. She took a moment to text Kid. *Add research on Barty Arnold and a possible Sheridan real estate development called Sheridan Hole. He's the one Glen was supposed to meet the day he died. Charity said Glen was considering investing or partnering. Also, she didn't confirm will, insurance, or pre-nup, or give any witnesses.*

Then she walked around back to see if she could raise a human.

Samson was expecting her after all. On the back patio, two burly men jumped to their feet at the sight of her, guns drawn.

She raised her hands. "Don't shoot. I'm Jennifer Herrington. I have an appointment with Mr. Samson. No one was answering the door, and I heard noise back here." Noise was the only way she could think of to describe the blaring rap music she'd last heard in Houston.

The security guards half-lowered their guns and traded a look. The burlier of the two said, "You here to see Sammy D.?"

"Um, if he is the same guy as Mr. Samson, then yes." Now that she was less in fear of her life, she took in the rest of the scene. Women in tight jeans bearing strategic rips and held together by safety pins, clips, rivets, and frayed threads. Breast-hugging sweaters. Uggs. She predicted frostbite. The scent of marijuana was probably going to give her a second hand high. Empty bottles and glasses littered every surface. *It's like Vegas in Big Horn, population 350.*

She became aware of a man's head rising out of what she now saw was a hot tub. In it was not only the man but several more women. Giggly and hopefully clothed. Of age, she hoped, but it was close. The man was a good twenty years older than them, even if they were of age. *Why? Why do some women demean themselves like this for the rich and powerful?* Because clearly this guy was rich and powerful.

He climbed from the hot tub. A cheetah print speedo was the only thing covering him, and it was nearly obscured by his belly. Steam rose from his body.

"Sammy D? This woman Jennifer Harringbone said she's got an appointment with you?" one of the guards said.

"Jennifer Herrington. We just spoke on the phone, Mr. Samson."

Samson took a thick towel from the other guard, who now was doubling as a valet. "I didn't imagine a woman your age would be such a looker. Call me Sammy D." The valet took the towel and handed Sammy D a plush black robe.

"Call me Ms. Herrington. Can we talk somewhere discreet about the WP Bar Ranch and Glen Trusk?" She repeated the pertinents of her visit, in case he hadn't retained them from their call. There was all that pot, after all.

"No secrets here. You want a swimsuit? Not that they're required."

"No, thank you."

"People all telling me to buy in Jackson Hole, but for my Benjamins, this the place to be. You feeling me?"

"Mr. Samson, I was told you tried to buy WP Bar Ranch?"

He snorted and snapped his fingers. The valet all but clicked his heels. "More Cristal for my ladies. Bring me a bucket of Onda Civics. One of each flavor. Don't skimp on the ice." He cocked his head at Jennifer. "Yeah. I tried but I got screwed by that white real estate agent. He dipped on me and took hella guap from Trusk."

Jenn tried not to look as confused as she felt. Dipped? Hella guap? She got the general gist, however. "That must have been upsetting."

He lifted both arms in a shrug. "It's just business, and I'm a businessman."

"Do you know Glen Trusk?"

"Never had the displeasure, but his reputation proceeds him."

"Sounds like Mr. Trusk kept you from buying the place on the mountain you had your heart set on."

He grinned, flashing a gold tooth or three. "This pad's pretty sick, though, don't you think? Be even better once I get the pool and waterfall in."

What was it with people moving into this arid water-poor state that was swimming-unfriendly for nine months of the year? "Have you been out to the WP Bar since Mr. Trusk bought it?"

"Nope." He winked. "I heard he's dead, Ms. Herrington. I also know you're representing the woman accused of killing him. If you think you'll exonerate your client by pinning his murder on the new black guy in town, you're going to be disappointed, and broke, because I have lawyers, too. It's a ridiculous theory. I own seven homes. That ranch meant nothing to me. I do know who it meant the world to, though."

Jennifer didn't want to seem blasé, but she'd heard similar from guilty parties all over the Houston metroplex. Still, he might hold important information for the defense. "Who's that?"

"Daisy Bean."

"And she is?"

"Her granddaddy sold to Trusk. Daisy wanted that place like a junkie wants smack."

Titters resounded from the hot tub and sycophants on the patio.

Jennifer fought down revulsion. "Was he selling because he needed money?"

"That's not what he told me. He said it was to keep it out of Daisy's hands. He disagreed with her lifestyle."

And yet he considered selling to this man? Misogyny, thou art a patriarch. Jennifer refused to ask for details about Daisy's lifestyle. "And do you know her?"

"I've met her a time or two." He waggled thick brows.

Don't make me ask. "Did she talk about wishing her grandfather harm?"

"That's all she talked about round me. I'm pretty sure she was giving the old man the finger when she dropped to her knees and gave me—"

Jennifer broke in as fast as she could. Some things you couldn't unhear. "Did she tell you she intended to kill him or give you any reason to believe she would?"

"She talked big but that was all it was."

"But she did *say* she wanted to kill him?"

Sammy D grinned. "I don't kiss and tell."

Jennifer highly doubted the veracity of that statement, but she'd gotten what she came for. She thought of one last question. "Do you know Barty Arnold?"

"A money-grubbing tool."

"You're not involved with him on any deals, then?"

"He wish. Tell him I said so."

"Can I get contact info for Arnold or Bean from you?"

"They call me, not the other way around, Beautiful."

She steeled herself not to react. "Thank you, Mr. Samson."

"Sammy D to my ladies. You're welcome." He took her hand as if to shake it, but instead brought it to his lips. She jerked it away. "If you ever get tired of those buttons and long sleeves, you know where to find me."

Jennifer fast-walked away from the backyard. She didn't escape the sensation of Sammy D's eyes on her ass until she disappeared around the corner. He might not have confessed to murder, but the painful visit had been worth it. *Daisy Bean, you're up next.*

CHAPTER FOURTEEN

Sheridan, Wyoming

Aaron threaded his fingers through the chain link kennel fence. Fifteen howling, wooing huskies and husky mixes were singing the songs of their people to him. "What an impressive place, Tommy." He could barely hear his own voice over the racket. He wondered how the neighbors liked the kennel in their semi-residential area. He doubted any of them made a stink. This was old Sheridan, and Wyomingites tended to live and let live.

Tommy Campbell rubbed at his ginger beard. Perry Flint had referred Aaron to him with his highest recommendations. The man stood a head shorter than Aaron. Fit but not in an obvious way. He looked like he could still crush a forty, though. *Wide receiver*, Aaron decided. In the Julian Edelman tradition, but not a guy who would have cracked a pro roster. "If you can stand the smell and the noise, dog sledding is the perfect sport."

"I'm already used to both of those things as a vet."

"So, you're going to keep those two malamutes then?"

"Yes. My wife and I love them." His statement made him hyper aware of Casey beside him. He was dreading the conversation he was going to have to have with her after this meeting.

"Tell me how I can best help you?"

"I'm hoping you can give me tips on how to train my dogs."

Tommy re-set his ball cap, giving Aaron a glimpse of bald scalp. Shaved? "I think the easiest thing will be to harness them in with one of my teams and see how they take to the sport."

"I'd love that."

"Me, too!" Casey said.

"How about next weekend?"

"Great!" Casey said.

"Let me talk to Jenn and confirm, but I'm sure that will work." Aaron half-smiled in a pained way. He was excited about Tommy's offer, but he dreaded walking things back with Casey. If the shoe was on the other foot, he wouldn't like Jenn hanging out with a handsome, overly attentive, and much younger man. For damn sure Jenn would be unhappy about Casey being here today. It had slipped his mind after Casey left, the day before, so he had missed the chance to tell Jenn last night or that morning.

Which meant he needed to be sure he was the one to explain it to her, before some other helpful soul in town decided to do it first.

Casey was speaking. "I hate to do this, but I have somewhere I need to be. Aaron, I'll text you. You know, in case your *wife* isn't feeling the dog sledding, and you want me to go in her place."

He realized another opportunity was slipping away. His window to set her straight. That would have been the sugar to help the medicine go down easier with Jenn. *Dammit.* He waved but didn't say goodbye or respond to her suggestion.

Casey shot him a disappointed look as he turned back to Tommy, whose eyebrows were raised almost to his hairline.

Disappointment was going to be the least of it. Aaron had a feeling Casey had the capacity for big emotions, like rage. He just hoped she wasn't into its companion—revenge.

CHAPTER FIFTEEN

SHERIDAN, Wyoming

JENNIFER DIDN'T USUALLY work in Kid's office on the weekends, but she had to drive into Sheridan for a therapy appointment and a grocery pick-up later anyway. Shopping the aisles was a distant, pre-pandemic memory. *One of the few good things to come from a terrible time.*

Jennifer stared at the drink station in the office. What to do to wake up her foggy, zombie-like brain? She checked the box of Keurig cups. No coffee, just tea. Was tea as strong as coffee? She could vary up her survival ritual. She just didn't get the instant rush from the smell of tea. She popped one in the machine and put her mug under the spout. Time to type up her notes from Sammy D and devise a plan of attack for the next few critical days on Betty's case.

The door opened with a gust of wind. Kid danced in and shut the door behind with his foot.

Jenn couldn't help smiling at him. "You're jaunty today."

"Yes. Things are good. Very good, thanks."

"Spill it."

"I had a good meeting with Black Bear Betty. She turned down the plea."

Jennifer smiled. "Not shocking. I think I'll hold off telling Ollie since he didn't specify an expiration date. But that can't be the reason you're jaunty."

Kid paused, looking like he was trying to hold something in, but then he grinned. "I had a date last night."

"With?" She braced herself for the name she didn't want to hear.

"Casey."

She shook her head. "Matches and gasoline."

"You can't talk me out of this. She's the most amazing girl I've ever met."

"She showed up at my house yesterday while I wasn't there. Be careful. She's paying too much attention to my husband."

"He's way too old for her."

Jennifer gave him an arch look. "In my experience, Aaron doesn't have upper or lower age limitations on his appeal."

"You're just upset because he took her to the dog sled guy's place today."

Jennifer's throat went dry. She hadn't known about that. She swallowed. "I'll admit I'm not a fan, but that's because of how she handled the hearing snafu." Kid's face darkened. "Let's talk about something else."

He waved her words off. "I have to go. I was just coming over to say hello."

"Don't go away mad."

He waggled his brows. "Just go away."

She was relieved at his quick recovery and laughed. "See you tomorrow." She wanted to update him on her interview with Sammy D and ask him about the progress he and Casey had made on their research, but now was not the time.

He left without the dance steps. *He's still a little mad.* Jennifer slumped against the back of her fancy chair. Aaron had taken Casey to Tommy Campbell's without telling her. Her dry throat gave way to burning cheeks. It had been bad enough with Casey showing up uninvited. *I assume she was uninvited.* This dog musher date was unacceptable. Anger cascaded in waves inside of her.

Her phone chimed. She glanced at the calendar notification. Mid-point of her cycle. Possible ovulation. If she and Aaron were going to try for a baby, tonight was the time to do it. Only she couldn't imagine baby-making when she was this mad at him.

Or am I just making an excuse to put it off another month?

It wasn't time to leave for therapy yet, so she forced herself to finish her work, then opened a blank document and saved it as "Book 2." For fifteen minutes, she fidgeted, avoided looking at the screen, and texted with Alayah. Worried about Betty and her case and ran through every option she could think of to get her friend out on bail, only to come up empty. When the time came to leave, it was a relief to escape the accusatory cursor blinking at her.

If it could talk, she knew what it would be saying. Writers write. You're an imposter. Writers write. You're an imposter.

She couldn't argue with the cursed thing.

"WEEKEND OFFICE HOURS. And from a Chaplain. Thank you for so much," Jennifer said as she smoothed her already-smooth jeans.

Dean grinned. "Think of me as a spiritual cheerleader. I think ministering to people's mental health needs is the Lord's work. I'll happily assist Him any day of the week. Speaking of which, how is your sleep going?"

"No improvement, unfortunately. On top of everything, my case isn't going well, and that is giving me something to recycle all night long. Our client is a friend. I think she's innocent of the crime she's charged with, and she's languishing in jail because the prosecutor over-charged her. She doesn't have money for bail. I'm tempted to put the money down myself."

"How much is it?"

She told him and explained the process. "In general, I've always thought it's not the role of a defense lawyer to bail out their clients. But this is Black Bear Betty."

"Do you think you can prevent her conviction?"

"You mean will I lose the money if I bail her out?"

He shrugged.

"So far, there's no evidence she did it, and there's no evidence that she didn't. Circumstantial evidence can be very damning without a solid alibi or a piece of exculpatory evidence. I'm a good lawyer, but I'm not licensed in Wyoming yet. My colleague is unseasoned."

He rubbed his chin. "And if you bailed her out and later learned she did the crime? How would that impact you?"

"Most times, I'd say that would be upsetting. To have helped a killer walk free, for however long. I'd be less bothered in this case because no one is mourning the supposed victim. And I mean no one."

"Murder is okay if we don't like the victims?"

"No, no. Forget I even said that." She sighed. "I would actually feel awful. I know I can't always have innocent clients, but the prosecutor in me believes in the rule of law."

"Seems to me like you have an ethical dilemma then. Act as her friend or as her counselor. Blurring the lines may make you less effective at each."

She nodded vigorously. "That's exactly the conundrum."

"What choice will help you sleep better?"

Damn, he's good. "Bailing her out."

"In my line of work, we call that gut instinct. I'd add that the gut is hard-wired to the brain by hormones and such."

"In my line of work, we consider it a weakness of the heart."

He laughed. "Just consider whether your instincts, no matter which organ they come from, are trying to guide you."

She nodded. The courts were closed on the weekend. She had

time to let her instincts process on the issue. In the meantime, she'd work the case.

"Still the nightmares about the shooting when you were a girl?"

"Yes." She picked at a cuticle, the tension from the conversation shift immediate.

"Since my suggestions haven't worked yet, what does your gut tell you will solve that problem?"

"Closure. Pootie Carputin charged and convicted."

"You're convinced it's him?"

"Yes."

"Because of his tattoo?"

"Yes. I'd never seen one like it before except in my nightmares about the shooting, which I now believe are memories."

"You got a good look at the shooter then?"

"Good enough to tell you that an aged-up Pootie with that tattoo fits all the particulars."

"Childhood memories are a tricky thing. Are you sure yours are accurate?"

"If they aren't accurate, why do they match exactly?"

"I can't give you a satisfying answer to that. But I have an idea. Sometimes we can banish night terrors by bringing them into the light of day, where they aren't as scary. Would you like to describe the tattoo to me?"

Jennifer shuddered. "I guess. I mean, it's like a Gadsden flag. The coiled rattlesnake but in rocks instead of grass. And underneath it is a D-T-O-M. You know, instead of the words spelled out. Don't Tread On Me."

"That's quite specific. What about the person it was on?"

"Caucasian man. Brown hair. I didn't notice much else because the shooting scared me, and the vision of the tattoo consumed me. In hindsight, he was very young. To me at that age, he was a fully grown man. But I'd guess not much more than twenty."

"That's not very much in terms of memory."

"I've thought about working with a sketch artist. Or doing dream regression or hypnosis."

"You believe in them?"

"They've helped me on a few cases. Other times they seemed like a bust. But they're highly suspect in court, especially to bolster a childhood memory. I only started remembering a few months ago, so I haven't made up my mind about next steps yet. But I actually hoped to talk to you about something else today."

"Oh?"

"A young woman who's showing too much interest in my husband, who I think should do more to discourage her."

"Has your husband given you reason not to trust him in the past?"

"No.. But he attracts a lot of female attention. He's too nice to the woman. Too subtle."

"Is this out of character for him?"

She couldn't help smiling. "He was raised to be kind and have manners. It's completely in character."

"So, what's the problem?"

Jennifer was stumped for a moment. "How it makes me feel. I want him to show me and other women that he is protecting our relationship."

"Aha."

"What?"

He held up a hand. "Tell me why this has come up today."

"My work colleague told me that this morning Aaron took this young woman with him to meet with a dog musher."

"I take it that's different from going to see a man about a dog?"

Jennifer laughed. "Yes. Both the same and different."

"What has your husband said about this?"

"I haven't asked him yet."

Dean threw his hands in the air. "Well, there you have it then."

"Have what?"

"What are the cornerstones of a good marriage, to you?"

"Open and honest communication. Kindness. Respect. Partnership."

"I am going to recommend you approach your partner kindly and respectfully and invite him to communicate with you openly and honestly. Because so far I'm hearing you only have third hand information."

His words made her feel ashamed. He was right. "Okay. Let's say he has a decent reason for taking her. He still took her. I'm still upset."

"Valid. And you can tell him that."

Her voice rose to almost a wail. "But I'm ovulating today!" She slapped her hand over her mouth.

"Aha."

"That word again."

"You're feeling pressure to have sex today."

"Well, maybe."

"And transactional sex is outside your comfort zone."

Jennifer paused, in thought. "I don't think we're to the point where we give up on it being making love."

"Because it's always been that to you before."

She thought of their long, hard spell. The infrequency with which they'd come together. But, yes, any time they had, it had been because she loved Aaron and wanted to try to be with him, to recapture intimacy in their union. It wasn't always fireworks. It was sometimes disappointing. Heartbreaking, even. The last few months, it had been very much about love. And the fireworks were back. She didn't want to backslide. She also didn't feel comfortable talking about it with Dean, whether he was a therapist or not. "It's very much that way to us now. I don't think I'm emotionally ready for it not to be."

"Fair enough. I'd suggest you have this conversation sooner rather than later then and handle it in such a way that you protect those love feelings."

"If possible."

"Again, that's fair. But assume a positive intent on his part until you hear otherwise. Listen with every bone in your body. You know, general communication tips for preserving intimacy."

She laughed. "I'm a litigator. A former prosecutor. I think you're assuming I have skills that have atrophied from lack of use."

"Well, we have fifteen minutes left. I can't think of a better way to use them—given the time sensitive nature of your condition—can you?"

It sounded worse than dental surgery without anesthesia to her. But her clock was ticking, in more ways than one. "Bring it on."

CHAPTER SIXTEEN

Sheridan, Wyoming

Kid arrived at his office Monday morning to find Jenn already there again. Two extra-large Java Moon coffee cups sat on his desk.

"One for you, one for me," she said.

"Who's the jaunty one today?"

"I just love their coffee."

"And that's made you *jaunty*?"

She blushed. Jennifer never blushed. "Aaron and I had a good talk last night. He's going to talk to Casey. Explain why she can't just invite herself to hang out with him."

Kid tried not to take offense. He liked working with Jenn. He respected her. She had already transformed his career with George's case and now Betty's. Things were brand new with Casey. He just couldn't help his feelings. They were unexpected. Powerful. Protective. "Good for you guys."

"I feel much better."

The door banged open. Casey walked in, similarly carrying two coffees. "Good morning, Wesley," she said. "Can you get the door for me?"

He hurried over and closed it behind her. "Good morning." He could feel his cheekbones in his smile. If Casey was any evidence, Tennessee women were lookers. But it wasn't just how pretty she was that intrigued him. She was smart and funny, too.

"I got you a coffee." She handed it to him, then said, "Oh, hi, Jennifer. I didn't know you'd be in."

"No problem."

Casey saw the coffees on Kid's desk. "You already had one."

"I didn't know you'd be in," Jenn said, her smile deceptively sweet. Kid had learned she was most lethal when smiling just like that.

Casey slipped out of her puffy jacket and hung it on a hook by the door. She stopped in front of Jenn. "While we're all here, I just wanted to say I'm sorry for how I handled our miscommunication last week, Jennifer. I want to put that behind us, if we can."

Kid beamed. Yes, he'd asked Casey to say this, stressing exactly the words she should use. The fact remained that she had done it, after initially expressing reservation. "What do you say, Jenn?"

Jenn's smile was gone but she nodded. "Apology accepted. We're here to represent our client. I'm all in favor of anything that helps us do that most effectively."

It was a nonanswer, but Casey took it in stride. "FYI, Glen Trusk was a complete ghost on social media. There was basically nothing about him online except charity donations and public events."

"At least you tried," Kid said.

Casey winked at him. "So, how can I help this morning?"

"I don't suppose you've heard from our alibi witness?" Jenn asked.

"You mean Will?"

"The one and only."

Casey pouted. Those lips. Kid was swept away to Saturday night. After Mexican food and margaritas, he'd driven her home and walked her to the door. He'd wanted so badly to kiss her goodnight. She'd leaned in and given him a one shoulder hug and a pat, then thanked him and gone inside. For long seconds, he'd stared at the closed door, hoping she'd reappear. *Please don't let her put me in the friend zone.* But it had been for the best that she hadn't come back. He could take things slow if that's what she wanted.

Casey was answering Jenn. Kid forced himself to focus on her words. "No, unfortunately. He's not super responsive."

"Okay. I have a few people to add to your list for thorough workups." She gave Casey two names—Daisy Bean and Barty Arnold —and a brief explanation of who each was. "I want to know everything about them."

Casey frowned. "Are they suspects?"

"Maybe."

"Okay. I'll see what I can find."

"Thanks. I like updates any time something looks particularly interesting as it pertains to our case."

"Gotcha."

"So, is there anything in that category yet?"

"Nope."

A look of frustration crossed Jenn's face, but she turned to Kid. "I want you to prioritize the financial details. Trusk's money, his wife's, and who stands to gain from his death."

"Three steps ahead of you."

"What?!" Jenn's eyes lit up.

"I got copies."

"How? Those aren't public records."

"I haff my ways." Kid quipped in a bad German accent and cracked his knuckles. "Actually, I think it was just a matter of lucky timing. The Mrs. filed for probate. It's almost like her legal team was anticipating this joyous event, because they had a comprehensive package. Everything was in it, so they're public records now, and I got copies."

"Don't keep us in suspense!" Casey was laughing.

"The widow had a prenup that left her pretty high and dry in the event of a divorce and completely barren for her own infidelity."

"Motive," Jenn said. "For her and her boy toy."

"The major beneficiary of his estate is a charitable trust. But Charity—the irony of her name should not be lost on any of us—gets his real property and a couple of million from his insurance policy."

"That's a ton of money!" Casey said.

"It's a fraction of his net worth. But it's ten times more than she'd have gotten for a divorce, at a minimum."

"What about other beneficiaries? Or business continuity issues?"

"It appears his business was mainly investing."

"Like in real estate development deals?"

"In the past, they've done well for him."

"What about Sheridan Hole?"

"Who?" Casey asked.

Jenn ignored her.

Kid said, "I haven't found anything linking Trusk to that project. Yet. But I do have a phone number and address for Arnold."

"Hello, somebody want to tell me what you're talking about?" Casey sounded a little whiney.

"You're the best. Can you—"

"Sent it to your email right before I came to the office."

Jenn blew him a kiss.

"What are you going to do?"

"Let's just say I've had a breakthrough. I know what I need to do next."

"Which is?"

"Very soon, I'll be tracking down Arnold. But first, I'm springing our client from jail."

"How?"

"I'm going to post bail."

Casey frowned.

Kid's expression matched Casey's. "Are you sure? You could be spending every cent we earn on this case."

"I'm not using that money. This one's on me."

Kid couldn't believe it of sensible Jennifer. He eyed her more closely. There was a twinkle to her eyes and a pink to her cheeks. *Oh, she and Aaron had a really good* conversation. And now he was the one blushing.

CHAPTER SEVENTEEN

Big Horn, Wyoming

Aaron whistled as he gassed up Demarcus Ware at the Big Horn Y. Last night with Jenn had been one of the best in his memory. As he'd feared, she'd already heard that Casey tagged along to Tommy Campbell's. But she'd listened calmly when he explained. He'd readily agreed the girl was taking it too far and promised to ask her to back it down.

They'd ended up in their king-sized bed. The sex had been lights out, but the best part to him was the laughter afterwards and falling asleep nose to nose, like in the old days. And they hadn't used protection. It hadn't hit him until afterward that Jenn had rolled the baby dice. He couldn't think about that. It was hopeful, exhilarating, and terrifying.

He'd been surprised, too, when she'd asked if he would be okay with her securing a bail bond to get Black Bear Betty out of jail. The old Jenn would never have done that. Moving away from the prosecutorial side of criminal law had revealed a softer, more caring side of her.

Bottom line, he was a lucky man to have his wife back. He leaned his head back against his vehicle. Not all marriages survived the kinds of lows theirs had. Wyoming had been magic for them in every way.

He turned and peered in the window. Two floofy dogs grinned and wagged their tails, watching him through the glass. Today he was taking the dogs to work. He hoped they'd enjoy the environment. He loved the idea of being the guy who took his magnificent dogs everywhere.

He heard a click. *What was that?* Inside the vintage Jeepster, Willett was standing with her paws on the driver's door armrest. His heart sunk in his chest. He'd left the keys in the car. He always did. Just like he always left the other doors in the locked position instead of leaning over and manually pulling up every lock.

He tried the handle. *Dammit.* Locked. And he couldn't even blame the dog. Not entirely. Unfortunately, he didn't carry a spare set in his hip pocket or anywhere on the vehicle. He had one at home, but he hated having to call his wife to drive him back up there. And in the meantime, the dogs were shut in the car. Aaron was afraid of someone breaking a window to free them. Because people sometimes went nuts about dogs in cars. The cold temperatures were perfect for the dogs, and there was plenty of air. In fact, Jennifer reminded him every time she rode in it that Demarcus was far from airtight. Any bystander rescue of the malamutes would just be a waste of window glass, which was hard to get and a bit spendy.

Perry Flint lived nearby. Maybe he could drop off a coat hanger, as that was all Aaron needed to break into his old ride. He patted his pocket. As if to rub salt into his wound, his phone rang... inside the car, where Sibley cocked her head and looked from the phone to him and back, like, "Aren't you going to do something about that?"

He went to the front door of the convenience store. A note was plastered to the glass. CLOSED FOR FAMILY EMERGENCY. BE BACK SOON.

"This is getting ridiculous," he said, to no one, because there was literally no one else at the station. Not a single vehicle at the pumps, which was unusual and probably due to the fact that the c-store wasn't dispensing coffee, muffins, and twelve packs of beer, which people bought at all hours of the day.

He looked around in frustration, searching for an idea. A solution. A savior. A little way up the road, he saw a man approaching, heavily weighed down by a backpack. *A through-hiker on his way to the foothills?*

When the guy was fifteen feet away, Aaron waved and shouted, "Hello, do you have a phone I can borrow?"

The man looked up. Aaron seemed to recognize Will Renwick at the same time as Will did him.

Aaron smiled. "Will!" Will was an odd duck, but he and Aaron had always had a decent rapport. Jennifer, on the other hand, not as much. Will rubbed her fur in the wrong direction and vice versa.

Without a word, Will turned and *sprinted* back the way he had come, across the road and onto a side street. He never looked back.

Aaron stood mouth agape. *What the heck was that about?*

He'd been standing there for a while, considering walking to a nearby house and asking to borrow a phone, when a sheriff's deputy truck pulled in for gas, a man driving. A man he recognized. Deputy Travis. He'd have a phone and everything they needed to get into the Jeepster.

He breathed a sigh of relief and walked over to ask for help. Three minutes later, Aaron was on his way. But not until after he typed Jenn a quick text. *I saw your alibi witness on foot near the Big Horn Y. He ran off when he saw me. What do you think that was about?*

She didn't answer immediately, and he drove on to his clinic, mind already turning to the patients he had lined up that morning.

CHAPTER EIGHTEEN

Sheridan, Wyoming

Casey's mouth fell open as she read the search results on her screen. That snotty bitch Jennifer had made it sound like the background check on Black Bear Betty would be practically a waste of time. But the conviction in front of her was anything but a waste. This was exactly the kind of information Jennifer wanted to know about.

Casey looked over her shoulder. Wesley was in the bathroom with the fan blasting. Probably after spraying half a bottle of Poo-Pourri in the toilet, too. She printed the records, then stuck them in an unmarked file. She closed the browser.

She wouldn't cross the street to help Jennifer Herrington. Hell, she wouldn't cross her legs for that woman. Besides, *he* would want her to keep this information a secret.

And she owed him. When no one else cared about her, he had helped her. Jennifer sure didn't care about her. The exact opposite.

A knock sounded at the door. She hurried over to it.

A teenage kid in a Speedy Courier shirt held out a package.

She put a finger to her lips.

"Uh, ok," he whispered. "This is for Wesley James and Jennifer Herrington, from the County Attorney's Office. Will you sign for it?"

Casey scribbled chicken scratch and snatched the package. In a low voice, she said, "Thank you."

She shut the door in the kid's face, but gently. She had to hurry. Kid had already been in the bathroom longer than she would have ever imagined.

She tore the package open. Evidence gathered from the tractor. Blah blah blah boring. Marijuana cigarette, unsmoked. She did a double take. Looked for any clue that they'd linked the joint to a particular human. She couldn't find anything. No fingerprints, anymore. Maybe they had sent off for a DNA test? But if it was unsmoked, there'd be no saliva on it. She exhaled. *It's all good.* The last few pages were crime scene photos. *Could these be important?* She smiled. Quite probably. At some point, Jennifer would realize they were missing. If nothing else, she'd raise a stink with the county attorney. That would be great.

Casey stuck them in the unmarked folder with Betty's criminal records, then buried the file at the back of the filing cabinet. Before she had finished, the bathroom door opened. Her heart went into triple time. Had Kid seen her? Would he ask what she was doing? What would she say?

He came out, looking pale and embarrassed. "Did I hear someone at the door?"

"Yeah. Missionaries. I told them you guys were lawyers and past saving."

He smiled a besotted smile that made her almost feel sorry for him. Almost. She had a mission. Nothing and no one could get in the way of it. "Good one."

She smirked as her heart rate returned to normal. He hadn't seen anything. Didn't suspect her. Was totally oblivious, just like she needed him to be.

CHAPTER NINETEEN

Sheridan, Wyoming

Jennifer regarded Peanut Hassenfratz over her cup of coffee at Buffalo Coffee, where there was barely any room to sit, since most of the space was taken up for t-shirt and bumper sticker sales. The weathered rancher was het up like a wet chicken. In point of fact, he looked more like a rooster, sitting on a low couch with his knees jutting, an oversized jacket contrasting with his skinny legs, and sparse electrified hair like a cocks comb.

"I thought this was about being a character reference for Black Bear Betty. I don't like the tone of your questions. Not at all," he said.

She nodded. "I apologize. Sometimes I'm direct to a fault. It seems like no one liked Glen Trusk. I just want to hear about your experience with him on the water issue."

"You just want to paint me as a suspect because me and him got sideways."

Yes. "Believe me, if everyone who got sideways with him was a suspect, the police would have half the town in jail."

Peanut stood, fists clenched, face red. "I ain't your huckleberry,

Miss Herrington. I've never even set foot on that worthless piece of land he bought. I was at my men's coffee club at Perkin's all morning."

Jennifer made a mental note. *Peanut has a temper.* And George could verify Peanut's alibi–or not—since he went to the Perkin's coffee, too. "I didn't expect you had. Thanks for meeting me. This was very helpful. Black Bear Betty will be most appreciative."

He huffed and strutted out.

Jennifer was glad she'd ordered her coffee to go. She preferred Java Moon's brew, but this meeting hadn't been a waste of time. She would actually have been more suspicious of the man if he'd tried to make his hatred for Trusk less obvious.

She glanced at her phone screen, checking to see if she'd missed a call and yawning. Coffee wasn't strong enough to keep her boosted anymore. No drinks were. But most other stimulants were illegal and out of the question, so she'd make do. Yesterday she'd secured a bail bond, but it had been late in the day before the funds had cleared. Too late for the bondsman to post it. Then she had this meeting with Peanut scheduled already for first thing this morning. Now she was waiting for a call telling her that bail had been made and Betty was free.

She couldn't wait to see her friend walk out of the jail and to give the woman a ride home.

Five minutes later, she stood in the lobby of the jail building waiting. And waiting. And waiting. The bondsman had told her to expect it to take an hour for them to release her after he posted at eight sharp. It was nine-thirty. She called the bondsman's office.

A reedy voice said, "Quick Release Bail Bonds. Charlie speaking."

"Charlie, this is Jennifer Herrington. I'm calling to check on the status of Elizabeth Jurgenson. You were going to post her bail at eight today."

"Hello, attorney. I went by this morning to pay it, and they told me her status had changed to held *without* bail."

"What?? That's not right."

"That's what I said. Waste of my time. And now I have to give you all the pretty money back."

"I'm her attorney. I would have heard if her status changed."

"Sounds reasonable, I'll grant you, but doesn't change anything. Can you give me a day to reverse your payment? I need your bank to fully fund it before I can deduct that much out of the account."

"What? Yes. Fine. Thank you." She hung up in a daze, forgetting to even say goodbye.

In another five minutes, she'd driven on a furious autopilot to the County Attorney's office, which was incongruously located in a quaint historic home with white trim and a big porch and balcony. She marched in on a head of steam. Ollie had the misfortune to be standing in the reception area talking on his cell phone. His eyes went wide, and he ended the call when he saw her.

"Jennifer. I didn't expect you," he said.

"Oh, I'm quite sure you didn't. What dirty trick did you pull to get Black Bear Betty held without bail?"

"Black Bear... Elizabeth Jurgenson?"

"Yes, Ollie. My client Elizabeth Jurgenson."

"No dirty tricks. At least not by me. But that's one way of describing what your client did. She shivved another inmate. Automatic loss of eligibility pending charges and a new bail hearing. The woman may die, which means another first-degree murder charge. She's over at the hospital in ICU."

"That's impossible. I wasn't informed."

"Just happened last night."

"Funny. My phone was fully functional then."

"I don't work twenty-four-seven. She was already in jail anyway. What difference did it make?"

"For starters, if she's going to be charged, I AM HER ATTORNEY."

"Correct. And you can meet with her any time."

"And it did matter because I had a bondsman posting bail for her at eight this morning."

"Oh, shucks. Yeah, too late. Your client messed that one up."

"Innocent until proven guilty."

"Lots of witnesses."

"There is nothing less reliable than a jailhouse witness. I can't wait to find which of them are receiving favorable treatment in return for their testimony."

"Listen, I get it you're upset, but this is all just the misfortune of timing. You haven't been wronged here."

Jennifer balled her fists. "Ollie, I have an innocent client in jail. A woman who has never hurt a fly. And you want me to believe she's suddenly on a killing spree?"

Ollie gave her a pitying look. "You should really background check your own clients. I'm surprised you didn't, Jennifer."

"Black Bear Betty is clean."

"Your definition of clean is a little different than mine. I call murdering her husband about as far from clean as you can get."

Jennifer clamped her jaw shut rather than admit her client had failed to disclose that tidbit and her team had failed to uncover it themselves. But inside, she was screaming and tearing at her hair.

CHAPTER TWENTY

Big Horn, Wyoming

Jennifer was too angry to go to Kid's office. Instead, she used the drive back to her own cottage behind the lodge to call Kid and fill him in. Her voice was hoarse from yelling when she was done.

"That makes no sense. Casey would have told you if she found something like that."

"So, she did finish Black Bear Betty's background?"

"Yes. At least she said she did."

"Is she there?"

"No. She went to run an errand."

"Do me a favor. Don't mention this to her. I'm going to do the background myself. I want to have the documents in my hand when I talk to her."

Kid was silent for a few seconds.

"Kid, I mean it. This is a performance issue."

His voice was clipped. "And I'm her boss."

"Then, with great respect, I am asking you to act like a boss and not a would-be suitor."

Clipped turned to cold. "I'm going to hang up now."

"Promise me you don't give her a heads-up until I finish my investigation. Please."

"Fine. I promise. I don't like it, but I promise."

"We'll talk to her together."

"That's better." Kid ended their connection.

Jennifer pounded the steering wheel so hard it hurt her hand. Why hadn't Betty told them about her past conviction? And how had Casey missed a public record? Chaplain Abel's communication coaching suddenly played in her head. Listen more than you talk. Assume a positive intent. It was too late for Kid, but she tried to apply it to the situation with Casey.

Okay. I'll assume she didn't get to it, although I asked her to do it first and she told kid she'd finished. I'll assume she's an incompetent boob who misrepresented what she was capable of. But Casey had handed off multiple criminal records on other witnesses in the last few days for Kid on other cases. He said she'd done a good job and gotten him exactly what he needed.

It wasn't a lack of skills.

The Grand Cherokee bounced wildly down the driveway, but Jennifer didn't slow her speed, not even when it fishtailed on the thin, slippery snowpack. She parked in front of the house and checked her phone before she got out. A message from Aaron that she had put off reading during her busy-turned-infuriating morning. Two messages actually.

The first had come in early. *I saw your alibi witness on foot near the Big Horn Y. He ran off when he saw me. What do you think that was about?* She pounded the steering wheel again. Will had been in town. And she'd missed him. She growled. Why hadn't Aaron gone after him?

The second text said *Willett locked me out of the car with my phone and keys in it. I couldn't go after Will.* He described the last location he'd seen him. But the messages were from two hours before.

A vehicle pulled up beside her. Jennifer looked over into the driver's seat of a Ford Edge and an unfamiliar woman's face. Silver gray bobbed hair, a dimple in her chin, and big, horsey teeth.

Jennifer gave a small wave and got out.

The woman met her in front of their SUVs, extending a hand, which Jennifer shook. "I'm Daisy Bean. I heard you're looking for me."

Jennifer's mind was so far away that it took a few beats before it registered. "Your grandfather owned the WP Bar Ranch."

"Yes, he did, the miserable old bastard. That's why I'm here. I'd like to talk to you about helping me get the ranch back, if this is an okay time."

"Oh!" Jennifer had never practiced real estate law. But she definitely wanted to talk to Daisy. "Well, I have an office out back. I don't usually see clients there." *Make that "ever."* "But if you don't mind the casual atmosphere, I can make you a cup of coffee and we can talk."

"Thank you. I'm not in the habit of ambushing people like this, I was just so eager to talk to you. My contact had your address but not your phone number."

"Sammy D?"

Daisy laughed. "Isn't he a character?"

That's not how Jennifer would have described him, but neither was it untrue. She said, "Mm hm."

Jennifer led Daisy along the shoveled path around the house and into the unshoveled walk across the backyard. "How do you know Sammy D?"

"We met when I tried to talk him into fronting for me to buy the house. I offered to pay him ten percent more than whatever he could contract it for."

"Did he agree?"

"He was considering it, but then it got stolen out from under him by Glen Trusk."

"Did you try to buy it outright from your grandfather?"

"He wouldn't even take my calls or calls from anyone associated with me. Literally, if he would see me in town, he'd pretend he didn't know me."

"Wow. That's harsh."

"Yes. And all of this because I have the audacity to love my wife."

"I'm sorry." She remembered Sammy D's intimation that Daisy had given him oral sex. Well, being gay didn't mean a woman was incapable of sexual acts with a man. It brought to mind her conversation with Chaplain Abel about transactional sex. *If you want something bad enough, what lengths will you go to? What lengths would Daisy go to?*

"My memories of that ranch as a child are golden. Before I disappointed the old man, anyway. I wanted to share it with Tabitha and our kids."

"How sad that he would rather it went to a stranger."

She nodded, lips compressed. "God, how I hated him."

"Did he pass?"

"Yes. A week after he sold the place. At which time I learned he hadn't made any valid changes to his will and that I inherited my share of his holdings. If he hadn't sold the ranch, I would have been able to horse trade for it with my sister and cousin."

Jenn let Daisy in the cottage ahead of her.

"Wow, this is cute."

"The previous owner squatted in here after he became a widower. I've done a lot of rehab."

"Poor George. He really loved his wife."

"Have a seat in the sitting area. Cream and sugar?"

"Just black."

Jennifer went straight to the Nespresso machine. She was too wound up for another cup but made one for Daisy and poured herself a glass of water from a Brita pitcher. Daisy had chosen the one armchair.

Jennifer took the couch. "You said you, your sister, and your cousin are the heirs. What about your parents?"

Daisy peered into her cup. "Both sets of our parents died in a gas leak. They were on a couples getaway together. We lost them all at once."

"That's horrible. My condolences."

"Thank you."

Jennifer plunged forward, past the sad topic. "Did you ever try to buy the ranch from Glen Trusk?"

"He'd finally agreed to meet with me, but he died before I got the chance. His wife hasn't returned my calls."

"It must have been very upsetting when Sammy D got cut out of the transaction, given your arrangement with him."

"Yes, although I can't honestly say Sammy D ever made me any promises."

"I understand." The man was slimy, that was for sure.

"My grandfather has never believed any rules apply to him. I'm sorry if I sound bitter. It's because I am. I used to love that man so much. *Nothing turns to hate so bitter as what once was love.* I think that's from Laurell K. Hamilton."

"Do you have a plan for getting the ranch back?"

"I'm hoping the sale can be voided for fraud. Then the estate returns the money, and we get the ranch back."

"The victim of any fraud would be Sammy D."

"Actually, I think it would be my grandfather's heirs. If he was purposely defrauding the estate."

"Was the offer unfair?"

"No, it was above market value."

"So, how did he defraud you guys?"

"By refusing to let us buy it outright."

"Did you have a right of first refusal?"

"Verbally, yes. He told that to each of us over the years. 'If I ever need money, you lot will get the first chance to buy it.'"

"Your sister and cousin will attest to that?"

She slid a folder out of her purse. "I already have affidavits from them, but they've offered to help in any way they can." She handed the folder to Jennifer.

Jennifer browsed the top affidavit. It stated the right of first refusal, that it wasn't honored, and as a result, the harm due to loss of a treasured family property. The other said the same. She closed the folder and left it on the coffee table. "Charity Trusk, Mr. Trusk's widow, has talked about selling it."

"That's my last resort. Now that our grandfather is dead and we don't have to fight him directly, we just want it back."

"I would imagine it makes millions of dollars of difference, if your new approach is successful."

"To me. The estate has the sale money so financially my sister and cousin are whole. Well, I am, too. But if I have to buy it, that comes solely from my pocket."

And now two parties to the alleged fraud are dead, opening up this opportunity. "Ms. Bean—"

"Daisy."

"Daisy, I'm not a real estate attorney. And I'm not licensed yet in Wyoming because I only recently moved here from Texas."

"You were a prosecutor, right?"

"Yes, although I've been doing criminal defense lately. I'm helping represent the woman accused of killing Trusk." She couldn't bring herself to say murder. One of their defense strategies would be accident, after all, and it was most probably how the man had died.

"That's why you're perfect. You have a background in combat, not discussing things over coffee with lawyers you went to grade school with."

Combat? She'd never called her career that before, but working her way up in the DA's office in one of the largest cities in the world had been that she supposed.

"And you don't have a history with me either. I want someone who'll take it on its merits, not because of my family's money, or *not despite its merits* because I'm not their cup of tea."

Jennifer tapped her lips with an index finger. "I work with a colleague."

"I don't mind that."

"I'll need to think about it and discuss it with him. I can't promise to take the case, but I do promise to let you know one way or the other by the end of this week."

"That's all I can ask. But do know I feel time is of the essence. If Mrs. Trusk is selling in this market, this case could become a whole lot more complicated quickly."

The two women traded contact information, stood and shook hands, and Daisy left.

Jennifer washed the coffee cup and glass. She hadn't been disingenuous about taking the case. It might be the right thing to do, in the end. Especially for Kids' sake. But that was assuming that she hadn't just met with a murderer. Because Daisy had as much motivation to move Trusk out of the way as anyone.

Jennifer made a mental note to follow up on the circumstances of her grandfather's death. And for that matter, the death of the original heirs.

Daisy didn't look like a serial killer, but then neither did Black Bear Betty. Maybe neither of the women were.

Or maybe one or both of them had multiple counts of blood on their hands.

CHAPTER TWENTY-ONE

Sheridan, Wyoming

Kid tried to twirl shrimp pad Thai noodles around a plastic fork. It bent near to breaking and the noodles slid off. He came to Black Tooth Brewery for the food truck at least once a week, weather permitting, and today was a sunny forty-five degrees with no wind. Perfect for winter al fresco dining under their patio roof, especially with the big fire pit burning a few feet away. The taproom was open, but he wasn't much of a drinker and never grabbed a beer with his food.

He'd never worried about how he ate his pad Thai until today, when he came with Casey, whose long hair was twisted into braids on either side of her face. It looked young and at the same time super sexy. In his discomfiture, he couldn't even remember how he usually got the noodles in his mouth. Maybe he'd just pick out the shrimp and veggies and take the rest home. It was a safer bet. He speared a shrimp and managed to get it into his mouth without mishap.

"How long have you known Jennifer and Aaron?" Casey asked.

Her blue gaze was direct and eye level across the outdoor table. He'd never gone out with a girl as tall as her.

Great. Now he had a mouth full of food. How could it take this long to chew and swallow one shrimp? He put a hand over his mouth and tried not to spit at her. "Since they moved here. Early last fall."

He felt uncomfortable with the subject of the Herringtons raised. It made him overly conscious of Jenn's instruction not to tell Casey about Betty's criminal record. He'd researched it himself after getting off the phone. Sure enough, one Elizabeth Jurgenson nee Bell had been convicted fifteen years earlier of vehicular homicide in Douglas, Wyoming after she ran over her ex-husband, although she'd claimed it was an accident. The transcripts included evidence of past domestic abuse, a la *The Burning Bed*, a movie he'd watched three times during law school. An oldie but a goodie. The fact that her husband had a history of beating her up hadn't bolstered her claim of accident. The foreman, interviewed after the verdict, said the jury found the victim despicable and would have entertained self-defense if there'd been evidence presented. They ultimately agreed Betty had taken the law into her own hands. The journalist had pushed it further, questioning whether it was a cold-blooded revenge killing. But months later on appeal, Betty's lawyers had successfully proved prosecutorial misconduct, and her conviction had been overturned with prejudice. *Wow—convicted and then unconvicted.*

But no matter the outcome, it had been a snap for him to retrieve the records and about seven thousand articles online about the case.

His hesitation while his brain had revisited Betty's record cost him the chance to change the subject.

Casey said, "Do you think they're a good couple? I mean, he's so nice, and she's, well... "

He rushed his words. "Yeah, he is the nice one. But he loves her. Tell me about your family." Immediately he regretted how he'd phrased his answer. Jenn was nice. She was awesome, in fact. Aaron was merely the more genial and friendly of the two. He wasn't going back to correct himself, though. He wanted off any topic related to the Herringtons and to stay away from the subject of Betty.

Casey took a bite of honey lime fried chicken and turned to watch a horse and rider clomping down the road. She covered her mouth with a hand. "Oh, my gosh. Is that normal?"

"It doesn't happen often in Sheridan anymore, but it isn't unheard of."

"I'd love to learn to ride. Do you have any horses?"

He nearly laughed. She'd seen where he lived. Where would he be hiding a thousand-pound animal? "No, but I have friends that do."

"Aaron said he just traded vet services for the fancy reining stud that Glen Trusk bought for his wife before he died. Maybe he'll let me ride him."

"Didn't you work as a stable hand at WP Bar?"

"Yeah."

"And you don't ride?"

She snorted. "No. But I'm good with animals. And what I didn't know, I faked in the interview. He wasn't hiring me for my experience anyway."

"What do you mean?"

"I mean he seemed to like having a young, pretty woman around. It's not the first job I've had where that happened either."

Her words made Kid feel squirmy. Wasn't he guilty of the same thing with Casey? But he wasn't an old perv taking advantage of her. They were nearly the same age. He was paying her well, and she was developing useful skills. If things didn't take off between them personally, that would be fine. He'd be a good boss. "I'm sorry."

"Don't be. He got what was coming to him. Karma, ya know?"

He wanted to assure her she had a bright future with his firm, but he just nodded. First he'd have to figure out how to afford her long term. And how to get her past the huge mistake she'd made with Jennifer. Casey looked off into the distance. Something in her expression worried him. Had Trusk done more than just admire her assets? Or had some other jerk she'd worked for in the past?

"Where did you work before Trusk?"

"I was a girl Friday for an old geezer."

"Back in Tennessee?"

"No. Wyoming."

He was working up his courage to ask her if Trusk or someone else had harassed her, when she stood and took her empty food container to the trash.

"Ready?" she said. "I'm getting a little cold. Southern blood, you know."

He jumped to his feet and snapped the plastic lid back over his mostly untouched noodles. They'd walked from the office. He took off his jacket and handed it to her. "Here. I'm warm. I don't need it."

She slipped it on, and he wished he could put his arms around her instead of his coat. *Stop thinking like that, you idiot.* Talk to her about work. Or about Trusk.

"Better?" he asked.

"Much. I need to run a few errands downtown. Thanks for lunch. I'll meet you back at the office."

His disappointment was sharp. He knew it wasn't a lunch date. He'd just hoped she would enjoy his company, like he enjoyed hers. Instead, she hurried the meal and bolted off alone. "Okay. See you there."

And she was off with a wave and a smile, leaving him feeling like a hungry fool. He sat back down and finished his lunch.

CHAPTER TWENTY-TWO

Sheridan, Wyoming

Jennifer and Kid sat across from Betty in a small meeting room in the courthouse the next morning. Last night had been particularly bad in the nightmare department. Jennifer rubbed her eyes and gave her head a little shake. No matter how tired she was, she had to do better than the walking dead for Betty's sake. *Come on, you can do this.* She exhaled in a huff that earned her a weird look from Kid. She ignored it.

"Well, let's get the hard stuff over with first. Although I don't know where to start," Jennifer said. "With the assault or you withholding information from us."

"I didn't assault no one. And I don't know what you mean about the other." Betty looked haggard. Dark, hollow eyes. Sallow skin. Lank hair. And she smelled stale. A little ripe. Her voice was even dulled.

"Let's start with the latter then." Kid had printed out all the old court documents as well as some articles. He slid the folder to her now. Jennifer chose one of the articles published in the wake of

Betty's conviction. She turned it and handed it to Betty. "This is you, right?"

Betty mouthed the words as she read. "Yeah, that was me. But my lawyers won the appeal. They told me it was like it never happened. That was what prejudiced meant."

"Prejudiced means you can't be tried and convicted again for that crime. His death happened. Your involvement in it happened. The records exist."

"You've read them?"

"Of course."

"You know he roughed me up good, then."

"I do. And I'm sorry."

"Don't know how he tricked me into marrying him. The world's a better place without him in it."

"Like Glen Trusk?"

"Yeah, sorta like Trusk." Betty seemed oblivious to how damning her answer sounded. "Only difference is that I ran over Jerry. I didn't mean to, but I did. I wasn't nowhere near Trusk."

"You can see how a past vehicular homicide charge could lead the cops and prosecutor to like you for this, under the circumstances? Since they believe Trusk was hit with a car, too, it explains why they're so keen on you. It's the kind of thing Kid and I needed to know."

"Well, now you do, and there's nothing else to tell."

"Is there anything else Kid and I need to know that you haven't told us?"

"Not about Trusk."

"Fine. Then let's talk about the assault." Jennifer had decided not to tell Betty how close she'd come to getting her bailed out. What was done was done.

Betty pounded her fist. "I didn't stab that poor woman. I don't care what those other women say. I'm getting railroaded again."

"Railroaded?"

"Like that judge did to me in my other trial. He and my husband were business partners. Friends first. But they owned little storage units. Where people unload their crap and leave it. Or sell drugs out of it. Or hide dead bodies. It was a seedy place."

Jennifer had read the transcripts and briefs from Betty's appellate hearing. Judge Clinton Arnold had refused to recuse himself when Betty's attorneys had raised the issue of bias early in the proceedings. Then there had been evidence that he paid an inmate to spy on Betty, and, when that hadn't borne fruit, he'd ordered her death.

"I saw where your attorneys thought the judge tried to get another inmate to kill you."

"He and Jerry owed a lot of money on that place. Jerry had a life insurance policy. I was supposed to be the beneficiary. But the judge was the secondary I think they called it."

"Contingent beneficiary?"

"Yeah, that."

"So, he wanted you convicted of your husband's murder or dead before you claimed the proceeds of the life insurance policy." Under the Slayer Rule, a beneficiary who murders an insured can't collect the proceeds of the policy. "And you hadn't filed a claim for the proceeds yet?"

"They threw me in jail the same day it happened. I didn't know about no policy. I only found out about it later. After the judge tried to get me killed. My attorneys wondered the same thing. I gave them permission to search our house. That's when they found it."

Jennifer turned to Kid, who had been writing as fast as he could. "You following this?"

"Yes. I read some of it in the articles about the appeal," Kid said, nodding. His eyes were bright.

"The judge was forced to resign after your appeal," Jennifer said to Betty.

"Right. And it wasn't enough, for what he did. They charged him, but the jury found him not guilty."

Kid looked up at Betty. "I read about suggestions of jury tampering, but that it was never proved."

Betty guffawed. "Douglas ain't no Jackson Hole. A little cash money goes a long way to keep lips shut tight."

Jennifer looked at the time on her phone. "We have to be in the courtroom in five minutes. Let's get back to the assault."

"I was in the john when four big women dragged me off from doing my business. There was this other gal, she was out cold, like someone had punched her. The biggest woman wrapped my hand around a shiv with hers on it and the others held onto me while she stabbed that gal with the shiv in my hand. Over and over." Betty shuddered. "Then all four of them started screaming that I'd killed her. I didn't even know her. Still don't even know her name."

"Helena Jones," Kid said.

Jennifer leaned forward, her heart rate speeding up. Maybe they had a defense. Maybe she could keep Betty from being charged and get her out on bail after all. "Why do you think those women would do this— to you and to Ms. Jones?"

"Maybe they don't like the looks of me. Maybe they're friends of Mr. Trusk, although I can't wrap my ahead around that man having friends. What I really think is maybe this is related to Jerry's case and his buddy the judge somehow. But I don't mind telling you, I'm scared."

"Add Judge Clinton Arnold, Helena Jones, and these other four inmates to the ASAP research and interview list," Jennifer said to Kid.

Kid turned to a new page in his notebook and took it down. "Got it."

Jennifer thought about Judge Arnold. His motive before seemed financial. But if Betty was right, this time sounded more like revenge against the woman that had cost him his career. If she and her attorneys had been right, he'd already shown he wasn't above contracting with violent criminals when it suited his interests. There was no time to investigate or gather evidence. The flicker of hope was fading and being replaced by worry. If the former judge was behind this, he'd started by trying to frame Betty. Would that be enough for him?

She said, "Do you want me to request solitary confinement?"

"Might be the only way to keep me alive long enough to get out of this place."

Jennifer nodded, lips pursed. She wasn't going to say it to Betty now, but the odds of her release were decreasing. If she wasn't convicted of Glen's murder, she'd still be tried for the assault. Or a second murder, depending on whether Helena Jones survived.

"And another thing. I have a medical condition. I need my treatments."

"You should have told us that from the beginning!"

"I thought you would be getting me out of here and it wouldn't matter. Now it does."

"What is the condition and what kind of treatment do you need?"

"I got IBS. I need THC."

Jennifer frowned. "IBS? THC?"

Kid translated. "Irritable bowel syndrome. Marijuana."

Betty stabbed the air with a forefinger. "It's a condition. That's my treatment. I'm feeling pretty shitty." She snickered. "I can get a doctor's note if you need it."

Jenn smiled with her lips. She was too stressed for toothy grins. "I'm sorry, but the state doesn't allow inmates to use medical marijuana, even with a prescription."

Betty's face seemed to spasm. Her spluttering response was interrupted.

A knock at the door. "Time for Ms. Jurgenson to go."

Jennifer faked an encouraging smile to her client. "See you in court."

Ten minutes after Betty was arraigned for aggravated assault with no bond—by an irritated Judge Ryan, who told Kid very bluntly to save his client's whiney arguments about being framed for trial—Jennifer took a seat in Ollie's office. His quarters were spacious and decorated with ornate antique furniture and Western prints. It was nice, and no different than from when his predecessor occupied it. She liked her mountain cottage far better.

"We have to stop meeting like this." He smiled at her.

She was in no mood for witty repartee. "As long as it's in the best interests of my client, I'll keep putting myself through it."

He rolled his hand for her to continue.

"We need her in solitary. She's in fear of her life."

"Afraid of paybacks, huh? She probably should have thought about that before she attempted to murder another inmate."

"Ask yourself why in the world she'd knife a woman she'd never met in jail, when there was no direct evidence she'd even committed the crime she's charged with? There was no history of bad blood, no beef."

"Jailhouse resentments build up quickly."

"You've read the transcript of the case against her that was overturned for judicial bias?"

"No. The only relevant part of that case was that a jury of her peers unanimously voted to convict her of vehicular homicide."

"The judge in that case was forced to resign after the appeal. He was charged with hiring another inmate to spy on her and ultimately to kill her in jail. Luckily, the assassin failed. But he lost everything when it all came out."

"So? That has nothing to do with her guilt."

"Or innocence. But it bears a startling resemblance to our case here. Black Bear Betty swears that she was attacked and physically manipulated by a bigger, younger, stronger woman who created the physical evidence to make it appear as if she stabbed Helena Jones, when she was in fact just another victim. Ollie, there is a connected former Wyoming judge with a history of similar actions against Betty, a serious axe to grind, and a golden opportunity to seek revenge—she's vulnerable when she's incarcerated."

"Do you have any evidence to back up this wild theory?"

"I'm not the one to be gathering it. That's the State's job."

"Come on. Four witness statements. I'm looking at an easy conviction."

"Just *investigate it*, please. That's all I ask. That and the protection of solitary confinement for my client. Trust me, you don't want to face me when I'm proving my *wild theory* in front of a jury of voters."

His face pinched. "Face you? I thought it was babyface James I'd be going up against."

She smiled. "I hope you're not suggesting I'm incapable of passing the bar exam?"

"A fair and *speedy* trial. Maybe too speedy for that to happen."

"Don't make me quote you when Kid seeks a reasonable period of time to prepare our case."

"Speaking of your case, our plea offer is withdrawn, given the new charges."

"Oh—did I not tell you? Our client rejected it." She stood. "I expect to get a call confirming solitary. On top of that, my client has a severe case of irritable bowel syndrome and is really suffering without medical marijuana. I'm hoping there's some alternative the medical staff can give her?"

Ollie beamed. "So, the joint in the tractor was hers."

Jennifer frowned.

"It's in your discovery."

"I must have missed that. And the crime scene photos. Last night I went through everything you sent over. The absence was conspicuous."

He squinted in confusion. "They were in there. I double checked it myself. I don't want any petty fights with you."

"I can assure you, I did not receive them."

Ollie pulled a file off his desk. "Here are the originals. I sent this to be copied and then I put the copies in the envelope myself." He drew out several color pages and waved them in the air. He hit a button on his phone.

"Yes, boss?" a woman said.

"Cheryl, can you make a few quick copies for me? Sorry for the rush, but I need to put them in the hands of opposing counsel."

"Sure, thing. I'm on my way.

"Thank you."

Jennifer nodded at Ollie. "I appreciate that."

"No problem."

Her anger at Ollie was dissipating, replaced by unease. The documents she'd reviewed had been scanned and put on their cloud server by Casey.

Casey, who'd been at the heart of everything wrong in their case so far.

She was beginning to wonder if Casey had a dog in this fight. Or was her fight only against Jennifer?

CHAPTER TWENTY-THREE

Sheridan, Wyoming

Jennifer stormed straight into the office waving the crime scene photos. The place smelled like the charred cast iron skillet style coffee beans a local shop used. "Casey, we need to talk."

Casey jumped like she'd been poked with a hot shot. She pulled earbuds out. "What?"

Kid's eyes were wide and slightly terrified. Jennifer motioned him over. He moved his chair like he was climbing steps to some gallows.

"I just came back from the prosecutor's office." Jennifer put the copies of the photos on the desk. "I asked Ollie where the crime scene photos were. He showed me the file copy of the documents that had been couriered over to us."

"Oh-kaaaaay?" Casey said, her questioning tone dismissive.

Jennifer pointed from Kid to Casey. "Which of you accepted the documents from the courier yesterday?"

Kid said, "Not me."

Casey raised her hand and wiggled her fingers. "I did."

Jennifer swallowed. She had to keep it under control, so Casey didn't make this about Jennifer instead of how the photos were handled. "Were copies of these photos in the package?"

"I don't remember. But I scanned everything I got into the cloud."

"Let's see the envelope and the contents."

Casey went to the cabinet against the side wall of the office. She pulled out a file and brought it back to Jennifer.

"Are they in there?"

"You're welcome to look."

Kid stepped in before Jennifer could jump down Casey's throat. "Casey, would you please look for them?"

"Fine." Casey flipped through the file like she was fanning the pages of a book. "Nope."

"That's very strange, because Ollie showed me the *copier* record, which shows these copies made and gives the correct page count for the batch including them. But I guess they fell out before they got here. Somehow."

"Must have."

Jennifer took a deep breath. She didn't believe for a second the copies had been taken out or lost between the county attorney's office and theirs. She'd have to search for them later, when Casey wasn't around. "Different topic. Have you completed the background checks on everyone on your list?"

Kid's eyes closed for a slow count.

"Yes."

"Did you know Black Bear Betty was convicted of vehicular homicide when she ran over her husband?"

"No."

Jennifer motioned for Kid to speak.

He cleared his throat several times. His obvious stall didn't work. "When Jenn brought this to my attention yesterday, we did separate background checks on Black Bear Betty. Her criminal records came right up. A quick search yielded reams of articles about her case, too."

Casey's eyes slitted and shot sparks in Kid's direction. "You've known since *yesterday* and you're just now telling me? Whose side are you on, anyway?"

Kid shuddered. Sweat marks dotted his blue dress shirt. "I'm on our client's side. This is the kind of information we needed. So, Jennifer and I agreed we'd chat with you together about this. I can show you the search I ran and where. I want to be sure you know everything necessary to do your job."

"I can do my job, Wesley. I just don't like the way she treats me." She jerked her chin at Jennifer. "Even you said she's not nice."

Jennifer folded her arms over her chest.

His voice cracked as he spoke. "I did not."

"Yes, you did. At lunch."

"That's a misquote. And out of context."

Jennifer stood. "Casey, please get up so I can sit in your chair."

"Why?" Casey snarled.

"Just do it."

Casey vacated her seat. Jennifer put her hands on the keyboard.

"What are you doing?" Casey sounded nervous for the first time.

The screensaver wasn't on, so Jennifer navigated to the open Safari browser. She typed ELIZABETH JURGENSON CONVICTIONS ARRESTS CHARGES in the Google search bar. She scrolled through the results, pausing to take a screenshot. "Kid, have you used this computer in the last few days?"

He shook his head. "Not since before Casey started."

"Neither have I." Jennifer turned the monitor to face them. "Why have all these articles about Black Bear Betty's conviction been clicked before?" The linked titles to the articles that had been opened were purple, while the others were blue.

Casey pressed her lips together.

Jennifer scooted to the side so she could see the screen, too. She opened the browser download history. She took another screenshot. "What's this one?" She pointed.

"How should I know?" Casey said.

"You downloaded it. I'd like you to guess."

After long seconds of silence, Casey hissed, "You know what it is."

Jennifer sighed and shook her head. She was very familiar with the download nomenclature for files from the service they used for background checks. Whether these were Betty's records, she wouldn't know for sure unless she opened the document, but Casey's response was telling. "Kid, you hired Casey. How you handle this is up to you."

He opened and closed his jaw several times. He pulled at his shirt collar. He licked his lips. Finally, he said, "Casey, I'm going to have to let you go."

Casey threw her long braid over her shoulder. "You're nothing but her puppet, Wesley." She grabbed her purse, coat, and traveling mug, then stomped out.

———

It was a short, tense ride from the office to the jail. Kid's thigh bounced as he chewed his nails. Normally, his odor was Axe body spray. If mowing the lawn in the height of summer had a smell, that would be his now.

Jennifer said, "It's been so busy we haven't had time for anything but Black Bear Betty's new charges. Did you get my email about Daisy Bean?"

The shops of Main Street flashed by quickly. The tall windows of her new favorite store, Jackalope Ranch. The beautiful stone building rumored to become an upscale restaurant. A little Mexican food place on the creek that she was eager to try.

"Yes. Thank you. I assigned the research on the deaths of Ms. Bean's grandfather and other family members to Casey. Obviously, I'll do those myself now."

"Thank you. After that's done, let me know your thoughts on Daisy as a suspect on any of the deaths—Trusk's or her family. Also, I'd value your opinion on whether we should take her case. It's a strange theory. She needs to hear back from us on that by the end of the week. I thought it might be a good one for you, if you want to take it on."

"No problem. And thank you." He turned in the seat. "Jenn, I just want you to know I didn't say you aren't nice."

"It's okay." Jennifer heaved a huge sigh, letting out tension from the confrontation with Casey. Some of it, anyway... "That girl is manipulative."

"She asked about you and Aaron as a couple—"

Jennifer snorted.

"*She* is the one who said you aren't nice. I said Aaron was definitely the nicer of the two of you, but I was kidding, you know, because he saves baby animals, and you're a tough criminal law attorney. Then I said you guys love each other and are great together."

"I understand. You're right, too. Aaron is the nicer of us." Jennifer pulled frontways into a parking space at the criminal justice complex. "Don't worry about it anymore. Case closed. Let's go show these photos to Black Bear Betty."

They walked the sidewalk together. Just before they entered the building, Jennifer stopped and put her hand on Kid's elbow. "I'm proud of how you handled Casey. I know that wasn't easy to do, but it was the right thing."

Kid nodded. His eyes were shiny.

"You understand that I couldn't because I'm not her boss."

"I do. But I don't think I like being a boss."

"Yeah. It was always my least favorite part of heading up the Homicide division."

Kid wiped his eyes. His emotions repurposed themselves into frustration. "I can't understand why she hid Black Bear Betty's history."

"Or the crime scene photos and joint."

"We don't know that she did that."

Jennifer arched her brows. "Don't we?" She released his elbow and held the door for him. "After you."

In a nondescript interview room fifteen minutes later, Jennifer laid the crime scene photos on the table and turned them to face Betty. If anything, Betty looked worse. Older. Smaller. Thinner. Ranker.

"Did you get me solitary?" Betty asked.

"I hope so. We'll know when we know."

Betty hugged herself by the elbows. "All right. What do you want to know?"

"Before we start, did you have a joint in the tractor?"

Betty cocked her head and closed her eyes. Then she shook her head. "Nah. I never brought drugs to work. I always figured it could get me fired."

Jennifer had reviewed the documents from Ollie in the parking lot after he'd given them to her. Not in depth, but with enough rigor to know he didn't have any physical evidence linking the joint to Betty. Just that damn circumstantial that was adding up too quickly. "Look at the photos. Do you see anything that could help us help you?"

Kid sat up straight and alert, pencil poised as Betty moved the pictures close to her then picked each up, holding it at arm's length, rolling her lips like she was putting on lip balm, and tilting her head from side to side.

"That's funny."

"What is?"

She shook her head and resumed her intense scrutiny. When she'd finished she nodded. "His chains are missing."

"Chains?" Kid said.

"Tire chains. I put them on his stupid truck myself. I told him he was gonna slide off his own damn mountain. And if they'd been on, he wouldn't'a went over the edge. Not in those conditions. It was hardly nothing that day. Just a little snow. " She shook her head. "The man was a knob, but he wouldn't have taken off the chains. Not after the rash I gave him about it. Plus, it woulda made his soft hands dirty."

"They say the tractor pushed him over."

She shrugged. "Without the chains, that would have been enough to slide his truck. But, if it did, I wasn't driving it. And I had the keys to it in my pocket."

"Wait, what?" Kid said.

Jennifer groaned. "That's the first time you've mentioned the keys." She didn't like that Betty was the last person with the keys. There were ways they could spin it, but those ways wouldn't look as shiny to a jury as the way Ollie would lay it out.

"I didn't think about it. They were still in my pocket when they locked me up. I had to give 'em up for one of those little bags they put your personal stuff in."

Jennifer stood and paced. "Who moved the tractor from beside the goat path?"

"Dunno. They wouldn't let me touch it after the, uh, accident."

"Was there another set of keys?"

"Mr. Trusk kept the spare on his own key ring." She guffawed. "In case he had an aneurysm and forgot he was allergic to work."

"Can it be started without a key?"

"Now that ain't easy. Somebody knowledgeable could do it in an emergency. But ya know, if someone had an M series Kubota, they could probably just use their own key in it."

"What do you mean?" Jennifer whirled, her mind racing.

"The key for a series of Kubota tractors is the same."

"Our M series tractor at the lodge—that key would work on the WP Bar Ranch tractor?"

"It should."

Jennifer said, "If the other guy's key fits, you must acquit."

Kid grinned.

Betty stretched and yawned. "Ya lost me there, counselor."

Jennifer pumped her fist. "We just need to find a suspect with an M series Kubota tractor."

Betty nodded. "I like your thinking. While you're at it, find out where those truck chains ended up. Let the cops fingerprint them. If anyone's besides Trusk's and mine are on there, there's your killer."

Jennifer drove home from the office an hour later on autopilot. Kid had still been at his desk, his face blue in the glow of his screen, vowing to knock out as much research as he could that night.

So much to process. It was dusk and lightly snowing. Six months before, she would have been terrified to drive on any amount of snow. How quickly she'd become almost indifferent about it. The smaller accumulations anyway, and as long as a deer or five didn't run out in front of her. The beautiful sheer white landscape and muffled sound gave her a sense of peace.

Tonight, she was even more confident than usual, which she attributed to Betty's case. She couldn't wait to find out about the death of Daisy Bean's relatives and to find a suspect with an M series Kubota. With a sinking feeling, she realized it was also time to investigate Casey's background. The girl's shady behavior might be jealousy toward Jennifer, or it might be something more sinister. She did have motive and opportunity, after all. She'd do the work herself. Kid didn't need salt rubbed into his wounds about the girl.

But what really had her jazzed up was Betty's last comment. "Find out where those truck chains ended up. Let the cops fingerprint them. If anyone's besides Trusk's and mine are on there, there's your killer."

Charity had ordered Jennifer never to set foot back on WP Bar Ranch. But the search had to start there. She'd grovel. She'd beg. She'd barter. Whatever was necessary to get in.

Her mind was elsewhere when she noticed the headlights in her rearview mirror. The vehicle was closing in on her quickly. The speed limit on this stretch of the road through Big Horn was thirty miles per hour, and she was going thirty-five. She pulled further to the right, her right-side tires over the outer white line, she was sure, although she couldn't see it under the snow. The fifty-five miles per hour sign flashed by, but she decided not to speed up. She wanted this reckless driver to pass her. Suddenly, lights bouncing off her mirror blinded her. The driver had turned on the high beams. But what could she do differently? She was practically off the road already. The vehicle was bearing down on her at a scary speed now, closing the last of the gap between them. From this distance, she could tell that it was large and had several inches of lift. Probably a truck, but maybe a large SUV.

Pass me, already.

She lowered her head and gaze out of the glare. Any second, this jerk would honk at her. She just needed to keep her cool. Maybe it was someone who had a family emergency. Or was driving under the influence. No reason to get upset.

WHAM!

"Oh my God!" The collision sent her pulse through the roof. She tightened her grip on the steering wheel. Had the driver not seen her? A change of strategy was in order. She sped up approaching the sharp left-hand curve at Bear Creek Road. All she wanted was out of the way of this menace.

WHAM!

The second impact shoved her Grand Cherokee forward. Her speed was too high, and the corner was coming up too fast. She pressed her brakes and held them as she turned her steering wheel to the left. Too late, she remembered never to lock brakes down on a winter road. How many times had George coached her and Aaron about black ice, impossible to see on the asphalt roads? He'd also made them buy snow tires. "Those folks in town may not need them, but you're living in a different world up here on the mountain."

Her SUV began to slide. Chains would be nice about now. Then in a graceful and terrifyingly fast maneuver, it began to spin. Until it sailed off the road, airborne over the ditch, where it landed ass over teakettle. She had a sensation of an explosion and pressure, then everything went very still.

CHAPTER TWENTY-FOUR

Big Horn, Wyoming

Aaron stopped at the Big Horn school to drop off the head football coach—and his best friend in Wyoming—Perry Flint. The two of them had just come from a dog sledding lesson at Tommy's. Tommy had harnessed the malamutes behind three of his seasoned dogs. It was immediately clear that between the two malamutes, there was only one puller, and it was not the dog with any sense.

"You can't let a dog like Willett lead, though," Tommy had said. "She's liable to run you off a cliff. Sibley will keep you safe."

"Safely in last place in any races," Perry had said.

"Ha ha. But Perry's right. She's sitting on the harness and making the other dogs pull her."

"A fair bit. But she might embrace it more over time. Keep working with her. Encourage her. Reward her. Show her there's nothing to be scared of. The other dogs are having fun. That may be contagious. But most of all, don't get frustrated. That will take the fun out of it for her. This is part of dog sledding. You're only as fast as the slowest dog on your team. Focus on what you can learn and do better to make it easier to communicate with them and lighten their load."

All in all, Aaron had learned a lot about mushing and his animals. And he'd laughed. Perry and he had eaten a lot of snow. As his old college coach would have said, it was about as much fun as you could have with your clothes on.

Now, Aaron and Perry walked into the head coach's office to talk a little football. Luckily, the tired dogs were welcome there, because Aaron didn't feel comfortable leaving them in the Jeepster. Not with Willett's mischievous, trouble-seeking nature, tenacious chewing ability, and titch of anxiety. She'd dismantle the Jeepster before he was out of the parking lot. And not with all the offers he'd had to buy Sibley, by passers-by. At lunch when he'd walk them together through town, they attracted a lot of admirers. Two floofs together were exponentially more floofy than two floofs apart. And Sibley's level of floof was near irresistible, it turned out.

The clinic visits would probably have to stop soon, though, unless both dogs changed dramatically. Willett required near-constant attention, and Sibley, it turned out, didn't suffer foolish dogs gladly. When she'd had enough of their chaos, she simply let them know in her own growly, toothy, doggy way that it would be wise for them to shut up and sit down. So far no blood had been shed, but he knew it was inevitable without close supervision. The smart move was to keep her out of situations that would flip her switch, and to show her it wasn't her job to control unruly canine behavior. That was up to him. But he couldn't do that if he wasn't with her, and he couldn't be with her if he was seeing patients.

It made him a little sad. He knew they were happy in their new home, though, and would be fine in the big dog run at his satellite clinic there. Willett had already established a routine in the mornings. At the first sound of his morning alarm, she jumped into bed with Jenn and him, burying her nose in his armpit for a power snuggle. Sibley was more reserved but stayed by Jenn's side whenever possible. He'd heard his wife cooing to the dog about how much smarter and prettier she was than Willett, and it made him happy to discover this side of Jenn.

"You with me, coach? Perry was standing at his white board with a dry erase marker in his hand. Around him, the office was chaos. Stacks of three-ring binders. Newspapers on the floor. Printouts of articles on the internet scattered across his desk. Three coffee mugs and several water bottles. He'd just finished outlining the offseason conditioning he planned for the team. "You looked like you were in La-La-Land."

"I was thinking about dog sledding."

"Dog sledding is over. Now we're getting the team in shape. They can't rest on their laurels. State champs back-to-back or bust."

"I have an idea. They can work out the dogs." Aaron grinned. "Kidding. Yeah, your plan looks good. We're losing a lot of seniors, though."

Willett rolled onto her back and tucked her front paws against her chest. Her tongue hung out like a red ribbon. Sibley looked at Aaron as if to say that Willett was the definition of *derp*. Their doggy odor was hardly noticeable over the ever-present scent of teenage boys' locker room. Neither smell bothered him at all.

"But the talent coming off the JV squad will make up for it. We'll have more speed in your secondary."

"We need it. That was our weakness last year."

"We're on the same page then." Perry capped his marker and took a seat. "I heard Jenn and Kid are working on Black Bear Betty's case."

"Yes. Can you believe they charged her?"

"I can't believe they didn't arrest Carolyn Barrett. She's been pretty vocal about his death being an upgrade to the neighborhood."

"He was a jerk, but that's harsh." Aaron remembered she'd been the neighbor who'd called Trusk to complain about his dogs chasing her cows.

"Yeah. She's not known for her sensitivity. She always demands players come help her stack her hay."

"I'm sorry, I don't follow."

"We give conditioning credit for manual labor in the summer. Haying is a big part of it."

"Oh, yeah, that's smart."

"Nobody wants to help her. She follows them around in a pickup and criticizes their performance, then doesn't want to give them breaks, feed them, or pay them after they work in the sun all day." Perry laughed. "Kind of like a coach."

"Do you think there's any way she had something to do with Trusk's death?"

"It's unlikely, but I never say never."

"I'll remind Jenn about their feud. Maybe she'll want to talk to her."

Perry motioned at Aaron's vibrating phone. "Do you need to get that?"

Jenn's name was on the screen. A phone call, not a text. She rarely called. And he'd had it silenced. How many messages had he missed that she'd been forced to call? The thought almost made him chuckle. "Yes, thanks." He accepted the call. "Hey, Jenn. What's up?"

Her voice was muffled. "Oh, nothing much. Just hanging upside down from a seat belt."

He leapt to his feet. "What?"

"I've been calling and texting. Somebody was ramming my car from behind. Then I hit black ice."

His fists balled. He could feel his adrenaline production kick into high gear. "Wait—ramming you?"

"Yes. And then drove off after my car flipped into the ditch."

He wanted to roar and then hunt down the person who'd done this to her and beat them to a pulp. But indulging his feelings wouldn't help. He had to take this step by step. She could die from exposure. Of internal bleeding. The list of possible horrible things was long and unhelpful. He made a chopping motion, as much to cut himself off as to symbolize what he wanted to do to the other driver. "Did you call 911?"

"Yes. Help is on the way."

In the background, he heard music. Maggie's new collaboration with Ava Butler. "Is the car still running?"

"Yes. The side window broke. I have plenty of fresh air. The heater is blasting, so I'm not really cold. Just stuck. And honestly being upside down isn't very comfortable."

"Where are you? I'm at the school."

"Less than a mile away." She described her location. "I had to hang up on them to call you. They wanted me to stay on the line until the first responders reached me."

He put his hand over the phone. "Jenn had a wreck," he said to Perry.

"Go, go." Perry shooed him with his hand. "Do you need help? I can come with you."

"She called 911. They should be there any second. She doesn't think she's hurt. Just trapped." A fireball exploded in his mind. *Please, God, no. No gas tank leak. No fire.*

"Call if you need me." He held up his phone.

"I will." Aaron sprinted from the office. It was only when he heard their paws on the ground that he realized he'd forgotten the dogs. They hadn't forgotten him though. "Are you really okay?"

"Things hurt a little. I'm crampy, which is weird. But the airbag saved me."

He opened the back door. "Kennel, girls." The dogs jumped in gracefully without breaking stride. "I'll be there in five minutes. I love you."

"I love you, too."

Please, please let her really be okay.

CHAPTER TWENTY-FIVE

Big Horn, Wyoming

Jennifer awoke the next morning with a headache, neck ache, and very sore ribs. She'd gone to the hospital the night before out of an abundance of caution, mostly because Aaron insisted. Deputy Travis had met them there and taken her statement. It had been all she could do not to throw up as the whiplash set in and the hospital smells assaulted her. Ammonia. Artificial pine scent. Dirty mop water. She held it in. This conversation was important not just for her own safety, but the safety of her client.

She'd explained to him that the driver behind her had rammed her and run her off the road deliberately.

"Did you get a license plate?" the big deputy had asked.

"No."

"Make/model, description of the vehicle?"

"Big. The lights were up high like it had a lift."

"Nothing else?"

She gave him some slant eye. "It was dark. It happened quickly, behind me. Then I was upside down in a ditch."

"I guess nothing about the driver, then?"

"No."

"Do you have reason to suspect anybody in particular?"

"Anyone associated with Pootie Carputin. He hates me."

"Any particular associate of his?"

"None have made threats against me. But you asked for ideas. So, here's another. Anyone who hates Black Bear Betty, anyone who wants to see her convicted or might be seeking revenge on her, anyone who was an associate of Mr. Trusk's."

"Why?"

This time she rolled her eyes. "Because I'm her attorney, and sometimes people believe if they eliminate the A team, that means the outcome will be different. Like if someone really did kill him, they might want to be sure the blame stays on Black Bear Betty. Didn't you hear what happened to her in jail?"

"I heard what she did."

"She was a victim of four women who attacked her and framed her in an assault. The threat is real, it's substantial, and it's ongoing. We've requested solitary for her own safety, but to my knowledge it has not yet been implemented. It will be on the State of Wyoming's watch—and Ollie Singletary's head—if Black Bear Betty is harmed."

"I'll check on the solitary. It can't hurt. Then I guess we'll see what Helena Jones says about the assault when she wakes up. If she wakes up."

"Yes, we will. And you're aware this isn't the first time something like this has happened to her?"

"Can't say that I am."

Jennifer had growled. "So much for Ollie taking things seriously and investigating."

"I don't know what you're talking about."

"I'm talking about how when she was in jail awaiting trial after the death of her husband, that she was spied on and ultimately an attempt was made on her life. Her conviction was thrown out with prejudice because of judicial bias and tampering."

"Are you talking about Judge Arnold? He was acquitted on all of that."

"There's this little thing called burden of proof. Beyond a reasonable doubt is a very high standard to deprive someone of their liberty. Failure of law enforcement to develop evidence or prosecutors to prove a case doesn't always add up to an innocent defendant. Something I am quite sure you're too familiar with."

Travis had sighed. "I am. Guilty parties get away with crimes far more often than I'd like."

"And innocent people get victimized. I need your help, Travis. My client is getting victimized, again. I was attacked tonight. I don't know who did it. But if you'll hand me your notebook, I'll write down all the names of the people who are suspects from my point of view in Trusk's death and I'll add Arnold just in case you forget we had this conversation."

Travis had looked at Aaron and said, "Is she always this feisty when she's been in a wreck?"

Aaron had taken Jenn's hand. "Consider this her softer side."

God, how she loved her man.

Later that night when they'd finally gotten home, Aaron had taken care of her like she was as fragile as her grandmother's china. Both dogs had glued themselves to her side in bed until she fell asleep, and they were banished to make room for her husband.

If I'd only known how much I'd be hurting this morning, I wouldn't have turned down the heavy-duty drugs.

She sat up, wincing, and propped pillows behind her. Time to pull it together, or, as Aaron would say *play through the pain,* something she'd hated in his football days, but seemed like the only option in her situation. Yesterday, she and Kid had decided he would track down suspects with access to M series Kubota keys, and that she would hunt for the Rivian's missing chains. Hopefully he'd finished his research the night before and could give her an update before they both got going on their respective tasks. Calling Charity was not going to make her head feel any better, but it had to be done.

As did getting in touch with Carolyn Barrett, who Aaron had reminded her about while they were driving home from the hospital, when she had in turn told him about Betty's theory of the missing tire chains.

Her husband appeared, blocking the light from the hallway with his big body as he stood in the doorway. "I wish you had slept longer. I tried not to wake you. How do you feel?"

"Like I rolled my Grand Cherokee. Is it totaled?" She pushed slowly to a seated position, groaning and pressing fingers to her head.

"No. The back end is smashed up pretty good from impact with the other vehicle. Your rear suspension and exhaust system will likely be messed up pretty badly, not to mention you'll need a new lift gate. The top is dented, but you weren't going fast enough to crush it, and it didn't hit anywhere else."

"That's good."

"Will you eat something?"

Just the words turned her stomach. Even coffee sounded awful. "Water."

He held up a glass and walked it over to her. "I guessed right."

She took it with a shaking hand. A sticky note clung to it. "I love you in right side up cars." She smiled. It hurt. "Thank you. For everything."

"You're precious to me."

"As you are to me." She sipped then gulped the water. She wasn't sure why, but she thought of Casey and her interest in Aaron. "I have to tell you something."

"Uh oh." He sat on the bed, taking care not to jostle her.

"We fired Casey yesterday."

His eyebrows went skyward. Both of them. "What happened?"

She held up a finger as she drained the rest of her water. "We caught her red-handed sabotaging the case and lying to us about it."

"Why in the world would she do that?"

"It's hard to fathom. I keep wondering if she's involved in this somehow. Or if she just hates me. Anyway, if she comes to you with a sob story, just know that it broke Kid's heart, but he pulled the trigger."

"Got it." He took her empty water glass. "I have a patient due in five minutes. Can I do anything else for you now?"

"No. But thank you. I've just got to face my day."

"Take it slow."

"I'm only a little battered, not broken. I have chains to find and witnesses to talk to."

His forehead wrinkled. "I can cancel my appointments and drive you."

"Oh, crap. Driving."

"I'm not just worried about you driving, I'm worried about the person who ran you off the road last night. Whether they're done."

"Ugh. I hadn't thought about that. But unless they're waiting for me outside our driveway, it won't be a problem. There's nowhere to hide up here. And it's broad daylight. Besides, I won't be in my own car, since it's smashed."

"I don't disagree, but I don't love it either."

"You're sweet, and as awful as it sounds, I can do it myself. Except for my lack of a ride."

"Take the Jeepster. I don't have to go anywhere today. And if something does come up, I can drive the old ranch truck."

"Aaron, I can't drive that enormous old thing!"

"Demarcus is gonna take good care of you."

"Let me take the truck."

"It doesn't have snow tires."

An image of the inside of the Grand Cherokee as it had slid, spun and flipped filled her mind's eye. "Sold. I'll put the Yellow Pages in the seat so I can see over the steering wheel."

"Do they even make telephone directories anymore?"

"Probably not. You know, if we have kids, they might be short like me. We should track down a few as boosters. It's what my parents always used for us."

This time he raised one brow. "Do you know something I don't?"

"Nothing to report. Idle chatter."

He leaned down and kissed her gently on the tip of her nose. "Be careful today. Keep me posted."

"Yes, sir."

He was smiling as he left.

Half an hour later, Jennifer had taken Tylenol, showered, and gotten as ready as she could. It was a decent hour—nine a.m. She texted Kid and told him about her mishap and that she wouldn't be in. He responded with the appropriate level of horror and sympathy, offering to take everything work-related off her plate. For a brief second she indulged a fantasy of binging the last season of *Castle*. But she declined, just asked him to be sure Carolyn Barrett was on the list for background research and asked him to type up the results of his research and email them to her.

And then she made the easier of two calls first. Or the one she assumed would be easier.

"Carolyn Barrett speaking." The voice was like machine gunfire.

"Ms. Barrett, my name is Jennifer Herrington. My colleague Wesley James and I are representing Black Bear Betty, who's—"

"I know who you are. I know what you're doing. I assume you're calling because you hope I killed that jackass Glen Trusk. I'm a busy woman, so I'll give you a short answer: I didn't. Goodbye." The call ended.

Jennifer stared at her phone. *Well.* She wanted to laugh, if she wasn't so sure it would hurt like hellfire. "Was it something I said?" Then she did laugh and discovered she was right. She winced and held her head until the pain passed.

After Carolyn, Charity Trusk wasn't as scary. Jennifer found the new widow's number and initiated a call.

The woman's caustic voice was instantly recognizable when she answered without a hello. "Tell me this isn't really the vet's little missus."

She's as unlikeable as ever. "Mrs. Trusk, a crucial piece of evidence has come up in your husband's case. Chains for the tires on his truck. Would you happen to know where they are?"

"No. And I'm in California and not coming back, so I won't be looking for them either."

"Would you be willing to let me search for them?"

"Good God, no."

"You could have anyone there with me that makes you comfortable. My colleague, perhaps? Or a deputy?"

Silence.

"Mrs. Trusk?"

"Shit. I don't suppose it makes any difference. Glen is dead. He's not coming back, thank God, so I don't care who gets pinned for the murder. If you find something that gets that old dyke out of jail, it won't change a thing for me. Knock yourself out."

Did she really just say Thank God her husband is dead? She might think it didn't change a thing for her, but she was still a suspect in Jennifer's mind. A suspect with plenty of money to hire people to do her dirty work. Or convince them to in other ways, a la ... barebacking, as Casey had put it to Aaron. "That's extremely generous and helpful of you."

Charity cackled. "Never thought you'd be saying those words to me, did you?"

Jennifer knew better than to fall for the bait. "You've been through so much. I hope moving back to California is the beginning of a much happier time in your life."

"Well, your mother raised you with manners. That was quite touching. Has your hot husband moved that horse yet?"

Jennifer bristled, thankful Charity already had her claws in Boot when Glen died and didn't feel the need to harass Aaron. "No. He plans to do it on the first day that it's safe to have the trailer on the ranch road. The snow has been relentless. But he's been over there twice a day caring for him and administering his treatments."

"Can't be soon enough for me. I have an interested buyer. I don't want a lingering animal to get in the way of a closing."

Jennifer would have to let Daisy Bean know about this development, if she and Kid took her case. "Thanks again."

And Charity was gone. Possibly before Jennifer had thanked her. *Is it the universe with the hang-ups or is it me today?*

She texted Aaron that she was heading to the WP Bar and trudged out to the Jeepster. Aaron loved this hunk of steel. He could have worse obsessions, but she didn't share his fondness for it, normally. Its shock absorption was subpar. Everything in it was manual. And it was a stick shift. She could barely reach the pedals.

She patted the door. "I'm hurting. Go easy on me today, Demarcus. Please." She hauled herself up and into the driver seat, blew out a few breaths as she recovered from the impact on her injuries, and cranked the engine. "I'll just turn back if the roads are bad. Or if there's anyone else on the road in a big vehicle."

For a beat she thought about getting the snowmobile. She'd be less recognizable in a helmet, but holy cow a helmet would hurt. It probably wouldn't be a smoother a ride, and Aaron swore the Jeepster was great in these conditions. She'd drive like a snail. All would be fine, as long as she didn't run into the creep who'd tried to kill her the night before.

CHAPTER TWENTY-SIX

Big Horn, Wyoming

After a blessedly uneventful if terrifying drive—Jennifer couldn't close her eyes when she was the one driving—she searched the stables and garage. She was drooping, but she hadn't found any tire chains. Or seen any other humans, which she counted as a huge blessing. She stood in the parking area between the garage and house, pondering the limits of her permission. She hadn't asked to enter the house, but Charity hadn't told her not to.

She tried the side door. It was unlocked.

"That's a sign." She pushed it open and braced herself for an alarm. If it sounded, she'd beg forgiveness.

But only silence greeted her inside.

The house was exactly as it had been the last time she'd visited it. Sterile, uncomfortable, out-of-place, and incomplete, smelling of paint and sawdust with subtle undertone of unloved neglect. She wondered what it had looked like before the Trusks had bought it. The bones were good. She'd heard a famous architect had designed the home. It was easy to believe, which made it even sadder to behold its current state.

She liked the layout, with privacy for the owner's quarters and easy traffic flow through multiple living areas. A long, deep sunroom facing the south was a standout feature. In it, a gallery of paintings hung, artfully arranged. She stopped to study them. While the art wasn't to her taste, it looked pricey. She peered closer at a few of them. They were not prints. And based on the famous signatures, neither were they reproductions. She felt her eyes widen. How much was the art in this room worth? And how could Charity leave it here without so much as an alarm system to protect it? These should have been packed away and stored under lock and key.

Down to business, Jennifer. The faster you finish work today, the sooner you can nap. In the meantime, there was always the extra Tylenol in her pocket. She decided to be systematic. And nosy. There weren't many places in here she could imagine someone stashing tire chains, but people did weird things all the time.

She started in the basement, opening every closet and drawer and even looking under the beds. More expensive looking paintings lined the walls. *You know you're art rich when your underground guest quarters looks like a museum.* She found nothing but a dildo in a fur pouch, which sent her scurrying up the stairs gagging like a cat with a hairball.

Next she attacked the single second-story room, which appeared as if someone had used it as an art studio. Here there were no paintings displayed. But there were no canvases, brushes, or tubes of paint in the specialty cubbies seemingly designed specifically for each type of item. Nor were there chains. The room was as barren as, well, Jennifer herself.

"Don't worry, old girl. You're perfect just like you are," she said aloud, before she went down the stairs.

A text notification sounded on her phone. Trish Flint. *My brother said you had a bad accident. I hope you're ok!!*

A feeling of warmth spread through her. It was nice having friends. Jennifer answered immediately. *Sore but fine. Thanks for checking on me. Coffee next week?*

Three dots appeared. *I'd love it. How about Monday morning at my place? I make the best in town and have a great view.*

Perfect!

Trish sent an address and time, and Jennifer saved it in her phone, then refocused on the task at hand. Back on the main floor, she worked quickly from the rooms she felt were least likely to bear fruit. The bedrooms. The bathrooms. The living and dining areas. The wet bar. The kitchen. All the hall closets. So, so many hall closets. Closet doors did cut down on hanging space for art, although the Trusks had still crammed in a good number of surely priceless treasures. The architect or whoever had designed this house apparently went by the adage of *more is more* when it came to storage.

Finally, she had only the laundry and mud rooms left. She stopped for a glass of water in the kitchen, where she took her next dose of Tylenol. Her headache was returning. Her body ached. Her stomach was growling. She checked her phone. It was noon already. How had so much time passed here already? She responded to texts from Aaron to let him know she was well.

Time to get this over with.

Her highest hopes were pinned on the mud room, so she searched the laundry room first. Again, a multitude of doors to open and shut. As many doors as paintings elsewhere in the house.

Laundry room done, she trudged down a long hall, closed her eyes and took a deep breath. After she finished this room, she'd head home and take the nap she'd promised Aaron and the doctor last night that she'd take in the afternoon. She pushed through a swinging, louvered door into the small space filled with cabinet doors and one large closet.

"Come to mama," she said.

She found absolutely no chains.

But something orange caught her eye. Orange and small and hanging from an incongruously rusty nail.

It was a keychain with keys. And it said KUBOTA on it.

"Yes," she shouted with a fist pump.

CHAPTER TWENTY-SEVEN

Big Horn, Wyoming

Jennifer scanned the snowy WP Bar landscape with binoculars. Kid was walking around, using a metal detector over the snow. She felt much less uneasy there today with him with her. It had been his idea to come back and search the accident site for the chains, and it was a good one.

She got credit for the discovery of the key chain, which she'd confirmed did in fact work with the tractor before she'd headed home the day before, holding it in a baggie. She'd conveyed it home and written up her notes on it—ignoring Kid's research email in her inbox —before crashing. She only woke up when she heard Aaron scream, "BAD DOG."

She smiled. *Which one? I'm betting Willett.*

A few minutes later, he peeked in their room. "Are you awake?"

"Sort of. What happened?"

"I was making wild-caught Alaskan halibut for dinner. Willett was in the mood for sushi. How do hot dogs sound to you?"

She chuckled. "I hope you're not talking about roasting anything that didn't come in packaging from the grocery store. A la Willett the dog in hot water."

"Ha. There's an idea."

The memory made her smile now. Smiling already hurt a lot less today. In fact, everything about today was better. Aaron had served the hot dogs on a bed tray with white wine and a vase of slightly tired grocery store flowers. It had been a romantic evening followed by a romantic early morning.

"I'm getting bupkis." Kid brandished his metal detecting wand like an old man with a cane. He was so cheery that she assumed he hadn't been in contact with Casey. *I hope so, anyway.*

"When did you become Jewish?"

"My maternal grandmother."

"Ah. Are you done? We can warm up in the Jeepster and go over your research."

"I've got about five or ten more minutes to go."

Damn. That meant Jennifer had to search the cliff face. She moved to the edge, fighting a sense of vertigo. She hated heights. But the accident site wasn't just the road. It was the foot of the cliff. It was the descent from one to the other. That meant she had to look down. She swallowed hard. Maybe Kid could do this part? But he had resumed working with his metal detector.

I can do this.

She looked down, felt herself sway, and jerked her eyes back up.

Dammit, Jennifer.

She tried again. Same result.

Maybe if I get closer to the ground?

She lowered herself to her knees and put one gloved hand in the snow. She tried looking over again. It wasn't great, but it was much better. She was in a good position, looking at the cliff and the base from the side. She trained her binoculars on the ground first. She didn't have high hopes for that area. The truck had been hoisted out. Real humans had been down there collecting evidence. But she had to rule it out.

Like Kid, she found bupkis.

Slowly, she panned upward with the binoculars. Her hands were shaking, and her breathing was rapid. She focused on slow regular breaths. Passing out was contraindicated in this situation. She continued climbing the cliff with her eyes.

And then she saw something. Something that didn't look like snow. That appeared manmade. She wasn't even sure why she thought that. Couldn't describe her impression other than the shape and color weren't like a rock or a bush. The colors—black, blue, red, silver—contrasted with snow, although whatever it was appeared to be buried in the white stuff.

"Kid, come here. I think I found something."

He crouched beside her a few seconds later.

She handed him the binoculars and pointed. "Halfway down. What do you see?"

"Holy moly. I see something that could be tire chains."

"I don't suppose you could climb down there and check it out?"

He snorted and handed her back the binoculars. "No way on God's green earth. Or white earth in this place and time. But I know someone who might. I can contact him as soon as I get back to the office."

She stood, lightheaded, and turned away from the cliff. It felt wonderful to have her eyes on terra firma, the horizontal kind. "Sounds good. I'll draft a motion to dismiss for prosecutorial misconduct." She ticked on her fingers. "Failing to collect this evidence. These and the keys. Also, for charging our client with unwarranted first degree to force a second-degree plea. And for failing to provide protection for her when we requested it. Ignoring the evidence we brought him. All of that. The kitchen sink."

"Have you read my email?"

"Not yet."

"We can go over that, too, then. There's a lot to talk about."

A horn honked from the direction of Red Grade Road. They both startled and turned. A Range Rover was creeping towards them. It honked again. Jennifer walked toward the SUV's driver's side.

The driver rolled down the window. "Excuse me. You're trespassing," the man said.

Jennifer gritted her teeth under a smile. "Actually, I'm not. I called Charity and got her permission before I came. My name is Jennifer Herrington. And you are?"

"Here to show the property to a potential buyer. Are you almost done?"

Jennifer wanted to say no. She wanted it badly. But the truth was, she and Kid had found exactly what they came for. She swept her hand toward the goat path. "It's all yours. We were just leaving."

CHAPTER TWENTY-EIGHT

Sheridan, Wyoming

Friday morning, Aaron rushed into the clinic, running late from the YMCA, which he'd recently joined. Actually, he'd been running late *to* the YMCA, and he had no regrets about how that had happened. It had been a great evening and morning with Jenn. But he was still excited about the gym, too. This had been his first really comprehensive workout in a long time. The pheromones and endorphins had him feeling like Thor. The only bummer was that he'd had to leave the dogs. They were shadowing George, who was delighted about it, since Liam had gotten too frail for the job.

All those good feelings came crashing down when he entered the lobby. His first sight was Casey, who jumped to her feet as two beagle puppies barked and lunged against the leashes held by a teenage boy. He hadn't talked to Casey about leaving him alone. There hadn't been a chance. He'd hoped he wouldn't have to. There was no way he was going to initiate contact to raise the issue. And now, here she was. He couldn't do it in the clinic.

She moved to intercept him. It was a small space. He wouldn't have been able to escape her if she'd been standing with her back against the wall.

"Aaron. Hi." Her eyes were bright. Intense.

"Hello, Casey. What brings you here?"

"Do you have a minute?"

He looked pointedly at the clock behind the reception area. "Less than. I'm late and booked solid."

"Thirty seconds is all I ask."

"She's been here half an hour already," Loretta said, her voice drier than usual and her expression disapproving. "Lon Early is bringing in his champion border collie with a suspected broken leg. He'll be here in ten minutes. We have patients waiting in every exam room. Doctor Taylor called in sick. You're all we've got."

The door behind him opened and he heard a loud hiss.

"Game and Fish called to see if the fox is ready for release."

"I'll call them back."

"And Mrs. Snell is here with her Maine Coon, Sugar Plum."

Casey's mouth tightened. "Can we talk outside?"

He felt the eyes of everyone in the lobby drilling into him. He could imagine the whispers this would start and wondered how long it would take for Jenn to hear about this encounter. Probably faster than Casey's thirty seconds. No way was he going outside and making this look like more than it was. "Here is fine."

She lowered her voice and turned her back to their onlookers. "I came to follow up on my application. Do you have anything opening up?"

"That's up to Loretta. She's the practice manager. Did you ask her?"

"Yes."

"My answer is whatever she said." He softened his words with half a smile.

"I need a job. Can you talk to your wife? She got me fired."

He stared at her without answering. By his estimation, thirty seconds was up. He made a move to pass her.

She blurted out, "Why don't you have kids?"

He couldn't believe he was hearing her right. And that the rest of his staff and patients were, too. "That's a very personal question."

"It's because of her and her career isn't it?"

"I don't like the direction this conversation has taken. I need to—"

"Just hear me out. You want kids, don't you?"

He held his hand up between them, no longer caring about their onlookers. "That's enough Casey. No more visiting my house or my clinic. No more personal questions. You're a nice girl. I wish you the best. But this is the end of these interactions. Do you understand?"

Her face went ashen. "I'll stop. Just... please don't cut me out of your life."

He shook his head, keeping his voice as low and kind as possible. "I don't know at what point you felt like you were in my life. I don't mean that unkindly. But I did not invite your attention. You showed up on my doorstep. I've tried to be understanding, but this has to stop. You have mistreated my wife and made me very uncomfortable. Please—don't make this hard. You need to move on. And now I have patients to see."

She gaped at him, eyes welling with tears.

He forced himself to nod at her and leave her standing in the lobby, although it made him feel like a shit heel. But it came down to a simple choice. Jennifer or the feelings of other women. There was no way he was letting her or anyone bad mouth his wife or try to come between them.

Never. No one. No how.

CHAPTER TWENTY-NINE

Sheridan, Wyoming

After Kid had sent a request to a climber friend to help them with chain retrieval, Jenn sat down with him to go over the information he'd gathered.

He stood and began pacing as he talked. "The death of Daisy Bean's parents and aunt and uncle was ruled accidental. I found some articles questioning that early on, but the police never ran with any suspects. The journalists talked to people who said there was bad blood and bad seeds in the family tree."

She rolled her lips. "Any particular branch?"

"All fingers pointed to Daisy, but no one had anything specific."

"Damn. Maybe a call to the police who handled it? See if there's anyone you can talk to about what they really thought."

"I'll put it on the list." He stopped pacing and spun to face her, holding up his hands and wiggling his fingers. "But the grandfather is the more relevant and interesting case to look at, I think."

She rolled her hand for him to continue.

"Gramps was ruled natural causes, for starters. He was old. But, again, the journalists dug up people who referenced that bad blood and bad seed again and claimed that he was in perfect health for his age. The direct beneficiary of his death is his heirs, who are limited to grandchildren since their parents had died. Some would say conveniently. Arguably, Daisy had the biggest stake since she was due to be cut out of the will."

"What do you mean, 'due?'"

"Insiders claimed he'd redone his will but not finished executing it yet."

"And we assume Daisy knew this, too?"

Kid shrugged dramatically. He was like a one man show. "Possibly. Or maybe people are jerks, and she knew nothing and did nothing wrong. I'll add the Sheridan County Sheriff's office to the list for follow-up."

"Good. Now, about—"

"Sheridan Hole or Judge Clinton Arnold?"

She laughed. "Dealer's choice."

"Let's start with the Sheridan Hole development. Good old Barty Arnold bought the old Bridgewater place about fifteen years ago. In our recent influx of outsiders to the area—"

"Like Aaron and me."

"Um, I wouldn't say that actually. You guys aren't building oversized new houses on razed-to-the-dirt former ranchland."

"True."

"Barty seems to be looking to capitalize on the people who want to be the richest people in Sheridan instead of the poorest ones in Jackson Hole. He's offering three, five, and ten-acre plots for large custom homes in a gated community with all the luxuries."

"Does he have permits and finances?"

"The articles I read seem to suggest he has the former and is struggling on the latter. He needs cash or credit in order to build out the infrastructure. You know, roads, water, power, and golf courses."

"Hence his relationship with Trusk."

"Right. And I can't confirm anything there yet."

"Okay. Are they selling plots or breaking ground yet?"

"Not yet." Kid beat his hands in a drum roll on his desk. "But here's the part that's going to blow your mind."

"It's still a little fragile from my wreck yesterday. Go gently on it."

"Barty Arnold and Clinton Arnold—"

"Are brothers!"

"No."

"Father and son?"

"No. Nor are they brothers-in-law before you go that route."

"Then what are they?"

He grinned. "The same person. Bartholomew Clinton Arnold."

"Gold!" Jennifer jumped to her feet and did a happy dance from her cheerleading days.

Kid's jaw dropped. "Were you just doing the macarena?"

She pointed at him. "Bite your tongue."

"Consider it bitten. Don't forget Black Bear Betty told us that her former husband Jerry and Arnold were business partners."

"Just like Trusk," she breathed.

"Minus fifteen years ago. Otherwise, yes."

"Holy smokes." The wheels in Jennifer's brain were spinning. "And Arnold presided over Black Bear Betty's trial."

"Tried personally to get her convicted and then tried to dead her."

"To get his hands on the life insurance money to pay off the money he owed on his seedy storage units."

"So sayeth our client."

"The theory works for me. You get back to work. We need a face-to-face with Barty Clint."

"An ambush or scheduled?"

She did one last four-count of moves from her dance. "I think ambush."

"I like your thinking!"

For the next few hours, Jennifer typed furiously on her motion to dismiss, breaking only to leave two messages. One for Ollie about solitary for Betty and an investigation into the woman's claims. The other to Travis, ditto about the investigation, but also to see if he'd made any progress on the person who had hit *her* and ran. Every word of her prosecutorial misconduct motion was a joy. She thought back to the times defense counsel had taken aim at her. It had made her so angry, and her assumption had always been that is was nothing but tactical. Maybe sometimes it had been, but it wasn't to her now. She'd never dreamed how good it would feel to be on the other side. Or how much she yearned to oust Ollie and take his seat. She couldn't even speak it aloud, but it was a feeling that grew every day, especially as she become more and more disenchanted with the way he was performing his job. She'd had high hopes. He was an upgrade from Pootie in so many ways. But in the end, Jennifer knew she could do it better.

At two o'clock, Kid whooped victoriously.

Jennifer tore herself from her document. "That sounded good."

"It is. My friend who ice climbs is going to meet us out at the WP Bar and get the tire chains for us."

"That's fantastic. When?"

"Now."

Her eyes stretched at his answer. She rubbed them. The print had been getting smaller lately, in proportion to how long she stared at a screen. But was it just strain or was she knocking on the door of—gasp—readers? How could she be thinking of a baby right when her body was entering its decline? *More yoga.* She'd made the cottage bedroom into her office, but she'd left the space by the fireplace for her yoga mat. Her mostly unused lately yoga mat. It had even been on Chaplain Abel's list of recommendations for destressing, better sleep, and less nightmares. "Just let me hit save and grab my coat and purse."

Thirty seconds later the two of them ran to their separate cars. Kid would be returning to town. Jennifer would head home after this.

"Be careful in that monster-mobile," Kid shouted, as he opened the door of his little tin can.

"I'm more worried about you. One strong gust of wind and you'll be airborne all the way south to Casper." Kid had bought a new-to-him Prius after George's case. He'd been safer when she met him, and he was driving his mother's Denali.

They were both laughing as they pointed their cars toward the mountains and headed to meet Kid's friend. Still, Jennifer could admit that driving through Big Horn gave her the shivers and had her looking in her rearview mirror. No strange vehicles drove up on her and rammed her, however.

When they reached the WP Bar Ranch gate, Kid pulled over and hopped in with Jennifer. "Do we have permission to be onsite?"

"Well, we did. I didn't re-up with Charity. Better to ask for forgiveness in this case."

"I just hope that nasty real estate agent isn't still out here."

"Seriously."

Kid gestured ahead of them. "That's Adam parked on the other side of the cliff."

Jennifer drove across the goat path and pulled to a stop behind Adam's old Subaru, roughly where the Kubota had been parked when she and Aaron had discovered Glen in his Rivian at the bottom of the cliff.

Adam was already out of his car and carrying coiled ropes and a few bags of gear out to the cliff face. He looked like he could be a classmate of Kid's, but whereas Kid couldn't grow whiskers, Adam was ninety-percent facial hair and the rest sinew. Kid jumped out of Demarcus Ware and bounded up to his friend. The two dapped knuckles and then bumped shoulders. Jennifer joined then, more sedately.

Kid made a flourish with his hand toward Jennifer. "Adam, this is Jennifer Herrington. The woman who is making a man out of me. I mean, a lawyer." His face turned splotchy red. "Sorry, that came out wrong. Jenn, this is Adam Carmichael. He was a year ahead of me at Sheridan High."

The young man's voice was Barry White deep. "Nice to meet you, Ms. Herrington."

She shook his calloused hand. "Jennifer. You, too, Adam. Thanks so much for coming."

The next few minutes were consumed with Adam's preparations. Kid tried to help but mostly got in the way. Jennifer stood back, amused.

Ten minutes later, Adam shouted, "I'm going over."

Kid hurried over to where Adam had anchored his rope, looking at it and then over the side at his friend.

Jennifer tried to picture what Kid would do if the rope came loose. Adam outweighed him by fifty pounds. If Kid was all Adam was counting on, then Adam was in deep trouble. She was no better choice, though. Kid outweighed *her* by fifty pounds.

Down to Adam, Kid shouted, "Do you need me to hold on to you?"

"Nah. It's tight. You can just holler goodbye if it gives way."

"Not funny," Jennifer said, as both men laughed.

And then Adam jumped back off the icy cliff. Jennifer's heart nearly stopped. From below them, she heard the rope sing, and she pictured it moving through Adam's hands. She had no desire to lean over and see it for herself. Watching him possibly die going after the chains was last on her list of things she wanted to do today.

A door slammed, then another. Jennifer hadn't heard a vehicle approach. She didn't want to see who was there—real estate agent? Daisy Bean? Sammy D? One of the angry neighbors? The person who had run her off the road? When she turned, it was none of them. Deputy Travis sauntered over, beside him a tall woman with green eyes like a feline. She was similarly dressed in law enforcement gear, but as she drew closer, Jennifer saw that her patch read KEARNY COUNTY.

Travis stopped in front of her. "Greetings. What do we have going on out here?"

The woman, who didn't introduce herself, walked closer to the cliff and stood watching Adam descend.

She crossed her fingers behind her back. "Kid's friend Adam is doing some winter rappelling and rock climbing. We came to observe. I've always been interested in the sport."

"Funny. I heard you may have found evidence in my murder case."

"From whom?"

"A little birdie with a strong sense of civic duty."

Jennifer hadn't told anyone but Aaron. Kid had told Adam. Adam had no reason to know why they were here or tell anyone. Kid suddenly found the sky very interesting. She took a few steps away from the law enforcement officers, herding Kid with her.

"You're still talking to her, aren't you?" she muttered.

"What?"

"To Casey."

"Some."

"And you told her about this?"

He flushed. "I was excited."

She balled her fists. She hadn't thought she needed to explicitly instruct Kid not to be dumb. And yet she had, and he'd contacted Casey today while in the office with Jennifer. How had she not noticed it?

"All right. What's done is done. Maybe this will work to our advantage somehow. In the meantime, you owe me. You get to file the motion for dismissal for misconduct against Ollie this afternoon. Be sure to drop a courtesy copy off with him personally."

"Oh, that will be fun."

She couldn't say she would mind missing those fireworks.

She moved a little closer to the cliffside to watch Adam. Kid stayed in lockstep with her.

"Hello, Attorney James," the policewoman said to Kid.

"Deputy Pace." His voice was respectful, but he turned his attention down to his friend instead of introducing Jennifer.

She started to introduce herself, but then Travis moved up to the edge, so she did, too—Travis closer than her—and peered over.

"Hey bud. I'm Deputy Travis." Travis gave a two-finger forehead salute.

Jennifer hated leaning over, too, but she couldn't help it. The bottom seemed to pull her toward it. *It's just an illusion. Your feet are on solid ground.*

Adam stopped, seemingly in midair. "Cool. Nice to meet you, lawman. Unless you're here about my traffic tickets?"

"Nope. I'm here to observe the collection of the evidence."

"I'll be back with the goods pronto."

Adam lowered himself at a speed that made Jennifer nauseous, his body nearly perpendicular to the wall. He hopped down in puffs of snow and mini avalanches like an abominable snow spider. His trajectory seemed too far to one side, until he pulled up short parallel to the set of chains she had spotted. He began inching across that cliff face toward it.

Suddenly, she understood. *He didn't want to risk burying it. And now he doesn't want to dislodge it.*

Slowly, slowly, Adam neared the chains, then reached out and snagged them. At the same time, his feet lost traction and his body went vertical. He faceplanted against the cliff with a muffled, "Oomph."

Jennifer stifled a scream. Was he hurt? Had he dropped the chains? They could be buried if he had. She didn't begin to know how many feet of snow was piled at the bottom of the cliff, both from the natural snowfall and from the snow pushed off the road by the plow.

Adam was dangling by his waist. An odd sound was coming from him. It took Jennifer a moment to realize he was laughing. He reached up with one hand and held on to the rope. With the other, he held the chains aloft. "Is this what you guys are looking for?"

Kid whooped, Jennifer shouted, "Yes," and Travis muttered, "Come to Papa," under his breath.

"We're the ones that found them," Jennifer said.

Travis tucked his thumbs under his arms. "Doesn't matter if they're evidence."

Kid said, "There should be another set. I thought I saw them about ten feet further down."

Adam nodded. "I'll stash these and go after them in a sec."

Jennifer thought about the keys she'd found and the ones in Betty's personal belongings locked up at the jail. If a defense attorney had withheld them from the cops and her, she would have socked them with an obstruction charge. If she and Kid had retrieved the chains and withheld them from the state along with the keys, it could have ended up that way for them. Ollie would be mad enough after her motion was filed. Best not to end up in jail with Betty. It was time to disclose the keys she'd found.

"I have another item you'll want, then."

Travis gave her an arched brow look. "I suppose you're going to tell me you didn't know any better."

"No. I only became aware of it moments before you arrived. You coming here saved me from bringing them to you."

He gave an exaggerated eye roll. "Don't keep me in suspense."

She shook her head. "First tell me what you've found out about the person who ran me off the road last night."

"Not a damn thing, unfortunately."

"No witnesses? No video?"

He snorted. "Where do you think you are? New York City? Or just still in Houston?"

"If it had been you or someone you loved, you'd have high hopes that the perpetrator could be caught, too."

"No doubt. But, seriously, no. No witnesses, no video. No physical evidence."

"What about the paint on my bumper?"

"We've got a dent. We've got some black paint. We don't have fingerprints or DNA. If we develop a suspect, we can try to match the paint to their vehicle. Not the other way around."

"Fair enough. Now, what about Black Bear Betty."

He groaned. "I talked to Ollie. He has four witness statements." She started to interrupt, but he held up a hand. "I'm going to see if any of the guards have ideas about who these women were in contact with. Maybe—just maybe—if someone outside put them up to this, we can trace it back."

"Thank you."

"You're welcome. Now, can I have my evidence, please?"

Their conversation had given Jennifer a chance to think about how she wanted to frame her discovery of the keys. "Betty took the only key she knew of with her when she went to the bathroom up at the house, before Trusk died. Since she wasn't allowed to move the tractor after, she still had it on her when she left that day."

Travis winced. "Bad oversight on my part. I appreciate the heads-up."

"According to her, anyone with sufficient know-how could hotwire that tractor."

"I don't know how to. Do you?"

"Neither of us is a killer. Anyway, her tractor key is in her personal belongings at the jail."

"Where they've been touched by God knows who all."

"You're welcome. And I found another keychain with keys to the Kubota up in the mudroom at the Trusk house... earlier. I took them in a baggie over to my home office for safekeeping, and I didn't touch them."

"How convenient that the defense discovers their own exculpatory evidence. I'll need an affidavit."

"You'll get one."

"Expect a vigorous argument against admissibility. What do you think this proves?" he said.

"Are you serious? A tractor that can be hotwired, an additional set of keys? Opportunity. For people other than Black Bear Betty. She also said, by the way, that any Kubota M Series key should start Trusk's tractor right up. I know you'll want to work up a list of people with motive and opportunity and see which ones had the means. Assuming you don't come up with evidence that blows the smash-and-push tractor theory out of the water."

He laughed. "Like what?"

Behind them, she heard Kid say, "Way to go, Adam. Want a hand over?"

She turned in time to see a hand appear on the rope, followed by another. Adam's head popped up. He was grinning ear to ear. "Nah. I'm good. But these chains aren't. Somebody cut the bungee fasteners right in two."

Jennifer bit down on the inside of her lip. Cut them? Trusk wouldn't have cut his own fasteners. That meant sabotage, which could be a sole or contributing reason the truck went over. As in *not an accident*. What would that portend for her client? Her fingerprints would be on the chains if she hadn't been wearing gloves.

It could be worse for Betty unless they found the real saboteur.

She glanced at Travis. The smug look on his face told her he knew it, too.

CHAPTER THIRTY

Sheridan, Wyoming

Sitting at a table in front of the dramatic two-story rock fireplace at the public library in Sheridan, Kid drummed his thumbs then switched to an imaginary piano and played a dramatic arpeggio. When he finished he looked up. A little girl no older than four with pigtails sticking straight up on each side of her head was watching him in awe. He bowed his head. She clapped and giggled.

If only he felt like his work was applause-worthy. Maybe he should ask the child's parents if she could follow him around and cheer! Yesterday had been exciting with lows equal to the highs. Finding the chains and retrieving them, then realizing that the sabotage didn't necessarily exonerate Betty. Her fingerprints would be on them, unless someone else had wiped them clean. Again, he and Jenn were left trying to disprove a negative: that Betty hadn't done something no one else had witnessed anyone else doing. He'd ended up facing down an irate County Attorney when he delivered the courtesy copy of Jenn's motion to dismiss based on prosecutorial misconduct.

But he was on to something that was sending a symphony through his nervous system. He had become sadly convinced that for whatever reason Casey had taken a dislike to Jenn it had resulted in her withholding information. He assumed that was to make Jennifer look bad in court. Or maybe Casey hated Black Bear Betty. He hadn't been able to figure it all out yet. He just knew he couldn't trust her work. He couldn't trust *her*. She had reported their conversation to the cops yesterday. Not that she didn't have a right to. Not that it would change what the evidence said. Jennifer had drilled into him from the beginning of their time working together that it was better to know everything and deal with anything that was bad than to be in the dark. So be it.

He was more concerned that if Casey had found something useful that would lead them to their most important alibi witness—Will Renwick—that she would hide it to frame Betty or make Jenn look bad. Will couldn't have gone far. He didn't have a job or a vehicle, last Kid knew of him. Aaron felt sure he'd seen him on the side of the road a few days ago. For all he knew though, Will had stolen a car and been the one to force Jenn off the road. Until they found him, nothing was certain.

He had to fix this and find Will. He felt responsible for the uncertainty. Jenn hadn't wanted to hire Casey in the first place. It had been his stupid idea. Her big blue eyes, long legs, shiny blonde hair, and whip smart brain had short circuited his judgment. *Never again*. He thought about their dinner and lunches. Time he'd hoped she thought of as dates, like him. Had she just been using him? All those questions about Jenn and Aaron bothered him even more now. She'd never shared anything about herself, either. Not really.

So, he'd come to the library to get out of the office that reminded him of Casey and of his humiliation. And he'd started from scratch building a profile on Will, hopefully one that would lead to someone or something pointing to his whereabouts.

And Kid thought he'd found it.

Will had been mentioned in the paper for a few criminal

escapades in his teens. Kid's follow-up in the databases showed his record had been expunged of his acts as a minor. But one of the articles mentioned his father—Harold—and stepmother—Priscilla—by name. Kid quickly found that Harold had died years before. After that, the stepmother fell off the face of the earth. He couldn't find a Priscilla Renwick anywhere. But when he traced back to the marriage license he found Priscilla's maiden name. That led to a second marriage license a few years earlier. She now went by Priscilla Kennedy and lived in Ranchester, just north of Sheridan.

Kid emailed the results to himself and Jennifer, slammed his laptop, and jumped up with it under his arm. Finally, someone who could possibly give them a glimpse into the past that had shaped Will. Because the best predictor of future behavior is past behavior. And it was this current behavior and where it had taken Will that Kid was interested in.

Two short hours later, Kid and Jennifer stood on the steps of a prefabricated home planted on a barren piece of dirt at the edge of Ranchester, waiting for an answer to his knock. Kid had been riding high on his discovery. Now that they were at Priscilla's home, he was more calm but still hopeful. It was a very good feeling after how down the situation with Casey had made him feel.

A woman's voice called out, sounding suspicious. "Who's there?"

Jennifer smiled widely—Kid had noticed she did this even when she was on a phone call, whenever she wanted to be nonthreatening. It showed in her voice. "Hello. My name is Jennifer Herrington. I'm an attorney in Sheridan. I'm looking for Will Renwick."

"He ain't here. He wouldn't be."

An even bigger smile. "That's what I thought. But you're his stepmother, correct? I would love to talk to you and see if I can learn anything that helps me find him. He's a very, very important witness in our case."

"I *was* his stepmother. I was married to his dad at least. Let me tell you—Will came by his crazy naturally."

Kid and Jenn shared a look.

Jenn said, "I've brought my colleague with me. Kid James. We'd really appreciate just a few minutes of your time and insight."

Kid heard a scratching rattle. Chain lock. Then the door opened. Heat and cigarette smoke hit him like a shock wave. He kept his expression steady.

Jenn was half a head taller than Priscilla Kennedy, which made the woman quite short. Actually, the women were quite similar, especially their mouths, which Kid thought were sort of bow shaped. Plus, their short blonde hair. Blue eyes. Petite frames. Priscilla could have been Jenn's mother or aunt. "Hello, Mrs. Kennedy. I'm Jennifer. This is Kid."

Priscilla pulled a heavy cardigan tighter around a frail torso. "Come in. I don't want the neighbors gossiping. It could get back to Will."

Kid motioned Jenn to enter ahead of him. "And that would be bad?"

"He didn't want me in his life then. He got me out of it as soon as he could."

"When his father died?"

"When he left for the Army."

They took seats on a couch—Priscilla—and armchairs—Kid and Jenn. Kid took a brief glance around. Lots of needlework homilies, lace curtains and doilies, and dried flowers. Very tidy. Furniture sagging and worn but clean. A strong odor of onions and garlic. Maybe beef stroganoff. He pulled his attention back from the house to the witness. His and Jenn's interview routine was well established by now. Kid started taking notes, including his observations. He knew he was welcome to jump in whenever he felt the need.

"Let's start at the beginning." Jenn gave a firm nod. "When you first met Will."

"I married his father. Harold. After his mother died. Will blamed me for his mother's death."

"Why?"

"His father and I, we'd been seeing each other before she passed." She took a deep breath. "I was Will's babysitter when he was little. That's how I met Harold."

"How did his first wife die?"

Kid knew. He'd read about it when he was looking for information on Priscilla. The first Mrs. Renwick had been strangled and left in a cattle pasture. A ranch hand had found her stomped and muddied body. It was horrible and had probably had a lasting impact on her son.

"Someone killed her."

"Was the murderer caught?" Jenn asked.

"No." Priscilla looked down.

"Who was it?"

"Some folks say it was Mr. Renwick."

"*Mr.* Renwick?"

"Harold. My ex."

Interesting she calls him her ex and not her deceased husband or something affectionate.

"Do you think it was him?"

"I didn't at the time. Later, I wondered. He, uh, he was different after we married."

"In what way?"

She gnawed on a fingernail.

"Did he hurt you?"

She nodded.

"Did he hurt Will?"

Another nod, more gnawing.

"And how did Will act? Was he scared of his father?"

"How is this going to help you find him?"

"I don't know yet. But it won't *not* help."

She nodded, terse. "He worshiped his dad."

"When did Will start rejecting you?"

"From the day we got married. And Harold let it happen."

"How old was Will then?"

"Thirteen."

"I read he started getting into trouble."

"He did. Because he acted like Harold."

"He hurt people?"

She looked at the ceiling. "I wouldn't say that. But he was destructive. Didn't care about nothing or no one."

"Did he hurt you?"

"He played tricks on me. Cruel things. But he never laid a hand on me."

Kid decided that was a yes answer and jotted down his impression.

"Like what?"

"Like... leaving my needles pointing the wrong way in my pincushion."

Ouch.

Jenn nodded, her eyes warm. "And then he went into the military?"

"Yes."

"You were still married to Harold?"

"Yes." She lowered her gaze.

"Do you know how it went for him in the Army?"

"I know he was a maintenance officer in Afghanistan. There was some trouble."

"Like in high school?"

"Yes. The same."

"What happened?"

She sighed. "He got sent to a doctor. They discharged him, for medical reasons."

"He came here?"

"Here, but not home. We lived in Wyarno back then. He stayed in Sheridan."

"Did you see him?"

"No. But he saw his dad. And his dad would repeat things Will said around me."

Kid said, "Who would his dad be talking to?"

"What?"

"You said his dad would repeat things Will said *around* you. Not to you"

"Oh. Well. To himself, mostly. He'd been ranting and raving for years."

"What did Harold tell you Will was doing?"

"Seeing a shrink through the Army. It upset Harold. The diagnosis. He said no son of his was crazy and neither was he."

"Do you remember the diagnosis?"

"Antisocial personality disorder."

Kid nodded vigorously, taking a few catch-up notes. A class he'd taken in law school covered mental illness in criminal law. He got ethics credits for it. People who suffered from APD had a total disregard for the feelings of others. They were likely to lie, act out violently, or break the law and show no remorse. It was relatively uncommon—a little more than half a percentage point of the population—but it was believed that forty-seven percent of male inmates and twenty-one percent of females inmates had it. Famously, Ted Bundy, John Wayne Gacy, and Charles Manson were diagnosed with APD, three of the most ruthless American serial killers of all time.

Jennifer said, "I've tried a lot of cases over the years against defendants who either had or claimed to have APD."

"Will told his dad that meant Harold had it, too. Will was angry about it. Really angry. Like his father had made him that way on purpose."

"What do you think?"

"Something was wrong with Harold. I don't know what to call it."

"Were you still living together as man and wife when Harold passed?

"Yes."

"How did he die?"

Her voice fell to a whisper. She looked away. "He got drunk and passed out and didn't wake back up."

"Was Will there the night it happened?"

Her eyes remained fixed on closed curtains. "No."

Kid was no lie detector but every cell in his body screamed that Priscilla was no longer telling the truth. Whether about how her husband died or about whether Will was there or something between the lines, he did not know.

He said, "Where did Will like to go, to get away from things?"

"I honestly don't know. Maybe he told his shrink. He didn't talk to me. Harold didn't much either."

Kid thought about completing the workup on Will as a witness. How was he going to get his hands on his military records? Did he have a prayer of obtaining anything medical? Probably not without a release from Will for either. First they had to find him. Then convince him that a release was in his best interests. In other words, the chances were slim to skeletal.

But then he had another idea. "Who were his friends? Back when he lived with you."

"Friends? He didn't make friends. He'd occasionally get fixated on some girl. That's the closest I ever saw him to being kind, is when he was trying to court a girl. Like Harold with me. But it always fell apart in the end. Then it was worse than if he hadn't liked the poor girl."

Jenn looked at him, a question in her eyes. He nodded. He was done. He put his pen and notepad back in his briefcase.

Jenn stood. "Thank you, Mrs. Kennedy. This was very helpful." She handed the woman a card. Kid added his to the woman's hand. "If you think of anything, no matter how trivial, please let us know. We think Will's knowledge could save our client from being convicted of murder."

Priscilla stared at the cards. "He won't care. Even if you find him, I mean."

"Do you think he's dangerous?"

"Just mean."

Kid didn't believe they were going to find Will from the information Priscilla had given them. On the other hand, he was even more eager to than before. APD? He wanted to meet this guy. See someone like he'd read about, only in real life.

If only he could think of some way to track him down.

CHAPTER THIRTY-ONE

Sheridan, Wyoming

Jennifer parked across the street from the county attorney's office in the lot. She was dragging, and not just because it was Monday or because of her nightmares. It had been a sad weekend. Liam had passed in his sleep on Saturday night. They'd had a small ceremony on Sunday for the sweet old St. Bernard. George was bereft, clinging to Jeremiah with tears on both cheeks. Jennifer had surprised herself by sobbing openly and even Aaron developed a sudden case of the sniffles. Because the ground was frozen, George put up a marker for Liam. LIAM NICHOLS. BEST FRIEND. BEST DOG. He let Aaron take Liam's remains to the clinic. Later, Aaron would bring the dog's ashes back for George. Even the malamutes had picked up on the mourning and somber occasion. Sibley hugs had helped Jennifer more than she'd expected. Willett had cuddled into Aaron and kept watchful eyes on him.

Jennifer tried to shake off her blues. She needed her game face. Think about the positives. Like that she and Aaron were in a sizzling place in their relationship, and that he'd told her about Casey showing up at his clinic, including that he had laid down the law with her about further contact, a fact verified by half the town. That thought helped. But was it enough to sharpen her up to face Ollie? If she were in his shoes, she'd be breathing fire at the sight of the defense attorney who'd filed a motion to dismiss for prosecutorial misconduct.

Ollie met her on the front porch and held the door open, like he'd been watching for her or someone. His face was impassive. *So far, so good.* "Why so blue? Did your dog die?"

Jennifer flinched. "Yes, as a matter of fact, he did."

He shook his head, gesturing her in ahead of him. "I'm sorry. I just assumed it was because you'd heard the results of the forensic tests on your new evidence. That was insensitive of me. My apologies."

She nodded acceptance and forced herself to switch gears. "The only surprise about that evidence would be if my client's fingerprints weren't on her tractor key and the tire chains she put on Trusk's Rivian to protect him." She sighed. "I got a message on my cell phone from Deputy Travis that the results were sent here. I'm just here to pick them up."

Ollie followed her inside.

"Good morning," a receptionist said in a chirpy voice.

Ollie nodded at him. Jennifer lifted a hand and smiled.

"It's her!" a woman's voice screeched.

Jennifer turned and saw the fragile figure and anxiety-ridden eyes of Melinda Carputin, Pootie's daughter. The woman's red hair was in wild disarray. "Melinda. How are you?"

"Terrible, thanks to you. You've broken up my family and ruined my father's reputation, all for a man who killed my sister."

Jennifer bit the inside of her lip. Melinda's claim that George had killed Sarah Carputin wasn't supported by the traffic reports on the day Sarah died in a collision with George. The police had found her at fault. But she understood the desire not to blame a loved one, and the need to find a reason for a tragic death. However, she absolutely refused to take responsibility for Melinda's parents' divorce. That had occurred after Pootie's conviction but Kid's successful defense of George—with Jennifer as his legal consultant—and their exposure of Pootie's crimes was a result of them, not a catalyst.

"I'm sorry to hear you're not well." Jennifer stopped there, unable to think of what else to say.

Ollie gestured with his head toward his office, and she followed quickly, with Melinda still grumbling behind them in the lobby.

In his office, Ollie motioned for her to sit. Jennifer didn't plan to be here long. She shook her head.

He shrugged. "Suit yourself. Sorry about Melinda. She comes by from time to time. She knows we can't release her father, but that doesn't stop her from making the rounds and asking."

Jennifer nodded. She remembered family members of defendants doing similar things in Houston, although it had been harder there for them to get past security.

Ollie picked up the phone and called his assistant Cheryl. He asked her to locate the documents and make a copy for Jennifer.

"Already done. I'm on my way," Cheryl said.

Why couldn't Cheryl have been the one who'd come looking for a job instead of Casey? As soon as Jennifer passed the bar, she'd need to hire someone. And set up an office downtown. She loved Kid, but she did not envision her office-sharing over his mom's garage for her law practice. But he could certainly relocate to hers, if she found good space.

Ollie picked up some papers and tapped them on his desk to straighten the corners. "Not to start Monday with a fight, but I don't appreciate your motion or having your errand boy drop it on me. That was a cowardly move."

Here we go. Jennifer rubbed her eyes. She was so tired and had been ever since she rolled the Grand Cherokee. Battered and bruised was a hard way to sleep. Harder even than usual. The only benefit was that if she was awake, she didn't have nightmares, just far too much time to think about everything else. "Cowardly? Try recovering from a car wreck I believe was caused deliberately by whoever killed Trusk. My client is in jail, so it wasn't her. And as I'm sure you gathered from the motion to dismiss, the lack of appreciation is mutual."

His eyebrows shot up. "For me doing my job?"

"I've done your job. I just want you to do it well."

Finally, she started to see his temper rise. It made her feel better. "You were an *assistant* district attorney. I am *the* county attorney."

"I ran the homicide division for Harris County. I had ten attorneys reporting to me. You have four. I do understand your job, I promise you."

He stared at her for long seconds, then his lips twitched, and he shook his head. "And you want it."

She smiled sweetly. "I want it to be done well. That includes things like taking inmate safety seriously and charging defendants ethically. I included a list in the motion. It's something of a primer, really."

"I highly doubt those *things* were that important to you before you became a defense attorney."

Cheryl walked in and handed a thin package to Jennifer with a smile. She was about Jennifer's age, but her polar opposite. Tall, dark haired, dark-eyed, with olive skin. Thick but certainly not heavy for her height. More just less curvy than Jennifer. A wide, straight mouth except for when it broke into that smile. Possibly Native American heritage. Even their style was different. Cheryl was dressed in black from her boots to her neck, except for a brilliant turquoise squash blossom necklace.

"Thanks." Jennifer tucked it in her purse.

Cheryl said, "No problem." She left without drama. Jennifer decided it wouldn't hurt to try to recruit her when the time came.

She returned to Ollie's last comment. "I was under a lot of public scrutiny. Possibly that was part of why I cared about them. Since my time consulting on the other side of the bar, I've definitely had my awareness heightened. Keep in mind, though, I'm not licensed and don't practice criminal defense law in the state of Wyoming. I'm an overqualified legal consultant to Wesley James. I'm the one who runs his errands and picks up his discovery. It was his motion, not mine."

"He may have signed it and delivered it, but he sure as heck didn't write it."

She gave him a smile as sweet as Cheryl's.

He stood and moved away from her to the corner of his office where he crossed his arms. "I got your client moved to solitary."

"Thank God." She couldn't believe it had taken him that long. "How about asking the sheriff's office to investigate the issues I raised about Judge Arnold?"

"There's no evidence."

"Because no one has looked for it. Besides, you can have my client's testimony on it. That's evidence."

"The words of a desperate defendant."

"The words of an innocent woman who has been framed and is in fear for her life."

"I have four witnesses. Defending her is your job."

She tucked the folder from Cheryl under her arm and angled toward the door. "We seem to have reached the same old impasse. I won't repeat the ugly truth."

Ollie sighed. "I want this job, and I want to do it well. It's not easy."

"That I know. And if I can ever help you in any way, let me know."

"Is that what your motion is? Helping me?"

She walked to the door then turned. "Actually, that would be a very good way to look at it."

"Wait. I forgot." He returned to his desk and shuffled papers, then picked up another file. "The medical examiner's report came in." He held it out to her. "This is your copy."

"Don't keep me in suspense." She took it from him but didn't open it.

"Died of injuries sustained upon impact. No stroke or heart

attack or other condition which could have caused him to veer off the road. No drugs or alcohol in his system."

"I wish the ME had a crystal ball to consult then we'd know whether it was inattentive driving or inability to handle inclement road conditions. You can't prove murder when you can't disprove an accident. You're in an overloaded eighteen-wheeler with no brakes headed straight toward reasonable doubt."

"We'll let the jury decide. We have the Kubota paint. You found the sabotaged tire chains for us. "

"Which my client told us should have been on the tires and prevented sliding. Would a guilty person who had sabotaged chains tell us to look for them?"

"She would if she thought it would make her look less guilty."

Jennifer shook her head. "It's pointless continuing this conversation."

Ollie shook his head. "How about this then: despite how poorly your case is going, I'll re-up the State's offer of fifteen years and second-degree and throw in the aggravated assault for free."

"You're dreaming."

"And you have a duty to submit my offer to your client along with all the other dismal facts of her case."

That was a truth Jennifer hated being reminded of. She stomped out to the Jeepster without another word, slamming the door with all her might as she got in.

CHAPTER THIRTY-TWO

Sheridan, Wyoming

"TOP YOU OFF?" Trish Flint asked. Behind her, a picture window displayed Sheridan County's picturesque skyline—the Bighorns anchored by the jagged edges of Black Tooth Mountain.

Jennifer held a hand over her mug. She needed to slow down on the caffeine, which she'd been pounding from the moment she arrived, seduced by the amazing smell of the coffee and homemade blueberry muffins. Now her hands were starting to shake, and she'd been running off at the mouth. She'd barely let Trish get a word in edgewise, except at the beginning when Trish had confessed the tall, dark, and handsome Ben who kissed Trish's blonde braid and left when Jennifer arrived was her former teenage sweetheart.

"That's a story for another day. Suffice it to say that after neither of us ever married, we're giving it another try. Thank God for Facebook or we might never have found each other again after all these years." Trish had smiled with a dreamy look in her eyes. Then she'd begun asking Jennifer questions, and the conversation had centered around Casey. Casey! With all Jennifer had going on with Betty's situation, her own baby dilemma, and the nightmares triggered by Pootie's escape from justice—the very thing that had caused her to realize she lacked friends in Wyoming—she had spiraled down the Casey rabbit hole. What kind of insecurities did that reveal, she wondered?

"It sounds like you've caught her red-handed and dealt with it, though," Trish was saying.

"Yes and no." Jennifer thought carefully about her next words. She couldn't disclose details of Betty's case. While she thought about her phrasing, she buttered a second muffin and took a bite. It was still warm. And the blueberries burst in her mouth. Nothing Jennifer baked ever turned out this luscious. "I have one more thing I'd like to verify. I think she sent me an email with false information then deleted it out of my inbox. I'm not tech savvy enough to look under the curtain, though, and see if it's still out there somewhere."

Trish's blue eyes twinkled. "I have just the person for you. I met a deputy in Kearny County recently—a couple of idiots set part of the national forest there on fire—who is a computer wizard. He said for me to call if I ever needed anything."

"I feel bad about you calling in a favor for me."

"He's not like that. I think it was a sincere offer. I also sensed he can be very discreet. And in your line of work, you need to be friendly with the opposition in neighboring counties."

Jennifer's mind briefly went to her secret desire to run against Ollie for Sheridan County Attorney. If she won, law enforcement wouldn't be the opposition anymore. Trish was right, though. Until that time came—if ever—she needed to be on good terms with people like her friend. "All right. I'd love an introduction, then."

Trish already had her phone out. She fiddled with it a few seconds, then put it to her ear. "Leo Palmer, this is Trish Flint with the National Forest Service. We met—" She paused, smiling. "Yes, nice to speak with you again, too. Listen, I have a friend who needs your computer skills. She's a defense attorney in Sheridan. Jennifer Herrington. I honestly think it's important for the two of you to know each other anyway. Could I connect you to work out the details? Great. I'll text you. And good luck on the election. If I was in Kearney, I'd vote for you." A few moments later, she said goodbye and ended the call. "He's heard of you and said he'd be delighted to see if he can help."

"Thanks! And he's running for sheriff?"

"He's the interim sheriff now. The last two sheriffs there have died on the job."

"Oh, my gosh!"

"I wouldn't want to sit at that desk."

"Me either."

Trish was typing rapidly. "There, I sent a text to him with your contact card and vice versa. He said he'll expect to hear from you."

Jennifer saved the contact card. On a whim, she quickly typed a text. *This is Jennifer Herrington. Trish said I should contact you about a problem I'm having. I'll be in touch soon!* She hit send.

No sooner than she'd finished, a text came in for her. Normally, she wouldn't have checked her texts when with a friend, but she couldn't help but read it. It was Kid. *Arnold is at the YMCA. Ready to ambush him?*

How do you even know this? She responded.

I was following him. Long story. Meet me there?

Jennifer's pulse sped up. *Game on*, she thought. "I'm sorry to have to rush, but I just heard from my colleague Kid. He's located an important witness. Time is of the essence."

Trish flapped her hand. "Go, go. I have Zoom calls starting in fifteen minutes and need to clean up my office. The unexpected issues of work from home days."

Jennifer stood, feeling a little awkward. It had been so long since she'd had a "first date" with a new friend. "Next time, my treat. This has been really lovely."

Trish pulled her into a hug. "The pleasure was all mine."

JENNIFER MET Kid in the sun-filled lobby of the YMCA. Luckily, Aaron had bought her a membership when he'd joined recently, so she wasn't going to have to wheedle her way past the front desk. Kid was pulling out a membership card, too.

"Do you come here much?" she said.

He held his card to the reader. "Nearly every day."

Jennifer copied his movement with the card. She was only a little surprised when hers worked and she was admitted for the first time. "What do you do?"

"Swim. I was on the swim team in high school."

She could see that. "Now where do we go? I don't suppose you know where he is?"

"No, but we'll find him. Follow me."

Jennifer fell in behind Kid. Together they searched the gym, several weight rooms, cardio machines, talking as they went. They entered the pool area.

"That's him in the hot tub. I recognize him from his pictures." Kid pointed at a ruddy-cheeked man facing their direction. His stomach sat in front of him like he was holding a cantaloupe on his knees. Strands of light brown hair lay across his head, with most of his scalp exposed.

"I'm not exactly dressed for this." She took off her shoes. "Do you have something to take notes with?"

"I'll do it on Notes in my phone."

She squared her shoulders, hung her jacket on a towel rack with her shoes below, and marched in her slacks and blouse over to the former judge. He was staring past her as she approached, but when she got close, he switched his focus to her and smiled in greeting. When she stopped beside him, though, he frowned.

"Mr. Arnold?" she said.

"Yes?" His gaze moved to Kid, who was now standing behind her.

She lowered herself to a seat with her legs crossed at the ankles

Indian style, or, as her nieces called it, criss-cross applesauce. The tile floor was dry, if hard. The chlorine in the air brought tears to her eyes and burned her nose. She put a hand on her chest. "I'm Jennifer Herrington." She indicated Kid. "This is my colleague Kid James. We were given your name by Charity Trusk."

His recoil was slight, but she saw it in the tightening of his lips and dilation of his pupils. "What is this about?"

"We have some questions for you."

His head whipped left and right. "Here?"

"Was Glen working with you on Sheridan Hole?"

"Yes. He was financing it."

Jennifer felt her face betray her with surprise. So, she went with it. "Really? That's not what his wife said."

He snorted. "His wife was not his business partner."

"Had he already funded you?"

"Sadly, for the people of our community, he had not."

"Where will the money come from now?"

"I'm actively courting potential investors."

Jennifer smiled. "Sounds a lot like what happened a few years back when your business partner Jerry Jurgenson died."

Arnold shot up from the water and scrambled out of the pool, belly swaying from side to side. "Charity Trusk didn't send you to me."

"Did you think she did? I said she gave us your name."

He started walking toward the men's locker room. With his wet feet, his progress wasn't fast. "This conversation is over."

Jennifer stayed right beside him with Kid on her heels. "If you'd have gotten that money from Jerry's life insurance policy, you wouldn't be looking for investors now, would you?"

In the empty entrance to the men's room, he whirled on her, his face almost purple with rage. He reached out with big, red hands and shoved Jennifer into the tile wall. Her head slammed into it with a snap. It was still sore from her wreck only a few days before, and the pain was sharp and instantaneous. She crumpled to the ground. *No.*

Show no weakness. But despite her best intentions, her body betrayed her, and she landed in a heap.

"Jennifer!" Kid shouted, falling to his knees beside her. He cradled her head with one hand.

"I'll be fine. Don't let that bastard get away."

Kid shook his head. "We'll let the police deal with him. That was assault, and you're injured."

CHAPTER THIRTY-THREE

Sheridan, Wyoming

An hour later, Jennifer had convinced Kid she was only stunned and just fine. What was the difference between her lightly concussed and her normal sleepwalking anyway? They had gone after Arnold, but he'd hightailed out of the YMCA so fast there was nothing but dust left in the parking lot in his wake. They'd agreed to make a police report after they visited the adjacent jail to give Betty an update. Jennifer had handed the keys over to Kid at his insistence, however, and they'd stopped by his office to change into dry clothes as they'd both gotten wet on the men's locker room floor. Jennifer was glad she always kept a change of clothes in her oversized briefcase.

"What's the matter?" she said, after they were on their way to the jail. "I really am fine."

Kid looked lost in another world as he accelerated down the hill in front of the courthouse on Main Street to catch the green light.

"I feel stupid."

Preoccupied, more like it. "Why?"

"Arnold ran off on us and assaulted you right in front of me."

"Not your fault."

"I haven't followed up on who has Kubota keys yet."

"Only twenty-four hours in the day. But I'd add Arnold to that list."

"Added." He nodded. "I can't figure out how to find Will. He's like a cipher."

"I can't either. Do you think I'm stupid?"

"No." He sighed. "But it's also Casey. I should have seen through her. She just did such a good job on everything for me that I couldn't imagine how she didn't for you. And I guess it's because she didn't want me to see it."

"You have an endearing tendency to see the best in people."

"Maybe." His voice was grumbly.

"And she manipulated you. Purposefully. Showed you what she wanted you to see. She was good at it."

"Which circles back to stupid."

Jennifer tutted. "Young. Infatuated. Human."

"Yes. Humiliated. Very."

"Wiser."

He drove in silence. Parked and entered the jail without further conversation. Checked in and followed the guard to the interview room without another word between them.

When the door had closed behind the guard, Kid said, "We don't have any good news for her, do we?"

"None. Not on the original case or the new one. But Arnold admitting Trusk had agreed to finance him and then assaulting me isn't bad news. It's just not fully developed yet." She hadn't told him about Ollie's latest offer. Or about the medical examiner's report. She barely had the energy to share it with Betty, so she decided to wait.

"Damn. I wasn't even thinking about the new aggravated assault case. I've been so consumed by the Trusk case."

"I'm becoming more and more convinced they're one and the same."

The door opened and Betty lifted her chained wrists and waved.

A guard escorted her in. Jennifer hated to admit it, but she'd rarely smelled anything worse than her client. It made her sad. Betty was usually fastidious about her hygiene, with the exception of her fondness for cigars. Some people found those pleasant, though.

"Remove the cuffs, please," Jennifer said.

The guard did. "I'll be outside if you need me."

"Thank you."

He nodded and closed the door behind him.

Betty rubbed her wrists. "Tell me some good news."

Jennifer gave her a sad smile. "If we had some I would."

"That's not what I'm paying you for."

"As I recall, you haven't paid us anything yet, but until that time comes, let me explain our role. It's to zealously defend you. I promise you, you're getting every bit of that and then some. While the news isn't good, we have plenty of it." She spread the pictures of the sabotaged tire chains on the table. "For starters, we found the tire chains. They had landed in two places on the cliff where Trusk's truck went over."

"Somebody cut 'em plumb in half."

"Correct. The state found your fingerprints on them and plans to claim it was you."

"I did no such thing. I put whole chains on, in one piece each. My only goal was that the numskull didn't go over."

"Which is what we will argue. I also found another set of keys to the Kubota."

"And?"

"No prints."

"Why not?"

"My guess is someone wiped them clean. But clean keys equals no evidence. We'll tell the jury they could have been the keys used to drive the Kubota to push the Rivian off the cliff. If it was even pushed and didn't just go over because somebody cut the chains."

"You've gotta find the person who cut the chains!"

"We've talked to everyone we can think of, and no one saw

anything remotely suspicious, including cutting tire chains on a car that later went off a cliff and resulted in the death of a man."

"Who've you talked to?"

Jennifer nodded to Kid. He pulled out their witness list and read the names, adding Arnold.

Betty pursed her lips. "That's a damn good list."

Kid said, "Thank you."

"How'd it go with Arnold?"

Jennifer touched the back of her head. "He said he and Trusk were business partners."

"Like with Jerry!"

"Yes. And he acted fishy when we asked him about Jerry's insurance money."

Kid crossed his arms over his head. "He assaulted Jenn."

Betty's eyes went round and wide. "I didn't see that one coming."

"And she was run off the road by someone last weekend."

Betty leaned toward Jennifer. "Is this because of me?"

Jennifer put her hand on Betty's. "No. This is because someone else murdered Trusk."

Betty nodded but her eyes were troubled.

"Anyone we're missing?" Kid said.

Betty chewed on her top lip. "I don't think so."

"Anyone on there seem guilty to you?"

"With the exception of Arnold, all of them as much and no more than me. Which is to say I couldn't imagine they'd kill him."

"Again, the fact that we don't know for sure *anyone* killed him will be one of our arguments. Number one: Glen Trusk died in an accident. Number two: Black Bear Betty didn't kill him and there's no evidence that she did. Number Three: Lots of people had as much motive and opportunity as she did. If he was murdered, one of them did it."

"You said we don't know for sure anyone did," Kid said, pausing from his notes. "Does that mean you got the Medical Examiner's report?"

Jennifer pulled it out of her briefcase and handed it to him. "We did. Ollie surprised me with it when I was there picking up the results on the chains and keys. It said Trusk died of injuries sustained from a truck going off a cliff." To Betty she explained, "It would have helped us if he'd died of natural causes. We could have argued accident with more authority then."

Kid added, "We'll get to see records of his phone usage soon. To know whether he was on it or texting when he died. Again, that would help us with accident."

Jenn nodded. "Not conclusive, but persuasive. But there's one more thing that I got from Ollie. A renewed and slightly improved deal."

"Why would I take a deal for something I didn't do?" Betty snarled.

"Because we haven't even talked yet about the risk that you'll be convicted of the aggravated assault."

"I told you I didn't do that either!"

"If we go to trial we'll do our darndest to convince the jury of that. We'll discredit the witnesses who say you did it as best we can. We'll investigate who could have been behind framing you. But there's no video. It's your word against theirs."

"The woman who got stabbed didn't die. Maybe she'll tell the truth."

"Would she know for absolute sure that you didn't attack her on your own?"

Betty frowned. "Maybe not."

"That's where this new offer comes in. You'll recall that the County Attorney offered you fifteen years and second degree in exchange for pleading guilty."

"He can stick that where the sun don't shine."

Jennifer held up a hand. "Now he said he'd include the aggravated assault in it."

"For how long?"

"Same. fifteen years. But it would cover two possible guilty verdicts."

Betty pressed her lips in a hard line. "Would you take it if you were me?"

"Kid's good in court."

"What about you?" Betty cut in.

"It won't be me. This case will go to trial before I get my license."

"Can't you stall?"

"'My lawyer isn't a lawyer yet' isn't going to work to slow the train. There's a limit to what we can do, especially in a case where there's not much left to discover."

"There's one witness you didn't talk to."

Kid nodded along with Jennifer.

"Will Renwick will tell you. I was up at the house."

"Will has disappeared. We can't find him to get his statement. But we did talk to his stepmother." Jennifer told Betty what they'd learned from Priscilla about the medical condition diagnosed by the VA psychiatrist.

"APD? There's a name for everything now. When I was growing up we just called it being a thoughtless jerk."

"You know him better than us. What do you think?"

"I expect it's right. He doesn't care about nothing or nobody much. I always felt sorry for him. Can't be a happy way to live. But he took a shine to Casey."

Jennifer shot Kid a sympathetic look. *He's not alone.* "She doesn't know where he is either."

Betty pushed back from the table in disgust. "How am I supposed to know whether to take the deal when we can't find the one person who can show I wasn't in the right place to do Trusk no harm?"

"We want to find him, too. But the very best he can do, from what you tell me, is narrow the window in which you could have killed Trusk. He can't say you didn't do it altogether." Unfortunately, the pictures from the scene didn't clear her. The tractor had been all over the road that day. Aaron and Jennifer hadn't helped matters when they'd pulled up in the Jeepster then traipsed back and forth in the snow either.

"But he knows I hit the truck with the tractor two days before all this happened. And who knows what he'll say about the day Trusk died. He might clear me altogether."

"What?"

"You don't know what he's gonna say until he says it."

Jennifer couldn't suborn perjury. But she wouldn't tell a witness to change a story either. Betty was right. Will could be even better for them than she hoped. *Or even worse.* "We'll find him. We won't give up until we do. In the meantime…"

"In the meantime, tell that county lawyer to get stuffed!"

She couldn't stomach the idea of her friend taking fifteen years for crimes she didn't commit. But even worse was the thought of Betty getting life in prison because Jennifer couldn't convince a jury to set her free.

She'd do what Betty asked, but she'd never been more conflicted on a case in her entire career.

CHAPTER THIRTY-FOUR

Sheridan, Wyoming

Kid decided he was an idiot before he even got to Casey's apartment on Tuesday. "You're demeaning yourself. She acted horrible. She's immature. She's not that into you. Or into you at all."

He parked and walked up to her door anyway.

He knocked and muttered, "Stupid, stupid, stupid."

She opened the door wearing jeans and a fuzzy pink sweater. A smile lit up her face. A wonderful flowery scent wafted out the door and settled on him like a powdery cloud of love. "Wesley. I am so glad to see you. I was afraid you'd never speak to me again."

She's beautiful.

He couldn't help but smile back. His goal to come here and get answers for why she'd sabotaged their case—or at least Jenn—and led him on all evaporated. "I just thought I'd see how you're doing. Make sure you're okay."

"Come in. But ignore the mess." She giggled and backed away. "I can't believe you're here."

Kid was feeling less stupid. More hopeful. "What have you been up to?"

"Job hunting." She rolled her eyes. "I found work as a night stocker at Walmart. It pays good but OMG it's so hard."

"I'm glad you're working, though."

"Have a seat on the couch. Can I get you something to drink? A Coke? A beer?"

"Coke. It's a workday for me."

"Right." She laughed. "Do you want ice in it?"

"Don't go to any trouble."

"That means yes to ice." She winked and disappeared behind a wall.

His heart stuttered. He was too nervous to sit. Maybe he should ask her to dinner again now that working together wasn't an issue? He paced around the living room, burning off his anxiety. He did a quick survey. No pictures. No knickknacks or art. Some clutter. It looked like she'd been to the laundromat, because a laundry basket was spilled onto the coffee table. *Lacy things. Look away, Kid.* He did and saw an Army green backpack sitting on the floor. It had a name stenciled on it. WILL RENWICK.

He stumbled backwards. Casey had Will's backpack? What did that mean? When did she get it? Then *Oh my God he's staying here with her!*

He heard the crack of an ice tray and ice tumbling into a container.

He went from dazed infatuation to wide alert and suspicious between breaths. He needed to look in that backpack. But he had to make sure Casey wasn't on her way back. "Um, what's taking you so long?"

"Chill. I'm going as fast as I can!" she said, in a teasing voice.

He had a minute, then. Only ice, no liquid yet. He kept his ears tuned toward the kitchen, hurrying so fast his hands shook. He unzipped the top and peeked inside. There was a note. CASEY, KEEP THIS UNTIL I'M BACK.

That's good. He's not with her.

He pulled out a book on surviving a winter on Walker Prairie. A receipt fell from its pages. It was from Sportsman's Warehouse and listed snowshoes and a lot of winter gear.

From the kitchen, he heard the crack and fizz of a can opening. He stuffed the book and receipts in the backpack and closed it up. Then he slung a strap over his shoulder and bolted from of the apartment before he could change his mind.

His emotions were cycling quickly now. He'd made it past shocked and was onto hurt. *She's betrayed us again. She's betrayed me.*

He'd almost reached his car when Casey came out. "Wait. Where are you going?"

Rage replaced hurt and boiled over inside him. "When were you going to tell me you were in contact with our missing star witness?" He held up Will's backpack then opened the passenger door and threw it on the seat.

She ran toward him. "It's not what it looks like. I've been staying with a friend for the last week while maintenance fixed my ceiling. Some pipes froze and flooded me out. I found the backpack outside my door when I got home this morning. I don't know when he left it. I promise. And I was working up my courage to call you and tell you about it before you showed up."

"After how you treated Jenn—how you treated both of us—I call bullshit."

"I know. I feel awful. But this time I swear, Wesley. I wasn't going to call Jennifer. But I was going to call you. I want you to take it now. I want you to find him. I'll help you if you need me to."

Kid ached with the need to believe her. Couldn't he just believe her a little bit and take a wait and see approach?

She closed the gap between them and put her hands on his forearms. It burned like fire where each fingertip touched him. "Please, Wesley. I like you. I thought you liked me, too. I thought when you showed up that meant we'd give things between us a try."

Kid felt a sensation of floating. Falling. Landing in something soft. From his pillowy resting place, the situation didn't seem as bad as it had before. She wanted to have a relationship with him. They could work this misunderstanding out. "Okay. We can talk about that later."

"Can you come over after work?"

"Maybe."

"I'd really like that."

He swallowed down his suddenly huge Adam's apple. He wanted to stay there forever, but he knew he needed to go. He peeled himself away from her fingers, almost one by one. Then he got in his car and drove away with Will's backpack. Halfway back to the office, he caught himself whistling.

CHAPTER THIRTY-FIVE

Sheridan, Wyoming

Aaron tried to give Jenn his attention on the drive to Tommy Campbell's, but without crashing Demarcus Ware. It was a delicate balance. The conditions weren't bad, but it was still a winding country road. And his wife was wired. More than wired, whatever that was. Jazzed. Supercharged. On fire. The subject du jour—Kid's discovery of Will's backpack at Casey's and what the contents revealed about the whereabouts of Betty's alibi witness.

She ran down her thoughts, hand karate chopping the air for emphasis. "Casey has been talking to Will this whole time. I just know it! But what in the heck is he doing up on Walker Prairie? It's the dead of winter. Remote, isolated. Up in the mountains. It's crazy!"

She'd basically said the same things four times so far. This time Aaron decided to answer her rhetorical questions, even though it was possibly a violation of her prime directive to *listen and be empathetic without giving me solutions.* "Maybe he's working on his survivalist skills."

She didn't react, probably mostly because she was barely registering anything outside her agitated mind. Throwing herself back against the seat, she said, "And Kid. What was he doing at Casey's house?"

"Aren't you glad he went, though?"

"I'm glad he found the backpack. I'm worried that he's going to fall for her act again."

"Maybe she really likes him."

"Maybe pigs fly."

"Come on. He's a nice guy. Smart. Fun. Kind. With a promising career."

"He's Big Bird with a briefcase."

Aaron had a sudden visual of Kid in the courtroom, yellow bow tie askew, tall and thin, gesticulating so assertively that his mass of hair flopped with his movements. *Yeah, she's not wrong.* "You don't think he's a nice-looking guy?"

"He is. But she's... bombshell."

"So are you, but you ended up with a punk like me."

"Ha." She leaned across and patted his knee. "Well, you're a pretty awesome punk."

Aaron parked and led Jennifer toward Tommy's house. She lifted her knees like she was marching because of the snow. Ahead of them, the first dogs to recognize their presence lifted their voices. A weird sensation surged through Aaron. An emotional sensation that nearly brought tears to his eyes. He wasn't sure why, other than the contagion of the dogs' excitement. "Did Kid say anything that made you think he's going to keep seeing her?"

"He didn't have to. It was written all over his face." She lowered her voice and said, "'But Jenn, she'd been out of her apartment for a week because it flooded. She just came home and found the backpack outside her door right before I got there.'" She sounded remarkably like her colleague.

"Sounds flimsy."

"Very."

They were close enough now to smell the kennels. Nearly twenty dogs came with a little stink. All of them were howling, wooing, and jumping on their chain link gates.

Jenn put her hands over her ears. "They don't even sound like dogs. What's wrong with them?"

He squeezed her shoulder. "They're talkers. And they're telling us they're thrilled we're visiting." He'd only thought their malamutes were talkers until he'd visited Tommy's kennels and heard real northern snow dog excitement.

Tommy walked to his front door and met them on the porch. His house was smaller than his dog kennels. "I heard the early warning system go off."

Aaron shook Tommy's hand, then pulled him into a shoulder-slapping side hug. "No one can sneak up on your place."

"I don't mind when it's the criminal element, but the pack has no discernment. They're this loud for squirrels, field mice, deer, cats, you name it.

Aaron put his palm in the small of Jenn's back. "This is my wife. Jenn, this is musher extraordinaire Tommy Campbell."

"Hi, Jenn. I sure do like those two dogs of yours."

"Nice to meet you, Tommy. We're hoping they can learn how to pull."

"Oh, that won't be a problem. They seemed pretty eager when Aaron brought them out . . ."

"About that," Aaron said. "You mentioned that you take your dogs up to Walker Prairie sometimes?"

"Yep. Snowmobilers shortcutting up the Soldier Creek Trail over to the groomed trail system blaze us a decent path. I like to do back-country workouts there. I was out there a few days ago, in fact."

"You didn't happen to see anyone camping up there?"

"I did."

Jenn jumped in with the subtlety of a shotgun blast. "Who did you see?"

Tommy took half a step back.

Aaron nudged Jenn. "I think you've startled our host."

She exhaled forcefully. "Sorry. I've got a lead on an alibi witness who might be camped up there."

Tommy said, "No problem. I can't say for sure who it was. Or if they were still there. I saw smoke near a good outfitting company's camping spot. I just figured it was a winter camper up for a few days."

Aaron watched his wife as he spoke. "We need to find Jenn's witness. Any chance you could direct us to where you saw the fire?"

"When do you want to go?" Tommy asked.

"Tomorrow," Jenn said. "I wish it could be right now."

Tommy shrugged, rubbing his ginger beard. "To get where I saw the smoke, we'd need dogs and a sled, snowshoes, and a snowmachine. It won't be fast or easy, but it will be a lot of fun. And a great training experience for the dogs."

Aaron tried to tamp down his glee. This was a serious work issue for Jenn. *But packaged in a helluva winter adventure.* "Can we bring our malamutes and work them into the team?"

"Teams. We'll take two sleds and at least one snowmobile. Your dogs would be welcome additions. But I've got to be sure you humans are outfitted correctly. Winter in the mountains is a good way to get yourself dead if you're not prepared. Let's go inside and work up your packing list."

Guilt twisted inside Aaron's gut. He'd be cutting out on his staff and patients in the middle of the week. He'd even scheduled Game and Fish to pick up the little fox, as it was now healed and ready for release. *But even I deserve time off now and then—and no way am I letting Jenn go up there without me.* He'd just have to put Game and Fish off a few days.

His wife flashed him a brilliant smile. He had concerns this trip was going to be more than she bargained for. And they might not even find Will. But on the bright side, he loved her determination to help Betty. *Bonus: she looks damn cute in a snowsuit.*

CHAPTER THIRTY-SIX

Big Horn, Wyoming

Kid put his car in park in front of the Herrington's lodge and turned to face Casey. Their talk that evening at her apartment had led them here. Sitting side by side with her on a couch that was basically a love seat, he'd told her Jenn and Aaron were heading up to Walker Prairie the next day to find Will, and she'd begged for a chance to prove herself to all of them.

"I've had time to think. I'm embarrassed, and I don't know how to explain myself. Honestly, I think I was jealous of Jennifer's life," she'd said.

Suddenly he was jealous of Aaron's. "Why?" *Please don't let her be attracted to Aaron.*

"Well, for starters because I want to be an attorney."

"I didn't know that."

"It's true. And she's so small and pretty. I've always felt tall and awkward."

"You're gorgeous." The words had tumbled out before he could stop them.

She blushed—actually turned pink in the cheeks—and he felt like his heart had stopped beating. "Thank you, Wesley."

He tried to say you're welcome, but no sound came out. He felt like a giant goober.

She took his hand. "Will trusts me, and he doesn't trust anyone. He'll talk to me, Kid. I don't think he'll talk to you or Jennifer."

"We're pretty persuasive."

"Honestly, Wesley, he doesn't like Jennifer." She'd looked up at him under her impossibly long lashes. "See... it's not just me!" Then she giggled.

He broke down and joined in her laughter.

Thirty minutes later, she'd been singing along with an old Luke Bryan song on the local country radio station on their way to the lodge.

He looked up at the structure in which his unsuspecting boss waited for him. It loomed in the dark. He hoped he hadn't messed up by telling Casey about the trip to look for Will. It had just leaked out of him. *Jenn is going to put me on a skewer and roast me in the fireplace.* He braced himself. "Wait here. I'll go prepare them for us."

"Didn't you tell them we were coming?"

"I told them I was coming. I thought it would be best to explain about you in person."

"Oh. How long do you think this will take?"

"I'll be back for you in five minutes."

She nodded, but she didn't seem to like the plan. *She doesn't have a choice. Not in this, not after what she's done.*

He left the heat and engine running and dashed to the front door. Loud animal noises on the other side announced his arrival before he rang the bell.

Aaron opened the door seconds later. "Kid! Come in. What are you doing up here?" It was hard to understand him over the dogs.

Kid shouted, "I texted Jenn."

The two fluffy huskies or whatever-they-were milled around him, tails wagging but showing no sign of turning off their warning sirens. Jenn and George were sitting at the dining table with their hands over their ears. Only Aaron didn't seem fazed by the racket. Kid followed him to the table. It smelled like an Italian restaurant. He didn't cook, so he couldn't name the herbs, he just knew that it made him think of lasagna.

Aaron and Kid each took a seat. The excited dogs jostled Aaron and Jenn's legs, their backs knocking into the underside of the table and shaking three glasses. One half-full beer, one coffee, and one glass of red wine with lipstick smudges on the rim.

Aaron said, "Okay, enough."

The dogs turned it up a notch.

"They'll stop soon," Aaron shouted. He pointed at a dish in the center of the table. "Would you like some eggplant parm? We just finished eating. Plenty left."

It was only then Kid noticed the plates in front of each of them. At least they were dirty and empty. Dinner was over. Maybe he wasn't interrupting at the worst time. "No. I'm good."

And as suddenly as the dogs had started their auditory assault, they stopped. The absence of sound felt dangerously awkward to Kid.

Aaron served himself the last of the parm. *Good thing I didn't say yes to it.* "Sorry. As you might have noticed, nothing shuts those dogs up. In fact, any attempt to quiet them is met with equal and opposite escalation."

"I think they're funny. I hope I wasn't interrupting anything."

Jenn went to the refrigerator. "We were just talking about tomorrow." She poured water from a Brita pitcher into a glass.

George grinned. "I was telling 'em I should be their trail buster and emergency ride out. I've got the most experience with snow machines of their crew."

Jenn returned to the table and handed the glass to Kid.

"Thanks." He sometimes couldn't believe Jenn didn't have kids the way she mothered him. Not in a bad way. He liked that she shared what she knew and kept him from committing malpractice, kind of like a mother would keep a toddler from running out into traffic. The thought amused him and loosened him up a little.

"You're welcome." She shook her head at George. "You only have one arm, George. Snowmobiling is a two-armed sport. Unless you've retrofitted one of your machines."

He sighed. "I have ideas. I just haven't made 'em a reality yet. It's hard to do the machine work with one arm."

"Dammit, George, you've got me here now, too. Let me help you. I don't want you missing the whole winter if we can make something work."

"I'll take you up on that."

The two men fist bumped.

Kid raised his hand. "I grew up on sleds. I'm pretty good on them, actually. But I don't have a snowmachine of my own anymore."

George slapped his leg. "Well, I can help there. I have a whole fleet of them."

"Do you have a two-seater?"

"Sure. You expecting to carry someone out? I guess that makes sense."

"Um, more like because I have someone who wants to come with us. Someone who is guaranteed to get Will to talk."

Jenn crossed her arms. His skin burned under her glare. "You didn't."

He chewed the inside of his lip. "She's the one he trusts."

Aaron gave Kid a look that basically said he was the dumbest man who ever lived, but that he had Aaron's sympathies.

Jenn was on her feet. Red splotches appeared on her cheeks and her voice rose. "Didn't you learn your lesson last time you trusted her?"

The dogs jumped up and ran to the door, sirens re-activated. *Casey! No... I told her to wait for me.* The door opened and the subject of their heated conversation strutted in supermodel style.

"Are we all set, Wesley?" She stopped and draped a hand on his shoulder.

"There is no 'we,'" Jenn said. "There's us and there's the person who's been working against us."

"I told Wesley I'm sorry." She criss-crossed her heart.

"Great for Wesley."

Casey drew in a lungful of air and stood taller which was quite tall. Her legs were incredibly long and—*stop it Wesley James you idiot!*

She said. "I am. I am very sorry, and I truly want to help."

"You've done the opposite of helping so far."

Casey popped a hip. Kid had known she wouldn't be able to restrain herself for long. Her dulcet tones gave way to a voice crackling with attitude. "Fine. I don't give a shit about helping you. I don't even like you. But I want to help Wesley. I want to make it up to *him*, because we're dating."

If Kid hadn't been sitting, he would have collapsed on the floor. *We're dating. We are dating. We are DATING!*

Aaron raised one eyebrow. "Points for honesty, anyway."

"Argh." Jenn shoved her hands into her hair above each ear. "The worst part of this is that she may be right. Will might refuse to talk to any of us." She pulled her hands away, leaving her hair sticking out.

Aaron reached for his wife's hand. "I promise I won't let this go sideways."

"You can't guarantee that."

Kid said, "I promise, too."

Casey raised two fingers. "And I promise not to mess it up."

Jenn said. "I just don't know."

She began to pace the kitchen, the living room, the hallway, and back, muttering to herself. The dogs watched her, heads cocked, faces concerned. No one spoke. Kid was practically holding his breath.

Finally, she shook her head.

A frisson of disappointment coursed through him.

Then she said, "I don't like it, but I think it's our best option."

Casey squealed and lowered herself into Kid's lap, linked her hands behind his neck, and planted a kiss on his lips in front of everyone.

CHAPTER THIRTY-SEVEN

Highway 14, Bighorn Mountains, Wyoming

Jenn drummed her fingers on the armrest. She was riding in the navigation seat because the winding road of Highway 14 triggered motion sickness. But it was a toss-up. Driving up-mountain on the passenger side robbed her of the forever view of open sky and white expanse out over Dayton and Ranchester far below and on toward Eastern Wyoming, which meant she couldn't tell whether Aaron was driving too close to the edge. He had a perfect record of never doing so, but there was always a first time, which could be the last time. Ahead of them, Tommy was driving his own truck and pulling a trailer, like they were. A snowmobile, two dog sleds, two teams, all their gear, a snowmobile, and five humans didn't travel light.

Giggles from the backseat derailed her thoughts. Casey, who Jenn did not believe for a second wanted to be dating Kid. The girl was leading him on. She just couldn't figure out why.

Or maybe she was just overly agitated already.

The whole thing with Casey and Kid made her miss Alayah. The two of them would have had fun dissecting the psychology behind this odd pairing. She couldn't imagine the same conversation with Trish. Not yet anyway. And Maggie would be great, but she'd probably embarrass Kid about it next time she saw him. Not to be cruel, but just because Maggie was aggressively funny and fearless herself.

She threw out a hand as Aaron approached a blind curve. "Slow down. Please."

He shot her a look. "I don't know how I manage not to die every time I drive without you here to coach me."

"I don't either. Seriously, I don't."

She heard Kid even though he and Casey where obviously trying to keep their conversation private. "Did I tell you we finally tracked down Barty Arnold and cornered him at the YMCA?"

Jennifer held off objecting to the conversation. She'd cut him off if he revealed anything too sensitive.

"What? Why didn't you tell me?" Gone was Casey's flirty, breathy voice and her giggles.

"Why would I? You don't work for my firm anymore."

"But I was the one doing that work. And, well, just because."

There were a few beats of silence. Then Kid said, "Wait. Do you know him or something?"

Jennifer leaned her head as far back against the seat as she could, trying to catch every syllable and nuance. What had Kid read on Casey's face that he asked that question?

"I just... "

"How do you know him?"

"Well, I mean, he got me the job at WP Bar."

Every hair on Jennifer's arms stood on end. Casey knew Arnold. She wanted to turn around and light into the girl. But first she wanted to hear what she had to say.

Aaron reached over and tapped her knee. "What, no more driving instructions?"

She didn't dare answer him, afraid she'd talk over the conversation behind her.

Kid sounded like he'd swallowed a live frog. "That wasn't what I asked. I asked how you know him?"

"He knew my family."

"In Tennessee?"

"Yes."

Aaron squeezed her knee. "Are you upset with me?" He looked over at her.

She put her finger over her lips and made wide eyes at him. He looked confused.

Kid's voice was rising. "You were friends?"

"I guess. More like with my mom."

The epitome of cagey.

Kid's cool broke. His voice cracked. "Casey, just tell me. Whatever it is, just tell me how you know the man!"

"He was my stepdad's brother."

"Your mom was married to his brother?"

"Yes. When I decided to come to Wyoming, he helped me find a job."

Jennifer couldn't take it anymore. She unbuckled her seat belt, turned in her seat, and said, "You knew who he was and how to get hold of him this whole time?"

Casey narrowed her eyes, then focused on Kid. "I wasn't going to lie to you. I just prioritized other work first."

Jennifer smacked the seat with her hand. "Casey, that's—"

Kid interrupted her. "Did you know about what he did to Black Bear Betty? Back when he was a judge?"

Casey burst into sobs. "Why are you interrogating me? He's a nice guy who helped me out even though my mom dumped his brother. I barely knew him."

Kid opened his arms and Casey dove into them, back heaving.

"Shh," he said. "It's okay."

But Jennifer could see the side of the girl's face. Her eyes were dry. And her lips were smiling.

CHAPTER THIRTY-EIGHT

Walker Prairie, Bighorn Mountains, Wyoming

The dog sled cut through an opening in a stand of spruce so narrow that Jennifer Herrington sucked in her breath. *Like that will do any good.* If it got stuck it wouldn't be because of her slight frame, or that of her enormous husband Aaron standing on the runners behind her. It would be the basket, which protruded several inches on either side of him.

Getting stuck wasn't even her biggest worry. It was the eleven half-crazed dogs pulling against the harness. She'd quickly learned that dog sledding was roughly one-tenth control and four-tenths influence. She wasn't a math genius, but she could do that addition. That left half, which was determined by their instinctual love for running, pulling, and chasing. Combined with the dogs' physical abilities, it summed to an exciting experience. An experience that had chased away the effects of her chronic sleep deprivation. It was hard to stress out on a sled, too. The dogs required all her attention. Well, she still felt some stress, after that scene with Casey on the drive up.

Casey. The way she'd manipulated Kid until he protected her

from Jennifer and disclosing the truth. The girl had withheld even more information from them than they'd thought. *Because she was grateful to Arnold or because she was protecting him?* And now she was with them as they tried to track down Will. She had no idea what to do about it. There was nothing they could do on the mountain. But when they were down, she was having a talk with Kid. Even if he hated her afterward, she needed his cooperation in getting the rest of the story from Casey. And she had to make sure Casey wouldn't be coming back to work on Betty's case.

But right now was all about right now. The dogs. Staying safe. Finding Will. She bit down on the inside of her cheek to anchor herself. Not with hard enough force to draw blood, but sufficient to jerk her out of her head and back into the moment.

And the moment required a lot. The team was basically acting like she and Aaron didn't exist, no matter how many commands they shouted at them. The other sled team didn't respond much better for Tommy, who was mushing ahead of them. Only the foot brake and snow anchor had any effect on their speed. At least they were quiet now, all their energy focused on the joy of running. Their frantic howling when they'd been hooked to the bumper of Tommy's truck had been almost equal parts ear-splitting and entertaining.

The lead dogs disappeared around a slight crook in the trail. The Herringtons' dogs attacked the curve, and their sled catapulted toward a rock outcropping. Tommy and his team had navigated the turn so effortlessly that Jennifer hadn't anticipated how terrifying it would be. Or how challenging. She and Aaron bent their knees and shifted their weight at the same time.

For a moment, the sled teetered. *No, please, no!* Tipping over would be a disaster. Sure, the dogs would stop because of the sudden drag, but if Aaron's weight didn't crush her or Jennifer didn't suffocate face first in the snow, she could die with her skull bashed in on a tree. But slamming into a giant slab of granite was no better. She eased herself back to center, hoping to correct the oversteer. Aaron's size and the muscle he still carried would provide enough counterweight.

Her pulse was so elevated that it felt like a continuous thrum instead of individual beats. The sled's right ski kissed the snow again, but the rock face loomed ever closer. Maybe the basket frame would provide some protection? But that was a ridiculous thought—it was little more than PVC pipe and wicker. The rock would pulverize it.

It was too late to brake. A strange squeaking noise came from somewhere. *Her*, she realized. It had come from her.

Jennifer held steady. What else could she do? The middle dogs disappeared into the turn. The sled fought toward the obstacle, pulled by centrifugal force away from the direction Aaron was leaning. Was it her imagination or was Willett pulling the wrong way against the others in mid-pack? This was her first major training run. She was supposed to be learning from the more experienced dogs, not working against them.

Jennifer stepped on the brake, hoping to use it like a rudder to pull them to the left. The rear dogs—the strongest in the pack—dug into their turn.

Why did we say yes to this crazy idea, like some Call of the Wild *wannabes? Maybe we could have found Will a different way. But probably not.* Her mind raced through regrets. That she hadn't tried her first official murder case in Wyoming yet. That she hadn't convinced the State to charge former prosecutor Pootie Carputin with the school shooting that haunted her from her childhood. Not seeing her first mystery novel published. The lost years of motherhood she'd squandered by putting off having a baby. Every minute she hadn't appreciated Aaron enough. If he survived and she didn't, other women would chase him even more aggressively than they already did, which he never seemed to notice.

I'm married to the best guy.

"I love you," she shouted to Aaron, then braced for impact, pulling her hands and arms tightly to her sides.

"I love you, too," he shouted back, his voice minus the terrified edge in hers.

There was a loud grating noise. The right ski scraped the granite and shuddered. The PVC supports bounced off the rock. Wicker splintered and peppered her face.

This is it. She closed her eyes, gritted her teeth. Sent up a prayer.

But then they were clear with the basket mostly intact. *It's a miracle!*

Adrenaline surged through her, and Jennifer whooped. She felt Aaron's body shaking with something.

"You're laughing!" she shouted.

"That was awesome," he yelled.

She leaned her head into his chest and laughed, too. "It was crazy!"

Sure, it had been a scary few moments but talk about a rush! Her whole body was electrified, except her weather-numbed toes. She'd fought to stay warm from the first freeze of the season. Maybe she didn't love everything about the Bighorn Mountains or living in Wyoming, but she'd never felt this alive back in Houston.

Aaron bent down and pressed his lips against her ear. "These dogs are amazing athletes. And Willett and Sibley are doing great!"

Their sled glided across an open expanse of white. Tommy and his team vanished into the forest ahead of them. They should be getting close to Walker Prairie now. She recognized She Bear mountain to the southwest from Tommy's description.

It felt strange to be off road in the dead of winter, in national forest backcountry. Jennifer wondered where the closest human was and how far away help would be if something went wrong. And things did go wrong in the mountains, even without deep snow, subzero temperatures, and over-stimulated dogs. That was why she, Aaron, and Tommy had emergency supplies, snowshoes, rifles, handguns, and equipment on both sleds as well as on the snowmobile with Kid and Casey. Self-sufficiency was the name of the game in the backcountry at any time of the year, but especially in this weather.

She sucked cold air through her teeth. The slight whistling noise and the schuss of the runners were the only sounds except the wind in her ears. Icy air froze the inside of her nose. Drawing a breath was difficult and uncomfortable. She could still smell the dogs, though. Damp fur. Exertion. It was all strangely pleasant under the circumstances.

They entered the forest, dense except for their trail. The quiet from before gave way to utter silence. Jennifer's body tingled from the pure earth magic around her. It beat writing trial briefs or arguing motions in court, and it rivaled her highest highs during successful closing arguments in capital murder trials. It was far better than studying for the Wyoming bar exam. But she needed that license. Betty's was her second Wyoming murder case as nothing more than a consultant. It was a waste of her skills. The courtroom was where she belonged. *The prosecution.*

The dogs burst out of the trees and into an open space that was probably technically a park but more like a good-sized meadow. *Like a scene from* Dr. Zhivago, *but more beautiful.* It was in this idyllic white wonderland against a backdrop of evergreens and an impossibly clear blue sky that all hell broke loose.

On the far side of the clearing, Tommy's lead dog let out a shrill yip, which was unusual. All she'd heard were howls and a-woos so far from the huskies. Whatever lay ahead was upsetting Tommy's dogs. She saw a tumble of fur then heard more dog noises and Tommy's shouts of "whoa" and "easy."

When Tommy's forward progress stopped, both dog teams started howling in chorus. It sent chills up her spine, all the way into her scalp and the tips of her ears.

"Whoa," she called. She stomped the brake, then released it. Stomped, released, stomped, released. "Whoa. Easy." Finally, she pressed and held the rubber cleat against the snow.

The dogs came to a noisy, agitated stop.

Aaron leapt off the sled and ran for Gizmo, a husky mix and their lead dog. Her husband's big feet kept post holing in the snow, so his progress was slow. Gizmo strained against the harness, panting, howling, and whining all at once. Finally, Aaron reached him. Bending over and holding onto the harness's hand strap, he spoke to the dog in low, soothing tones that Jennifer could hear but not understand. When the dog had calmed somewhat, Aaron straightened.

Behind them, the snowmobile engine turned off. Kid called, "Are we stopping?"

Aaron had a deep, carrying voice that didn't require shouting most of the time. "Tommy? What's up?"

"Son of a bitch." It was Tommy's voice, but his words weren't in response to Aaron's question.

Is one of Tommy's dogs hurt? Jennifer sank the anchor. Between it and Aaron holding onto Gizmo, the other dogs would stay put. Probably. Maybe. She hopped off the sled and fought her way forward through powder. Her feet planted on packed snow below it. She was half Aaron's weight, so she didn't break through the lower layer. Her progress was easier, which was not to be confused with actually *being* easy.

"What is it, Tommy?" Her breaths seared her lungs. The altitude here was over seventy-five hundred feet—about one thousand feet higher than their Big Horn Lodge.

A drift trapped her foot. She toppled like felled timber, and her body sank. Gaining high ground was a monumental struggle. Her muscles shook. How were the dogs able to stay on the surface of the snow? Their light weight, she guessed. The heaviest huskies in the rear of the team couldn't have been much more than fifty pounds, although their malamutes were twenty-five pounds heavier. Jennifer was small but muscular, which made her heavier than she looked.

She paused on all fours to catch her breath. Perspiration soaked her sweater, and snow had crept into her coat at the collar and cuffs. She was muttering words that would have irked her southern mama. She tried to stand but sunk again. She gave up and crawled, head toward the ground, spitting frozen hair out of her mouth.

"Jenn, stop." It was Aaron, his voice a whisper.

Gladly. The break allowed her to look up and around. She'd closed more ground between their basket and Tommy's than she'd expected. In fact, she was only ten feet away and slightly uphill from it, which gave her a good vantage point of him—in his red wool cap and black winter gear—as well as the sled, the dogs... and a giant bloody mass of dark brown fur. Her insides flipped over.

"What is that?" she asked.

Tommy answered without looking back at her. "Moose."

"Is it . . ."

"Dead. Yes."

"Do you think a bear got it?"

"No. A black bear won't take on a moose, and we don't have grizzlies in this part of Wyoming."

This grizzly-free claim had always struck Jennifer as wishful thinking. There were no bear-proof fences between western Wyoming, where grizzlies were commonplace, and the Bighorns, where they weren't. Yet. "It doesn't look like it died of natural causes."

"I don't believe it did. Someone gutted it."

"Gutted but didn't harvest it?"

"Correct."

It was well past hunting season. Killing a game animal out of season—or without a license during season—was poaching. But poachers usually harvested at least some part of the animal. Not many people gutted the carcasses of animals they found already dead either. A queasy unease settled over her. Poachers got high fines and jail time, and criminals didn't like to be caught, something she knew well from her years prosecuting them as an assistant district attorney in Harris County, Texas.

"A little information back here, please," Kid shouted.

She licked her dry lips. "Who do you think would do something like this?"

Tommy pointed. "I don't think, I know. Him."

Jennifer couldn't see anyone. But then a figure moved closer, coming toward Tommy, his lead dog, and Jennifer. Effortlessly. Like walking on water. *Snowshoes. Dang it—I should have taken the time to get mine.*

Cradling a rifle.

Jennifer wished she'd stayed with Aaron back at their sled.

"That's close enough," Aaron shouted.

The figure stopped a few feet away from Tommy's lead dog, with Sibley—Jennifer's favorite of their two malamutes—only a few spots behind her. The lead dog went into a frenzy. Snapping, growling, and lunging. The person raised the rifle and pointed it at the dog's head.

"No!" Jennifer screamed.

CHAPTER THIRTY-NINE

Walker Prairie, Bighorn Mountains, Wyoming

The figure didn't lower the rifle. Aaron tensed, strategizing. He couldn't risk rapid movements, but he needed to get between Jenn and this nutjob. But if he started moving now, would it trigger a shot, either at the dog, him, or—worst—his wife?

"Enough," Tommy said. "We don't care about your moose. A man's gotta eat."

"Call off your dog."

Aaron recognized the voice. A man's voice. Will's voice. *We've done it. We've found Jenn's witness!* He relaxed a fraction. When Will realized who they were, he'd calm down.

Tommy said, "The dog is harnessed up. It's not going anywhere."

"Will," Aaron said, keeping his voice friendly and soothing. He lowered the balaclava covering his face. "It's Aaron Herrington. Everything's good. We're no threat to you."

"Who's with you?" Will pulled up his face mask exposing angry red skin patches.

"That's Tommy Campbell on the first sled. Behind me on the

snowmobile, that's your friend Casey from the WP Bar. With her is Kid James. He works with Casey and my wife Jenn, who's right in front of me."

Will stared at each person in turn, looking extra-long and hard at Casey and Jenn. His voice sounded hissy. Snakelike. "What are you doing up here?" His gun was no longer pointed at the dog, but it wasn't pointed at the ground either. While Will's attention was spread around amongst them, Aaron began working his way slowly toward his wife. *Micro-motions. Noiseless. He seems volatile.*

Jenn raised her hand in greeting. "We want to talk to you, to verify Black Bear Betty's alibi. She's been charged with killing Glen Trusk, but she says she didn't do it, and that you can vouch for her. I'm hoping you'd talk to Kid, Casey, and me about it. I'd hate to see her or anyone convicted of something they didn't do."

Will's rifle came up again, aimed roughly at Jenn's knees.

"Whoa, whoa," Aaron said. "How about keeping that thing pointed at the ground?"

Will ignored him. "I'll talk to Casey. Only Casey. Alone."

Jenn turned to the snowmobile, looking past Aaron, then faced Will. "I don't feel great about that."

"I don't feel great about you tracking me down, Priscilla."

"Priscilla?"

"I meant to say Jennifer."

"Who's Priscilla?"

The name sounded familiar to Aaron. But he probably knew a bunch of Priscillas. Did he know one who had something to do with Jenn? Or with Will?

Will shook his head back and forth rapidly. "I just messed up your name. Enough blather. Make up your mind. It's Casey or no one."

"I'll talk to you," Casey said. "We're friends."

Will sneered. "But you led these assholes up here to find me. You're the only one I told where I was going."

"I didn't tell them. They figured it out. And they only want to help Black Bear Betty. Not hurt you."

Will's breathing had sped up. His chest heaved. His eyes were restless to the point of over-stimulated.

"Take me to him, Kid," Casey said.

Kid cranked the snowmobile engine and began gliding toward Will. Aaron ran through the deep snow toward his wife, using the snowmachine and its movement as distraction and cover.

With the dog sleds blocking what little semi-packed trail there was through the clearing, Kid had to veer wide around them. It went fine at first. He gave the machine gas and stayed upright on the powder. But just as he passed Tommy's lead dogs, he let off the throttle. One of the snow sled's runners ran up on something hard and elevated. The other dipped under a drift.

Aaron reached Jenn. He couldn't believe how out of breath he was.

The snowmobile toppled over, Casey screamed, and the two of them were dumped at Will's feet. Kid was sprawled with a leg trapped under the chassis. Casey was thrown clear. Before she could even get to her feet, Will stomped forward and yanked her up. He pulled her toward him and wrapped an arm around her neck with her back to his chest. The other arm still held the rifle, and he managed to point it roughly at Jenn.

Aaron stepped in front of his wife and held his arms out.

"Aaron!" Jenn hissed.

He spoke just loud enough for her to hear him. "I'm not taking a chance he shoots at you."

Will began backing away, pulling Casey with him. She was stumbling and would have fallen if he didn't have hold of her.

The snowmobile engine stopped. *Flooded, I bet.* The silence boomed with menace.

Aaron had always thought Will was a little off, but now he realized he'd underestimated that by many orders of magnitudes. The closer glimpse he'd had of the other man a few minutes before had showed eyes wide and black from enlarged pupils. Will was living on a barren prairie high in the mountains in the coldest, snowiest season of the year. Pulling a gun on strangers and acquaintances. And, from all appearances, kidnapping Casey.

Yeah, he's completely unhinged. From a quick whispered conversation with Jenn before they'd departed the vehicles on the dog sleds, he understood that her suspicions were squarely on Arnold, the former judge. Casey's admission that she'd led them astray in the investigation to keep them off Arnold made it seem like she might be involved, too. So, why was Will losing it, other than his illness—Jenn had told him about the APD—and the side effects of camping at altitude alone in the winter? Definitely he'd been exposed, by the chilblains on his face that Aaron had seen a few minutes before. Hypothermia could cause confusion. Had Will lost his sense of reality? He had been calling Jenn by the wrong name.

Aaron called after him. "Where are you going, Will? Can't you talk here? No one's going to eavesdrop."

Kid had wormed his way out from under his snowmobile and began bear crawling toward Will and Casey, below Will's line of sight.

When Will didn't answer, Aaron said, "At least let her stand up and walk."

"What's it to you, Daddy?" Will screamed.

Aaron frowned. *What does that mean?* "I just think in this weather and this terrain, Casey should stay where we can see her."

"Are you afraid I'm going to hurt your daughter?"

"Will, no!" Casey said.

"Shut up, Casey. It's time he learned the truth. About you and about his nasty wife."

"Aaron?" The question in Jenn's voice was trusting but concerned.

He met her eyes and shrugged. He was completely confused. Keeping Will talking was important though. He strode toward Will, hands up. "What are you talking about?"

With all of Will's attention on Casey and Aaron, Kid had nearly reached the tip of Will's snowshoe. Aaron hoped he wasn't about to do something extremely foolhardy. Kid was no match for Will. He moved his head side to side at the young attorney, trying not to make his no obvious to Will, who still seemed to have no idea Kid was near him.

Will shook Casey. *He's not moving her anymore, at least.* "Tell him, Casey. Tell them all what you told me."

Casey drew in a shuddering breath. She looked completely stricken. "It's true. You're my father, Aaron."

Aaron frowned so hard it hurt his forehead. "I don't understand." He looked at the tall, blonde woman. Guesstimated her age. Calculated when she would have been born. When her mother would have conceived her. And then he groaned. "Amy."

"Yes. Amy. My mother. The girlfriend you dumped when she found out she was pregnant with me." Now Casey's eyes held a challenge aimed at him.

Aaron held both hands up, advancing another five feet. "That's not true. She broke up with me. I wanted her to keep the baby. She said she couldn't. That she... she... "

Casey snapped, "Got the abortion you ordered her to?"

"No! I begged her not to. I couldn't change her mind. She wouldn't see me. I finally had to leave for college. She never returned my calls again."

"That's not what she said."

"If that was true, why didn't I know about your existence? If I left her with you, I would have known she had a baby. I believed what she told me she was going to do."

"Aaron?" It was Jenn's voice again. This time it didn't sound confused. It sounded hurt.

Jenn. Jenn who knows nothing about any of this, the saddest, darkest time of my life. He turned toward her. "Honey, I'm sorry I didn't tell you. I had no idea."

"Oh, right," Casey said. "You didn't know. You didn't tell her.

Mom told me the whole story. How Jennifer stole you away from her when she needed you most. If she hadn't broken you up, you and Mom would still be together. I would have had a dad."

Aaron's eyes were still on Jenn's.

Hers were shocked. Heartbroken. Her voice was soft. "I don't understand. You didn't trust me enough to tell me?"

Before Aaron could answer, he heard Will scream. "Son of a bitch."

The sound of a rifle shot ripped through the air.

Aaron flung himself at Jenn, knowing from the sound of the rifle and his reaction time that he was too late.

CHAPTER FORTY

Walker Prairie, Bighorn Mountains, Wyoming

JENNIFER STRUGGLED to get the words out under Aaron's weight. "It didn't hit me. I'm fine. What about you?"

"Thank God," he said against her forehead. "I'm fine, too."

With all that was going on around them, the thought that Aaron hadn't told her his high school girlfriend had gotten pregnant still intruded. The sadness was heavier than Aaron's bulk. *I thought we told each other everything. Maybe not for a while when we had problems, but for fifteen years before that. And lately. Oh, Aaron.*

She heard a groan. *Who's hurt?* Then a shout. Aaron's deception slipped from her mind. He eased his weight off her.

"You're lucky I fired a warning shot before I clubbed you. Next time I'll put a bullet through your forehead." Will's voice.

But not like the voice of Will who she'd known back in Big Horn. That Will was entitled, combative, and unpleasant. This Will was crazy. This Will matched the antisocial personality disorder diagnosis his stepmother had told her and Kid about. But it was more than that.

She ran through everything she knew about him in relation to this case. From the sketchy details about his Army discharge to his teenage years, filled with run-ins with the cops. His inability to hold a job. To find a place to live. His stepmother's evasiveness about him, yet her fear of him. His beef against Trusk for firing him. The fact that no one's alibi painted a clear picture of Will's whereabouts when Trusk died. Not for the entire time frame, anyway.

And now his complete disregard for all of their wellbeing, most surprisingly Casey.

How the heck does this all fit together?

Aaron whispered, "He's still got Casey, and I saw Tommy crouch down behind one of the sleds when I dove for you. He was too far away for Will to club him. I think it's Kid he hit."

Jennifer felt like her heart seized. Her colleague. Her partner. *Do I really want to be a prosecutor and leave him behind?* "Will, is Kid okay?"

"He'll have a bump," Will said.

"Kid?"

There was no answer.

"Is he unconscious?"

"Looks that way."

"Can I come help him, please?"

"I don't want you anywhere near me. Stay right where you are, *Priscilla*."

Again, Jennifer's mind went to Will's history. His early family life had been tragic. A mother murdered. An alcoholic father. And a stepmother. Priscilla Renwick. Will was associating her with his stepmother. But why? It didn't sound like he meant it as a compliment. Priscilla said that once upon a time young Will had loved her, when she babysat him, and that the love had turned to hate when he lost his mother and she married his father.

She understood all that. But what had Jennifer ever done to him that he associated her with his stepmother? *It doesn't hurt to ask. I hope, anyway.* "Did I do something to upset you?"

"I won't let you trick me this time. You pretend to care about me, but you don't. I know what you did. What my father did. I know why my mother is dead."

Aaron squeezed her hand and spoke under his breath. "He doesn't seem to know who you are. I don't like it."

"I don't like who he thinks I am."

"Who?"

"His stepmother. Who he hates."

"That's not good." Aaron shook his head. "We need our weapons from the sleds. I've got a knife, but I can't get anywhere near him as long as he's trigger happy. I hate to leave you, but I also want to be able to protect you."

Aaron was right. They needed those weapons. He was the logical choice to attempt to get them. But the thought of him becoming a target for Will was terrifying. The thought of his large, comforting presence gone was worse. "I'll keep talking to him. Maybe it will be enough to distract him."

"Be careful."

"You, too."

"And Jenn?"

"Yes?"

He pressed his face to hers, nose to nose. "I'm sorry. About not telling you. I'll explain it all when this is over. No secrets."

A lump formed in her throat. All she could do was nod. "Hurry back."

"I will."

He began a slow crawl toward the dog sled. Jennifer knew he'd have to move fast. Will's attention was on Casey at the moment, but he would realize Aaron was up to something soon. She strained to hear their voices. She couldn't make out words. Then the sound petered out.

Jennifer glanced at Aaron. He was far enough away now that Will wouldn't see Aaron if she drew his eyes to her. She shouted,

"Hey, Will, I don't understand what you mean. I'm Jennifer. I'm married to Aaron. I didn't know your mom or dad."

"You're married to my father," Will said.

"Aaron is not your father."

"But he's mine," Casey said. Will still had hold of her, but she didn't look scared. Whatever their conversation had been, it seemed to have resolved the tension between them. "Will and I have a lot in common. He told me how his stepmother stole his father away from his mom. And how she ended up dead because of it. My mother might as well be dead. You took my dad and her life was over."

There was a lot to unpack and a lot riding on how that went, if Casey was really Aaron's daughter. *That would make her my step-daughter. And she hates me.* But then Jennifer had a thought. What happened to her mom getting married to Arnold's brother? It didn't sound like her life had been as awful as Casey was making it out to be.

She decided there was nothing to gain by engaging her.

Kid still hadn't made a sound. If Will had hit him in the head, that could be dangerous. Casey wasn't helping her so-called boyfriend. That left it to Jennifer.

She stood slowly with her hands in the air. Her hands were shaking, and she felt sweat rolling down the side of her cheek. *Fear can do strange things.* "Will, I'm coming to help Kid, now. That's all I want. To make sure he's okay and get him to safety."

"I've heard that before. From Trusk." Will's voice changed to a nasal pitch. "Renwick, you can't be sleeping in my barn in this weather. It's not safe. I won't be liable for what happens to you out here. Little people like you see someone like me as a meal ticket. You keep taking and taking. Well, that's over. You're fired. Get your ass to town and don't come back."

Casey was nodding. "I hated him, too, Will. He was the worst. I'm glad Black Bear Betty killed him. If she hadn't, I'd have wanted to. The way he treated you. Me. All of us."

Jennifer bit her lip and kept advancing toward Will, Casey, and

Kid. What game was Casey playing now? Betty was innocent. Wasn't she? But Jennifer stopped herself. She had to keep Will's eyes on her. "Casey, how is Kid?"

Casey gave a flippant shrug. "Will didn't hit him that hard. I'm sure he's fine."

Rage replaced Jennifer's fear. Casey had used Kid. She didn't care a whit that he was unconscious in this frigid wilderness. Was she just self-absorbed, callous, or something worse? Again, she resisted the urge to go deep into analysis. There would be time for that later. Time to figure out what Casey's role in all this was.

She reached Kid and knelt beside him, hyperaware of Will and his rifle less than ten feet away. She probed Kid's neck and found a strong pulse in his carotid. "Kid, can you hear me?"

He stirred. She hated that he was up here because of her. He was lying here injured because she'd insisted on this trip to find Will, under the misguided notion that Will would want to help Betty. She'd been wrong. Wrong about more than that. *Aaron has a child. A grown woman child.*

Kid's eyes blinked open. He croaked out a few words. "Big City."

She smiled at him. "Where does it hurt?"

His eyes crossed. "My head. The side."

Jennifer's medical knowledge was minimal. Kid wasn't bleeding. She recalled from one of her cases—a man hit his girlfriend, she'd died of a closed head wound, and Jennifer had secured a second-degree murder conviction—how dangerous closed head wounds could be. The skull trapped swelling inside the cranium with the brain.

Will's rifle stock against Kid's head could be lethal.

She looked up at Casey and Will. He no longer had hold of her at all. She was speaking softly to him. Soft and fast. She snuck a glance back toward the dog sleds. Aaron had disappeared. *Good.* She didn't see Tommy either. They had to have the guns by now. Were they behind the sleds? Or flanking Will? But even if they got into a position where she and Kid weren't in the line of fire, they'd still have Casey to worry about.

As if reading her mind, Will put his arm back around Casey's shoulders and pulled her against him again, like a shield.

"Why do you have to do that?" Casey said, struggling against his grip for a second. Then she stopped, looking resigned but relaxed.

Jennifer stood. "I have to get Kid on that snowmobile and drive him out of here."

Will snickered. "What do you think I shot a minute ago?" He pointed the rifle barrel at the snowmobile. "Pow!"

"You shot it?"

"A kill shot. Right into the engine."

She almost asked him why, but the answer wouldn't matter. They now had only two dog sleds for six people to make the trek down. It wasn't enough room. Some of them would be walking. One of them was injured. One of them, at least, she hoped would soon be in restraints.

But Will hadn't checked to see whether the snowmobile was truly disabled. "I'm going to see if I can start it. He needs to get to the emergency room." She knelt again and patted Kid's shoulder. "I'll be right back." Then she leaned down and put her mouth close to his ear. "Stay down. Really low. Aaron went for our guns. I think Tommy's with him."

His smile was weak. "I'm not going anywhere."

Jennifer crawled to her feet then began the short walk to the snow machine. The drifts were thigh high. Her full snow suit restricted her movement and made it hard to lift her feet completely out of the snow. She was panting and sweating in three steps.

"Don't do it," Will said. "I still have plenty of ammunition."

Jennifer considered stopping. Then she thought about Kid dying because she let Will bully her. He hadn't shot any of them so far. And if he trapped them up here, they would eventually die of exposure. She kept up her slow march.

POW.

A bullet whizzed by her head. The sensation was unreal, like she was watching it happen to someone else in a movie. *This is what it feels like to almost die.*

PING.

It ricocheted off one of the sled's skis.

She turned back to Will, trying not to let her voice quiver. "Okay. I won't try to start it. But we have a medical kit in the under-seat compartment. Can I get that?"

"What else is in there?"

"Sandwiches. Gatorade. A thermos of hot chocolate."

Will whipped Casey around in a circle, her feet dragging. The girl screamed, but it sounded more angry than scared. "Where did Aaron and Tommy go?"

Jennifer was only surprised it had taken him five minutes to notice they'd disappeared. Between her distraction and whatever Casey had been saying, Will had been oblivious. But not anymore. Now he was distracted *looking* for them. His attention was off her. It was her chance to get herself out of the way in case Aaron or Tommy needed to fire their weapons. She ran the last few steps to the upturned snowmachine, catching her foot on the exposed ski tip and falling face first beside it.

None too soon, either.

CRACK.

The report of a rifle sent her scurrying on her belly behind the chassis. She leaned her back against it, panting, as more shots rang out.

Aaron shouted. "Will, cease fire. We're not shooting back."

Jennifer eased up and peered around the side of the snowmobile. Kid was still prone. Will was aiming the rifle using both hands. Casey was on her hands and knees on the ground beside him.

"You're trying to sneak up on me!" Will screamed.

"Drop your gun and let Casey go."

Will planted a foot on Casey's lower back.

She fell on her stomach. "What the hell?"

He pointed the gun at her head. "Come out or I'll kill her. I swear I will."

Will had the upper hand. Not just because of Casey. Kid was only a few yards away from him, too. Aaron and Tommy wouldn't do anything to jeopardize them.

So, what can I do? There had to be something. And it had to be soon.

A flash of inspiration struck her. Will was scared of dogs. The Great Pyrenees at WP Bar. Tommy's lead dog earlier. Could she use that against him? But how? And which was worse, risking their own lives or the dogs, too?

I have no idea. But I do know the dogs are quick and Tommy has a limited number of bullets in that rifle.

It was the only advantage she could think of, and if she was going to use it, it had to be now, while Will was still engaged with Aaron and Tommy. Staying low, she crawled as fast as she could to Tommy's team, her vision blurring with exertion and altitude by the time she reached them only thirty seconds later.

She paused by the dogs to catch her breath. They crowded her, licking her face, and blessedly staying quiet for once. Will was still screaming instructions at Aaron and Tommy. Aaron was answering in a calm voice.

She reached for the lead dog's harness and fumbled to unfasten it from the line. Her gloves were in the way. She ripped them off and they fell into the snow. *Dammit.* She couldn't worry about them now. She'd come back for them. With her hands bare, she worked the lead dog free, then moved on to the next. One after another, she released the dogs. They milled around her, uncertain what to do. The emotional energy given off by the humans had to be confusing for them.

She reached Sibley. Her hands were already so cold it was almost impossible to unfasten the latch. "Hey, sweet girl." Sibley's golden-brown eyes were deep and expressionless. Her usual doggy smile was absent from her face. "Want to help me out here?" She finally managed the latch, then rubbed Sibley's ears. *So warm on my hands.* "I need some zoomies. A lot of chaos. Some loud barking. Just please don't get yourself shot."

Sibley nosed Jennifer's hand, then spun and ran straight for Will, whose back was turned. Only Sibley didn't zoomie. She didn't a-woo, howl, bark, or growl. What she did was far more instinctual. Far more terrifying.

Without a sound, the dog bounded through the snow, staying low to the ground,. The other dogs responded to her alpha drive and arrayed behind her, like a canine jet fighter squadron. They were poetry in motion. But a horrible thought struck Jennifer, worse than Will shooting at one of them or one of the loose dogs. The other team was harnessed and anchored. The loose dogs could scatter and evade him. Not Willett's team. They were sitting ducks, helpless to run away.

Still gloveless, she took advantage of the tamped down snow where Tommy's team had passed and ran pell mell for the other team. "I'm sorry. I'm hurrying. I'm sorry," she said over and over, teeth chattering, as she somehow unbuckled each dog, despite having no feeling in her fingers.

She'd just released Willett when she heard Will shout. She turned in time to see him fall to the snow, a mass of black and white fur pinning him to the ground as his gun fired.

CHAPTER FORTY-ONE

WALKER PRAIRIE, Bighorn Mountains, Wyoming
Five minutes earlier

FROM HIS VANTAGE point in the tree line, Aaron kept his rifle pointed at Will. As athletic as Aaron was, he had no delusion that he could charge Will across deep snow and survive the assault. Will could kill Casey, Jenn, or Kid and cut Aaron and Tommy down with time to spare before Aaron could reach him.

Knowing that and accepting it were two different things, though. His wife was in danger. His daughter was in danger. *The daughter I cannot believe I have.*

By comparison, he was safe up here in the trees. And it made him feel like a coward.

"Don't do it," Tommy said.

Aaron stayed in position. "Do what?"

"Run out there and get yourself shot. You're no use to anyone dead."

Aaron grunted.

Will was spewing the same things on repeat. Come out or he'd kill Casey first and Jennifer—who he was still calling Priscilla —slowly.

"Something has to give," Aaron said. "Eventually he'll make good on one of his threats."

"I have an idea. He expects to hear you up here."

"Right."

"How about I work around to his other side and make a rush for him." Tommy had on his snowshoes. Aaron wished he'd grabbed his. *Greenhorn mistake.*

Tommy's plan made sense. "All right. But hurry. I don't know how much longer we've got until he snaps." *And starts shooting my family.*

"10-4. Give me five minutes." Tommy hurried off along the tree line.

Aaron raised his voice loud enough for Will to hear. "Put your gun down and let Casey up," Aaron said. "There's no need for any of this."

He searched for Jennifer. Last he'd seen her, she had taken cover behind the snowmobile. She wasn't there now. He became a little frantic. *Where are you?*

A streak of movement in the clearing caught his eye. What he saw made no sense. Tommy's sled team, led by a burly black and white dog, was racing across the park at Will. *Sibley. Our Sibley's going after Will.*

With Casey under Will's boot and Kid prone, that left only Jenn to have unleashed the dogs. He shot a glance back at the sleds in time to see her at work on their team, too. *That's my girl!* Twenty dogs. The ultimate distraction. It was brilliant. And he knew how hard the run to those sleds was, as he'd done it to get the guns, with his much greater leg length and muscle power. More than that, though, it required bravery.

Get down now, Jenn. Get down!

Like magnets, the charge of the dogs pulled his eyes away from

Jenn. To their dog, Sibley, leading the pack. Sibley was only slowed a little by the snow. She hit Will blindside like a battering ram. His rifle flew in the air as she piledrove his body into snow that exploded upward from the force of their bodies.

The rifle fired and spun just as he saw Willett running like a black streak across the snow.

No, no, no!

It was impossible to tell the trajectory of the shot. His eyes cycled through each member of their party, starting with Jenn and all the way through the dogs, ending with Willett. No one seemed to be hit, although he couldn't see Tommy. Finally, his eyes landed back on Sibley. She'd pinned Will and her silent attack had given way to vicious snarls. The message was clear—the dog would rip his throat out if he tried to get away. The other dogs stayed back, acknowledging that she had the situation under control. Closest to her was Willett, a-wooing and leaping around her. Sibley whipped her head from side to side, holding the back of his neck.

I can't let her kill him defending us. It's not fair to her. He ran toward the clearing, calling her off. "Sibley. Whoa. No. Sibley!"

But his wife beat him to the fray. "Sibley. No. Off. Come."

The dog looked up but didn't let go.

Jenn closed the last few steps between them and grabbed the harness on Sibley's back, showing zero fear of the attacking dog.

"No, Jenn!" Sibley could spin and latch onto Jenn in the heat of the moment. "Let go. I'll get her."

Jenn yanked the harness. Will shrieked.

"Sibley, LET GO!" Jenn commanded, deep and loud.

The dog loosened her grip and quit shaking her quarry.

"Sibley, let go." Jenn's voice was calmer.

Sibley finally relaxed and relinquished her grip. To Aaron's utter surprise, there was not a drop of blood on Will's neck. *Talk about all bark and no bite!* Also shocking was how fast Will moved away from the dog and toward where his rifle had landed.

Shit! Aaron had been so afraid the dog was going to tear Will apart that he'd forgotten about the gun.

As fast as Will was, Casey was faster. She dove into the snow and came up with a white-tipped nose and two-and-a-half feet of lethal force.

He held out a hand. "Good job, Casey."

But she turned the gun on him.

CHAPTER FORTY-TWO

Walker Prairie, Bighorn Mountains, Wyoming

Jennifer looked up from rubbing Sibley's ears and stopped whispering words of gratitude and praise to her heroic dog.

Casey had pointed the rifle at Aaron, whose own rifle was hanging at his side. "Back off, *Daddy*."

Jennifer's heart seemed to freeze and expand in her chest. She hung on tight to her dog, who was growling and lunging at Casey now.

"Casey?" Aaron said.

"Just back off and give Will time to get out of here."

"I don't understand."

"He had good reason for what he did. He doesn't deserve to be punished for it. That man was evil."

"What?" Jennifer said.

Casey glared at her. "You stay out of it. You've never had to suffer, not like Will and me."

"What are you talking about? What did Trusk do?" Aaron said.

"Fired both of us, treated us like dogs, and... and... "

Jennifer realized that in that moment, Casey was nearly as deranged as Will. She couldn't let this go any further. She had to stop her. Because there was no way Aaron was going to raise a hand—or a gun—against the young woman he believed was a daughter he'd never known about. Would Sibley protect her a second time? Everyone would be expecting it. Jennifer didn't dare let go, though. Casey would fire point blank into Sibley's beautiful, loyal, black and white chest. She searched frantically for an alternative weapon.

Aaron's voice was gentle. "And what?"

"And he... he expected things of me."

"What do you mean?"

"Sexually. He was a pervert. He *forced* me. And I told Will. I didn't know it would be the last straw for him with Trusk."

Jennifer felt sad for the girl. She'd never gone through anything like it, and she'd always been grateful not to work in sex crimes, because she thought the repetitive exposure to that trauma would destroy her. But being abused didn't give Casey the right to threaten them with their lives. She glanced at Will. He was sitting up now but slumped to the side. The snow below him was bright red. *Oh, my God. Did Sibley hurt him after all?* But he was holding his side. Low, near his hip. Sibley had never touched him there. *The rifle.* The bullet from the spinning gun. He'd shot himself.

He wasn't in shape to mount another attack. But if—when—they subdued Casey, they had two injured people to get down the mountain, and no snowmobile.

Kid! She sidled over to him, moving behind Casey. His eyes were closed. She lifted his wrist and felt for a pulse.

His eyes popped open. Voice low, he said, "Bear spray."

She spun, looking for the predator, her worst fear about dog sledding realized. "What? Aren't the bears hibernating?"

He had the strength to roll his eyes at her. "I have bear spray on my hip. Spray her."

She was glad Kid was all right. She was even happier he had a weapon.

She dug under Kid's coat and released a canister from the holster at Kid's side. She pulled the pin and put the canister behind her back with a finger on the trigger, just as she'd practiced with George's expired cans a few weeks before. As she slunk up behind Casey, her heart was hammering in her chest. She felt the wind on her face. It was blowing in the wrong direction. Jennifer was liable to get a face full of spray, too. And in order for any to land on Casey at all, Jennifer had to get the woman to turn toward her.

She walked in an arc around Casey, getting in a better position vis a vis the wind. Tommy appeared from the tree line, gun raised and pointed at Casey. For a moment, Jennifer considered backing off and letting Tommy take the lead. But shots could miss.

She was almost ready now.

"Hey," Will shouted. "What's that bitch Priscilla doing behind you, Casey?"

"Jennifer, no!" Aaron shouted.

Casey spun.

Jennifer lifted the canister and pulled the trigger. No spray came out. *No! It's not working!* Casey lifted the rifle and pointed it at Jennifer's chest at point blank range.

Jennifer winced and closed her eyes. *I love you Aaron.*

Casey pulled the trigger. Jennifer heard the click. But nothing happened. *I'm not dead.* Her eyes popped open. Casey stood rooted to the ground for a second, then she swung the rifle back and sprang toward Jennifer.

Jennifer pulled the trigger on the bear spray again. This time, the full contents emptied into Casey's face when she was only five feet away.

Casey's shriek was hair raising. "You bitch, you bitch, you bitch," she shrieked.

The rifle fell into the snow.

Jennifer backed away from the drifting cloud of burning spray, dropping the canister. Tommy grabbed Casey by the wrists. Aaron scooped up the rifle. Will buried his face in his hands.

And Casey kept screaming, shrill enough to trigger an avalanche.

CHAPTER FORTY-THREE

WALKER PRAIRIE, Bighorn Mountains, Wyoming

AARON HAD THOUGHT NFL training camp in August heat had been the hardest physical test he'd ever been through, until he had to snowshoe out of Walker Prairie. The only thing that kept him from complaining was Jenn and Tommy working just as hard alongside him. The dogs, too, strained under the loads. Casey and Will were strapped to one sled and Kid to the other. The tired teams needed almost as many breaks as the tired humans and didn't mind going slow enough for the snowshoers to keep up. It seemed like it was uphill the whole way, but he didn't remember it being downhill on the way out. And rocky. Lots of obstacles and hazards to catch snowshoes just under the surface. At least it was gorgeous with a clear blue cloudless sky. It smelled like pine tree heaven, too.

They were about halfway back to their vehicles at a rest stop when Casey broke. Will, almost delirious and half unconscious with pain, let her tell their story.

But she told it to Aaron, like there was no one else around.

"Aaron. Dad. I'm sorry. I'm so sorry. I don't know what came over me. I just—Will—he's damaged, like me. I didn't want to see your wife put him in jail."

His wife had piped up. "I'm a defense attorney, Casey. I only want to see Betty *not* go to jail. I don't put people in jail."

Anymore, Aaron thought.

Casey kept her eyes locked on Aaron. "I feel responsible for what Will did. If I hadn't told him what Trusk did to me, he might have let him go."

His own guilt weighed on Aaron. If he'd known about Casey and been a father to her, would her life have turned out differently? If nothing else, she wouldn't have come chasing after a father she'd never met halfway across the country with no money. She wouldn't have been vulnerable.

Will lifted his glazed eyes and looked over at Aaron. "I didn't need her help. I did what I did because Trusk had it coming."

That sounds an awful lot like a confession. From the look on Jenn's face, she thought so, too. It had *Black Bear Betty's going to walk* written all over it.

Jenn said, "Casey's an accessory after the fact if she knew about it and hid that information from the authorities."

"I didn't hide it. No one asked me." Casey's voice rose an octave.

"The law isn't on your side here, Casey."

"I didn't know."

"Again, not on your side."

"He had it coming. I'd do it again." Will's voice sounded raspy and spent. He reclined with his head back.

"Including framing Black Bear Betty?"

He mumbled, "That wasn't on purpose."

"Jennifer," Aaron said. "A word."

JENNIFER WINCED. Aaron called her Jennifer. He hadn't used the long form of her name in months. Not since things between them had gone back to good. Before then, he'd told her he loved Jenn, but he didn't like the woman Jennifer had become. She didn't blame him. She hadn't felt very likeable.

It bore ill portent that he called her Jennifer now.

"I'll move the teams along," Tommy said. "They're too tired to run off anyway." He mushed the dogs. The soft schuss of the sled runners was the only sound.

Jennifer walked slowly beside her husband until they were ten yards behind the sleds.

Aaron stared into the distance, not speaking.

"What?" she asked, unable to stand the silence any longer.

"Casey is so young."

"She's not a minor. She's not a child."

"She's only guilty of not telling anyone what Will did. You can see how guilty and responsible she feels for what happened."

"She worked for Kid and me. At a minimum she knew that keeping silent would endanger Black Bear Betty."

He smiled, flattering her. "But she knew that Black Bear Betty had a great team of lawyers."

"And she did hold a gun on us and fire at me. If it hadn't been out of ammo, she would have killed me, Aaron." The long declaration stole her breath, and she panted to catch it.

"That was fear. Heat of the moment. Self-defense, since you snuck up on her with a weapon."

"Oh, come on."

"You can see it. I know you can see it. If she was your client, you'd find a way out for her."

"She's not my client."

"But what if she was?"

Jennifer tripped and Aaron caught her by the elbow. She righted herself and kept walking. "Aaron, what are you not saying here?"

"I'm asking you to take her on as your client and keep her out of trouble."

"If I take her on as my client, I most certainly will counsel her to come clean and throw herself at the mercy of the authorities."

"But she could make up her own mind on that."

"Yes."

"And you wouldn't have an obligation to report her actions. Actions that you don't even have personal knowledge of. We're taking her word and Will's word, and frankly, Will is scary nuts."

"You sound more like a lawyer than me."

"Please, Jenn."

At least now he was calling her the name he loved her by. "This compromises my ethics. Aaron, I am considering running for county attorney against Ollie." She watched for his reaction, expecting it to be unfavorable.

Aaron bit his lip and went silent.

Well, the cat was out of the bag, whether he was happy about it or not. "If she ever ratted me out, my prosecutorial career would be over."

"If you're thinking about a prosecutorial career again, she may be the only child I ever have."

"What?"

"I don't want to have a baby if you're prosecuting. That job consumes you."

"I can't believe you're saying this. You've been wanting a baby for a decade. I'm not the same person I was. I'm much more balanced now."

"Forget I said anything."

"I can't just forget it."

"At least let's wait to talk about it when our subjects aren't all tangled up. I'm not even sure what I mean. But I do know right now I need your help."

"You mean you need me to put myself at risk, so she doesn't bear the consequences of her actions. At no risk to you."

He stopped and took her by her arms, gently. "Jenn, she's my daughter."

She jerked away. "And there's that. The fact that you lied to me all these years."

"I never lied. I blocked it out."

"You lied by omission."

"But she is my daughter. My *daughter*."

Jennifer wanted to sob and beat his chest. *I am your wife.* "Yes. But that doesn't change her actions."

"I am asking you for a favor. A huge favor. I am asking you to help my daughter."

Rage flared inside her, even though a part of her knew that she should be feeling empathy. Compassion. Even pity for the situation Aaron was in. Some of it spilled out. *I'm only human.* "Whose daughter? Your daughter? I've been your wife all these years, and she's just *your* daughter? I'm what—a bystander? Someone to manipulate into helping you and her? You and I both just found out about her. But if we'd always known, what would she be to me, Aaron?"

He hung his head. "Your stepdaughter. I'm sorry. Yes, she is yours, too."

"At least her stepmother. Maybe also her friend. Her confidante. Someone who took her to school and cooked her favorite dinners on her birthday. She would not just be yours. So why is she just yours now?" Tears welled in her eyes. *Dammit. Be strong.*

"It's different. You know it's different."

Jennifer wiped away the tears. "Yes, and you know it's different than you're making it, too."

"Touché."

Jennifer started walking again. Aaron fell in step beside her. They marched on in silence, snowshoes slapping the trail left by Tommy, all the dog paws, and two sleds.

Finally, Jennifer said, "You're asking me to risk my career on crazy, murdering Will keeping quiet about this? And on volatile

Casey—who has made it clear she hates me—not using this against me later?"

"When you put it like that, it's nuts. You're right. Forget I said anything."

Jennifer held up a hand. "I just want it to be clear between us. What the consequences are for me if this goes sideways. Both of us need to acknowledge the ask."

"I'm not asking."

"You did ask. I can't unremember the ask."

"I'm sorry. I love you. I'm—"

"Yes, Aaron. Yes, I will do this for you. I will do this for who this young woman should have been to me all these years. I will put it all on the line and try for the best outcome for her and pray it doesn't come back on me, in the hope that she will get her shit together and that someday we will all have a normal, loving, family relationship. Because if I don't do this, we never will, and deep in my bones, I fear it may cost me you. Not now, not tomorrow, but someday."

"It would never."

"It might. And I can't risk that." She looked up at her enormous husband. It was his eyes filled with tears now.

"Thank you. I love you."

"I'm not sure if I forgive you yet, but I love you, and I'm your partner. She is mine if she is yours."

He took her hand. "You are the most wonderful partner I could have ever imagined."

Jennifer didn't disagree with him. She also didn't have it in her to say anything else at the moment. Her head was already deep in legal strategy, and she hadn't even officially signed her new client yet.

CHAPTER FORTY-FOUR

Sheridan, Wyoming

"All rise," the bailiff said.

Judge Healy billowed into his seat almost before Jennifer could get to her feet. In a sonorous voice unlike his usual tone, he said, "State versus Jurgenson. Two cases actually. First-degree murder and aggravated assault. This is a little unusual, but I'll roll with it. Are we ready?"

Jennifer couldn't contain a smile. The assault victim, Helena, had woken from her coma and pointed the finger at the so-called witnesses, not Betty. Then the witnesses turned on the person who'd put them up to it. The dominoes cascaded in a line until they toppled former judge Arnold. The state would get another chance to hold him accountable for what he'd done to Betty, at least this time.

Kid said, "Yes, your honor," almost in unison with Ollie.

"Are we in agreement to drop the charges against one Elizabeth Jurgenson aka 'Black Bear Betty' in both cases?"

"Yes. We agree. Very much so," Kid said.

"The state does not object." Ollie gave a magnanimous nod.

Judge Healy cocked his head at Ollie with eyebrows furrowed. "I should hope not." To Betty, he said, "Ms. Jurgenson, all charges against you are dropped in these matters. You're free to go." He banged the gavel.

Betty, who was standing knee high to Kid between him and Jennifer, said, "About durn time." She saluted Jennifer and Kid and strode out of the courtroom muttering about this whole mess *ruining her business.*

Jennifer turned to watch her go, amused. The gallery buzzed with low laughter. Just before Betty reached the door—where Aaron was waiting to give her a ride home—she whirled around. "I don't suppose I could get a letter to take to my clients?"

"Like an excuse slip?" the judge said.

"More like a 'I ain't gonna murder you' note. That I got outta jail free."

Judge Healy paused, eyes twinkling. "Yes, I can put something together if you'd like."

"Should I just wait outside for it?"

He chuckled. "Come by for it in the morning. In the meantime, just tell folks I can vouch for you. In fact, I think I've got a few projects at my place I'd like you to bid on."

She nodded with a touch to an imaginary cap on her head and disappeared. Aaron caught Jennifer's eye and widened his. Jennifer matched his expression. Things between them had been strained. The secret he'd kept from her hurt. She turned back to face the judge and chewed on the inside of her cheek. Aaron's decision to hide his past was made long ago. She didn't like it. She wished he'd opened up after he'd matured. But if she dug deep in herself, she wasn't sure she would have done things differently than him. She hoped she would have. She just didn't know.

No matter what, though, their lives were changing. Jennifer would be sharing her husband with a grown daughter, as he tried to make up for a lifetime not knowing Casey. Jennifer was representing Casey and keeping her out of jail as she'd promised, but the girl wasn't happy about it, and her attitude toward Jennifer had not improved much. Glacial to icy cold, at best. Aaron was between a real-life rock and hard place. But then, so was Jennifer. Kearny County's interim sheriff, Leo Palmer, had taken mere minutes over a Virtual Private Network connection to retrieve the sent email that Casey had failed to delete off their server, the one where she had deliberately given Jennifer the wrong date and time for Betty's arraignment, even though she'd been able to get in through the saved administrative password on the computer she was using and delete it from Jennifer's inbox. The girl couldn't be fired twice. Jennifer didn't know what to do with the information, other than file it mentally as evidence of the lengths Casey would go to against Jennifer. She certainly wasn't going to tell Kid, who'd forgiven Casey for her actions on the mountain. It seemed like everyone had.

Everyone except Jennifer.

Judge Healy was speaking. "Bring in our next contestant, please, bailiff. Mr. Renwick."

Just hearing Will's name gave Jennifer goose bumps. She'd always thought something was off about him. How right she'd been.

After their group had come off the mountain, Will had asked for Kid to represent him, signed a confession, and been arrested and jailed. She'd had doubts about Kid taking his case, but Kid had been keen, so she hadn't stood in his way, especially after Will had signed a medical and military records release. Because of the raft of potential legal conflicts between Casey and Will, Kid and Jennifer were representing their clients alone. Luckily, Kid didn't have to take on Arnold as a client. That case would be contentious and difficult. Arnold had hired a fancy pants Jackson Hole attorney to take his case. *More power to him.*

Aaron had reached out to a highly-placed Army buddy about Will's records. Magically, they'd appeared overnight in Jennifer's inbox, and she'd passed them on to Kid. *It's all about who you know.* She knew she shouldn't, but she read them anyway. After a few incidents of escalating revenge violence he was reputed but not proven to have committed, he received a medical discharge for psychiatric reasons and was sent home to Wyoming. There were notes to the effect that it was for the safety of his supposed victims, who were terrified of him. He began treatment through the VA Hospital, where he first received the APD diagnosis. Jennifer had nearly fallen out of her chair when she saw the name of his treating physician: Chaplain Dean Abel. And when she read in police records that Priscilla Renwick Kennedy had sought restraining orders against her stepson on repeated occasions, starting in his teens and as recently as three months prior, she felt a chill race up her spine.

Kid turned to Jenn. His face had paled. "It's a first-degree murder charge. I don't feel ready."

"You've got this," she said. She believed in him.

Will shuffled in, eyes down, and stood beside Kid. He didn't speak or look up.

This was the man who had squatted in their barn, scaring Jennifer on many dark, early mornings. This was the man who would one day snap out of his fugue state and blame Kid, Jennifer, and Aaron for his incarceration. She wished she had pushed back harder on Kid not to take this case.

Jennifer walked toward the swinging gate that separated the gallery from the court.

Ollie frowned. "Where are you going?"

She shrugged. "Everything is set for the plea deal, right?" Will had agreed to the deal Betty had rejected. It was a good one for him and for the community, given his long history and worsening trajectory of APD and violence.

"Pending a psych eval. Given his condition, I don't disagree he needs treatment and is dangerous, but so is half the population in the prisons. Whatever the outcome, he needs to be locked up."

"I agree. You and Kid will figure the details out. In the meantime, I have an exam to take."

"What's next for you after that?"

"We'll see."

His expression didn't flicker. "You're going to oppose me in the election, aren't you?"

"I haven't decided. I've got a lot going on at the moment." It was true, but she knew she wanted his seat. She wanted to pursue justice, and she didn't feel bad that in her mind that included Pootie and the school shooting that haunted her. Aaron's words on the mountain still stung—that he didn't want to have a baby if she was going back into prosecution. They'd been festering ever since. Soon it would be time to lance that boil. She couldn't fault his objections based on the woman she was before. She just hoped he'd trust the one she was becoming to keep balance in their lives, whether there was ever to be a baby or not.

Judge Healy said, "If the two of you are done, we can commence with State versus Renwick."

Ollie faced the judge. "Ready, Your Honor."

Jennifer slipped out the swinging gate. She almost stayed to watch, but she'd meant what she said to Kid. He had this. Next time she entered this courtroom, it would be as a duly licensed Wyoming attorney, not a muzzled second chair. A consultant. An overqualified paralegal. She wanted to return to this, to litigation. It was in her blood.

"I understand the parties wish to present a plea agreement after arraignment?" the judge said.

Kid cleared his throat. "Yes, sir, Judge Healy." His voice cracked. "Yes, sir," he repeated, sounding strong.

Jennifer smiled and pushed her way into the hallway and away from the formal process of committing Will Renwick to fifteen years as a guest of the Wyoming State Penitentiary. She had a husband to find. A new stepdaughter to talk to. But those would come after a long overdue appointment with Chaplain Abel.

CHAPTER FORTY-FIVE

Sheridan, Wyoming

Jennifer arranged herself into the big armchair in Chaplain Abel's office. For a moment, her mind's eye fixated on the notes in Will's medical records. Antisocial personality disorder. Dean's signature on the diagnosis. Had Will sat in this chair? Had Dean been afraid of him? The coincidence of seeing the same psychiatrist was unsettling.

Dean said, "Has your sleep improved since we last spoke?"

"Not really." She related all that had happened, from Aaron's unexpected daughter to the young woman's anger toward her, and on to Betty's case. She left out everything related to representing Casey or the girl's involvement in the case. Medical privilege only went so far, and she had to protect attorney-client privilege.

He gave his head a few rapid shakes. "Wow. You've had a lot to process."

"I saved the best for last." She watched Dean closely as she told him about Will Renwick. "He pleaded guilty to second-degree murder. The state is cooperating on psychiatric evaluation and treatment."

Dean didn't react. It was like he'd never heard Will's name. Even if he'd forgotten Will was his patient, surely he'd seen the news over the last few days? But maybe not. Some people didn't watch the news. Like Aaron. She couldn't wean herself off of it, even if she felt like no matter which channel she tuned into, she was being manipulated toward an agenda.

"He attacked you?"

"Threatened us and our sled dogs. Fired shots. Knocked my associate Kid James out with the butt of his rifle."

"Unbelievable."

"But after all that he asked Kid to represent him. And he signed over all his military and medical records."

"Standard operating procedure, I would assume."

"Yes. That's how I came to know you provided his treatment through the VA and diagnosed him with APD."

Dean went preternaturally still, his face impassive. After nearly a minute, he said, "If you have the records and Will pleaded guilty, then you don't need to talk to me about him. And I don't talk about patients without a court order." He smiled, but it was rigor mortis stiff. "Most of my patients value discretion. Wouldn't you agree?"

That rubbed her fur in the wrong direction, as her grandmother used to say. But he spoke the truth. "I would."

"Now, about your sleep... "

"You're going to think I'm nuts, but with all that's going on, the thing occupying my mind in the wee hours of the night is the school shooting from my childhood. The tattoo. Pootie Carputin. The absence of justice."

"Justice and closure is how you're wired."

"Yes."

"I could write you a prescription for something to make you sleep, but that won't give you peace."

"I don't want to take anything that could be discoverable later." *Or might harm a baby. Although if I pursue prosecution, that may be off the table.*

"Then how about good, old-fashioned therapy? I'm a great listener and occasionally have advice that resonates."

"I'm open to that."

"But before we dive into the details, I'm going to start with my advice from 50,000 feet."

"Okay. And what is that?"

"Focus on the things you specifically can control."

"Meaning?"

"Your career, your marriage, and any family planning. Babies can bring great joy."

"They can also add stress."

He waggled his brows. "I know this firsthand. But deciding one way or the other about whether to have one decreases it. Then you can create joy with your husband. Focus on the joy. Luxuriate in deep cleansing breaths as you step into a settled future."

"Not really settled, given our new situation."

He did a funny motion that was part shrug, part nod, and part headshake.

The problem was that nothing was even close to settled. Aaron and Casey were at lunch together now, getting to know each other. She was a little jealous about it, but in a different way than she'd been before she knew who Casey was to Aaron. She was happy for them, but Jennifer needed to forge a relationship with Casey, too, or risk becoming the odd person out. She was starting from a deficit and fighting her own resistance.

You need to make room for Aaron's joy about Casey.

Assuming they could resolve the prosecution issue and decided to try for a child, would Aaron feel the same way he did about Casey about a child of their own? He'd broken down in tears the night before about Casey's babyhood and childhood.

Of course he'd feel the same.

But would Casey be jealous and possibly interfere or sabotage in some way, like she'd tried to do with Jennifer's case and marriage?

It was a strong possibility.

But in a blinding flash she knew that all her surface fears were camouflage for what lurked underneath. The nightmares. The memory of her own childhood. The shooter. Hank's little body protecting hers. The children who'd died.

Tears rolled down her cheeks, her nose, her mouth, her chin. "How can I bring a baby into a world like this? All the dangers. All the horrible people. My own parents couldn't protect me. No one was able to protect those other kids who died around me." Her crying turned to sobs.

Now that she'd uncovered the real issue, she couldn't believe she hadn't connected the dots before. This had been the stumbling block all along. Every moment of every day in her job she saw horrors. Children in the middle. Children hurt. Killed. Traumatized for life, like her. She'd experienced it firsthand and knew the lasting impact. She knew monsters like Pootie Carputin and Will Renwick were real.

"None of us can fully protect one another from all the bad possibilities that exist. But would you rather have not been born? Experienced love? Experienced joy and life in all its messy wonder?" He handed her a tissue from a box beside him.

She mopped up her face and blew her nose as she mulled over his questions. Thought about all the pain, fear, and mistakes. "I wish some parts had been easier, but I wouldn't have missed it."

He smiled at her. "The human condition carries with it illness, injury, trauma, and death. We're programmed for suffering. But we also have the capacity for joy, hope, love, peace, and many other wonderful things. We don't know which of us is marked for more suffering than others. Or more joy and love."

She nodded slowly. "I'll think about it."

"Then get out your number two pencil and a notepad." He mimed writing. "You've done good work so far today, but now class is in session. You're going to start helping yourself get better."

Back in Jennifer's cottage, two malamutes lay pressed against the door jamb where cold air leaked under, as far as possible from the crackling fire. Outside, the wind howled, and snow blew. When Jennifer first got home and let Willett out of her crate, the dog had run zoomies in the snow for fifteen minutes. Willett was now crated every time they left her in the house without humans, even though she screamed like a banshee as soon as the crate door latched. Their ears could survive that, but the house could not withstand the temporary, destructive schizophrenia that overcame the dog whenever Aaron and Jennifer left. Sibley behaved like a lady when they were gone, so she didn't have to stay in a crate. She'd participated in the zoomies, though, mostly to tackle Willett. Both dogs were happily exhausted now.

She walked over to them and massaged each pair of ears. "You girls were amazing up at Walker Prairie. Especially you, Sibley." She'd put her life in danger to protect her new family. They'd worked hard pulling the sleds back to the vehicles. As much trouble as they were, they were adorable, and they'd found their forever home.

Jennifer went back to the couch and her bar exam review materials. Within minutes her eyes were blurring as she read a page for the third time. Wills, trusts, and estates had never been a particular area of interest for her, except as they related to motive for murder. She shut the book and looked at the screensaver on her laptop. Aaron and her on their fifteenth anniversary, during a trip to Bora Bora. She'd insisted they return to Houston halfway through their planned week because of her trial schedule. Looking back, it had been the beginning of the tough times for them.

She was so glad that period was behind them. She couldn't let issues with Casey derail their relationship. Or conflicts over what type of job she held and whether that would disqualify her as a mother.

She ran her hands over the keys. Her fingers reached out without a conscious decision to do so. She entered her password and opened a blank Word document.

The dog sled cut through an opening in a stand of spruce so narrow that Jennifer Herrington sucked in her breath. *Like that will do any good.* If it got stuck it wouldn't be because of her slight frame, or that of her enormous husband Aaron standing on the runners behind her. It would be the basket, which protruded several inches on either side of him.

She took a deep breath. Where had that come from? The words came faster and faster. It was a rush almost as powerful as the scene she was writing about their confrontation with Will on Walker Prairie.

It was well past hunting season. Killing a game animal out of season—or without a license during season—was poaching. But poachers usually harvested at least some part of the animal. Not many people gutted the carcasses of animals they found already dead either. A queasy unease settled over her. Poachers got high fines and jail time, and criminals didn't like to be caught, something she knew well from her years prosecuting them as an assistant district attorney in Harris County, Texas.

"A little information back here, please," Kid shouted.

She licked her dry lips. "Who do you think would do something like this?"

Tommy pointed. "I don't think, I know. Him."

Jennifer couldn't see anyone. But then a figure moved closer, coming toward Tommy, his lead dog, and Jennifer. Effortlessly. Like walking on water. *Snowshoes. Dang it—I should have taken the time to get mine.*

Cradling a rifle.

Jennifer wished she'd stayed with Aaron back at their sled.

"That's close enough," Aaron shouted.

The figure stopped a few feet away from Tommy's lead dog, with Sibley—Jennifer's favorite of their two malamutes—only a few spots behind her. The lead dog went into a frenzy. Snapping, growling, and lunging. The person raised the rifle and pointed it at the dog's head.

"No!" Jennifer screamed.

Her phone rang, pulling her fingers away from the memories she was stirring. The elation was still pulsing through her. Her writer's block had broken. She had started her book.

She checked the screen. It was Joe. Almost like her productivity had summoned him. "Hi, Joe. How are you?"

His New Jersey accent was buoyant. "I couldn't be better because I'm calling with good news for my favorite writer."

Her happiness escalated into the scariness of hope. She crossed her fingers, closed her eyes, and said, "I like good news. What do you have?"

"I have not one but multiple editors vying for your book. It's become a bidding war."

The beating of her heart in her ears was thunderous. "What does that mean?"

"It means your book is going to get published, that you're going to make me a lot of money, and that they all want to know when your next one will be ready."

"Really?"

"Really! We'll have a deal in a day or two. Congratulations!"

"Oh, my God. Oh, my *God!*"

Joe laughed. "Now, about that next book?"

"I just finished a chapter."

"The first one?"

"Yes. But it's a good one."

"Tell me all about it."

And so, she did, short of breath and with tears of that joy that Dean had urged her to find earlier.

CHAPTER FORTY-SIX

Big Horn, Wyoming

Aaron walked into the bathroom to find Jenn crouched over the toilet. "What are you doing?" Two floofy dogs wrestled in the hall behind him, nearly taking him out at the knees. Having malamutes was even more awesome than he'd ever imagined. "I made us a reservation at Frackelton's. We're celebrating my wife, the soon-to-be-famous author tonight! You can't be sick."

Jenn set a white stick on the bathroom counter. "Your wife is off her birth control pills. I'm supposed to start today but I haven't yet. I thought I'd be better safe than sorry when the champagne is flowing."

"You think you're pregnant?" He kept his voice light. He was surprised that instead of feeling excited, he felt apprehensive. How would Casey handle the news? He didn't want to hurt her feelings. She loved being his only child, and he imagined she would be blind-sided, since he and Jennifer were on the older side for first-time parents. Then there were Jennifer's aspirations to return to prosecution. He had lived through that before. It was hard on their marriage and would probably be even harder with a baby.

"No. Just being careful."

"Gotcha." He backed out of the bathroom. "How long until you're ready?"

"Five minutes."

"I'll be getting the pets ready for our departure." Only six months before, he hadn't had a pet since he'd left for college. His marriage was back on track, he had a wonderful vet practice, a fun side gig coaching football, this wonderful lodge, the animals, and now a daughter. There had been so many wonderful changes for them in Wyoming.

He refilled Katya's feeder and ran water for the dogs. Jeremiah was chittering away on George's shoulder. Liam's absence loomed large. He missed the little red fox he'd nursed back to health, too. Game and Fish had asked him about his interest in helping them with wildlife, and he had given them a resounding yes. He couldn't wait to see what that entailed.

"You're working late." Aaron scooped food into bowls. George normally headed back to his place before dark, especially on stormy days.

"Damn contractors. Show up late, end early, leave a mess. I was finishing up everything they should have done. Black Bear Betty can't help me out either. She's busy on a bunch of new projects, too."

"I thought her incarceration would be bad for business, but apparently it's having the opposite effect. Aren't you worried about the conditions? You may have trouble getting back to your place." Aaron put the dog food bowls down. He held up a hand for the dogs to wait. "Sibley." He pointed to her bowl. She ambled over and started gobbling. "Willett." He pointed to hers. Willett sprinted to her bowl and ate daintily.

George looked out the window. "I lost track of it, to be honest."

"Just stay here tonight. I don't want to be hunting for your frozen carcass tomorrow."

George grinned. "I suspect that's the right thing to do. I'd thawed a steak though."

Aaron took the cat her bowl on top of a roll-top desk. The malamutes hadn't made an attempt on her life, despite her taunting them, but he felt better with her beyond their reach while her attention was on her food. "Thaw one of ours here. Our freezer is your freezer."

"Now you're talking."

Jenn swept into the living room. She looked stunning in tall furry boots, bundled in a fluffy knee length parka. A tiny, pretty abominable snowman. "I'm forgetting something."

"You've got your purse and phone?" Aaron asked.

"Yes."

"You've got gloves and a warm hat?"

"Yes."

"We're good to go then." He held his arms out to Jenn like he was introducing her, hyping her for George. "My wife just got the news that her first mystery is going to be published. She's an author now!"

"Congratulations. I don't read much, but I'm looking forward to this one," George said. "I heard there's a heroic, good looking mature gentleman in it."

Jenn laughed. "Something like that." She stopped to coo to Jeremiah and stroke his neck before putting her hand in Aaron's and walking out with him.

———

The drive to public parking in town was easy, thanks to recent plowing. The snow had stopped falling, too, which bode well for their drive home.

After they parked and he'd turned off the Jeepster, Aaron took his wife's hand. "I love you."

"I love you, too."

"No, I mean, I really, really love you. I'm so proud of you. It's not just the book. I'm excited for you about it, but I always knew it would be a success. It's so good."

"It's not anything yet, but we're closer. I don't want to jinx it."

He smiled. "It's going to happen. And what you've done for our friends. Keeping George and Black Bear Betty on the right side of the iron grates. You're such a great attorney."

"Now all I need is my license."

He looked deep into her eyes. "But most of all, I'm proud of you for the changes you've made and how they've impacted our relationship. You picked us, Jenn. I can't tell you what it means to me to have you back. And I'm sorry about what I said up on the mountain. I believe in you. Whatever you decide to do."

She leaned across the seat and nestled into his shoulder. "Thank you for that. I love you, Aaron."

"And now, your support about Casey. When that could have gone so badly for us. I hate that I never told you. It was a dark time in my life. But now to have Casey here with us, and you helping her, it's everything."

Jenn shifted against him, pulling back slightly. "I'm... happy for you."

"I know it's weird, but it's like we're a complete family now."

Jenn shivered. "I'm getting cold, Aaron."

He laughed. "Sorry! Let's go in."

They held gloved hands as they walked the snow-dusted sidewalks. Aaron felt something off about Jenn's mood. Maybe she was nervous about her book deal. He opened the door for her. The host recognized him. Most people in town already did. He was hard to miss, he knew.

Inside the restaurant was buzzing and cozy. Like a scene in a snow globe, with the snow outside. The smells were heavenly, too. It was the best place for steak or lamb chops in town, and he could smell them both sizzling in the kitchen. His stomach rumbled. *Way past my feeding time.*

"Mr. Herrington, Ms. Herrington, right this way." The woman gestured toward a table for eight, half-filled already by three people.

Jenn's steps faltered. She glanced up at him. "I thought you and I were celebrating."

"We are. With your family and mine."

Maggie saluted with her drink. Hank stood and slow clapped. Casey smiled at Aaron and twirled a straw in a glass.

"Congratulations. Next stop the bestseller's list!" Maggie said, loud enough to turn every head in the dining area.

"Hardly! Thanks, you guys!" Jenn hugged her cousin and smiled at Maggie and Casey.

"And congratulations on gaining a daughter," Maggie added.

Hank nodded at Casey. "She looks just like you, Aaron. We've had the best time getting to know Casey tonight while we waited on you."

"Yeah, weren't you going to be here like half an hour ago?" Casey pouted at Aaron.

"It took us a little longer to get ready than we'd anticipated," Aaron said, remembering Jenn over the toilet and the pregnancy test. He assumed it was negative since she hadn't mentioned it. But she hadn't been feeling well. Maybe that accounted for what he was noticing in her demeanor.

Casey rolled her eyes.

A waiter approached. "Drinks for you two?"

"Shit!" Jenn said. "I forgot to check my test." She took one of the empty seats.

"Test?" Maggie asked.

Aaron sat beside Jenn and took her hand. "Call George and have him look. He's spending the night."

Jenn pulled out her phone. "I'll be right back."

Aaron asked the waiter for a Blacktooth Brewery Copper Mule. The creamy lime ginger ale had become his favorite. "She'll order when she gets back."

"How about some appetizers in the meantime?" Hank said. "Calamari? Mussels? Gnocchi?"

"What kind of test?" Casey asked.

Aaron held his arms out. "The celebration is on me tonight. Black

Bear Betty's charges are dropped. We survived Walker Prairie. We've gained a daughter."

"You have," Casey muttered.

Ignore her. She'll stop that once she sees it gets her nowhere with you. "And Jenn is going to be published." Aaron beamed.

"Is anyone going to tell me what kind of test?"

Jenn sat heavily. Her face was as white as the snow outside the window. "One I failed."

Aaron frowned. "Negative? But isn't that a good thing?"

"Positive." She held up a finger. "Iced tea for me please."

"You're pregnant?" Maggie squealed, jumped up, ran over, and hugged her. "That's so exciting. I'm going to be an aunt!"

Casey's expression was dark. "You already are one."

"Way to go, Aaron." Hank was sitting beside him and clapped his shoulder.

Aaron looked at his daughter. Her face was tight and angry.

"Aaron?" Jenn's voice tore his eyes away from Casey.

"Yeah?" Aaron said.

"Do you have anything to say?"

Oh, shit. "Sorry. You shocked me speechless."

Jenn looked close to tears. It was a punch to the gut. He'd hurt her feelings. He wasn't used to having two women's feelings to consider. It was overwhelming.

He grabbed her by both hands. "It's wonderful news. The best. Talk about a celebration! But I thought you said you didn't think you were pregnant?"

"I didn't. I was clearly wrong."

Aaron became conscious of Maggie, Hank, and the waiter— he'd forgotten the man was even still there—turning their heads back and forth to watch Aaron and Jenn like a Wimbledon match. "Well, I love you." He kissed her nose. "I love our growing family."

She gave him a smile that was a little watery. *Better, but not there yet.*

He pulled her into his chest and whispered in her ear. "You will be the best mother ever."

Jennifer whispered back. "Thank you. You'll be the best dad."

He sat back and they smiled at each other. Her eyes were shining, but this time they looked like happy tears.

"Aren't you a little old to have a baby?" Casey said.

Jenn's mouth fell open.

"I mean, I'm the right age to have babies. You could be a grandmother!"

"Okay, okay," Aaron held up a hand.

Jenn's face splotched red. She leaned toward Casey. Her hand shot out like she was going to point at Casey, but it knocked over an ice water. It spilled across the table into Casey's lap.

"Hey! Watch it!" Casey jumped up and shouted. "You owe me new pants if these are ruined. God!"

The waiter, who'd just arrived with Aaron's beer, grabbed every napkin on the table and began mopping up the water before Aaron could do it. *Casey's behavior to Jenn is unacceptable. Ignore her now, focus on Jenn. Talk to her later.*

He started to reach for his wife. She jerked back like she'd been snakebit, pointing at the waiter's shoulder. Her mouth was moving but no sounds were coming out.

"What is it?" he asked.

She staggered to her feet, grabbed her bag and coat, and ran— literally, ran—to the door.

He didn't bother explaining himself to the table, just went after her, not catching her until she was on the sidewalk.

He took her hand. "Honey, what's the matter? Was it Casey? Or is it that I was slow on the uptake? I'm sorry about that. About all of it. I love you."

Jenn shook her head, scattering her tears. Her mouth opened and closed, forming words with no sound. Her pupils were dilated, her eyes wide, her nose running. He'd never seen her like this. It was like she was panicked.

"What is it?"

She tapped her shoulder. "The waiter. His tattoo."

Aaron tried to remember it. He had noticed a tattoo, but it barely registered. Some yellow. Red. Black. Other than that, he drew a blank. "Tell me what you mean, okay?"

She could barely get the words out, sobbing between them. "The snake. Don't Tread on Me. The one Pootie has. The one the *shooter* had."

"Oh! Oh my, God." All Jenn's nightmares. Had she really seen it? If so, he could understand her reaction. "I'm sorry. Would you like to ask for a different waiter?"

Kid James walked up at that moment. "Am I late? Congratulations, Jenn!"

Jenn turned from him, hiding her wrecked face. Kid looked at Aaron, perplexed.

Aaron waved him on. "Sorry. We'll be back in a minute. Everyone else is inside."

"All right." He mouthed. "Is she okay?"

Aaron smiled at him.

When Kid was inside, Aaron put his arms around his wife. She felt as fragile as a baby bird. "Talk to me."

"I'm—I'm—I'm having a baby, and he's still out there."

"Pootie?"

"Or whoever shot up that playground. I was so sure, Aaron. So sure. But the same tattoo. It could be anyone with that tattoo. I have to find out who it is. I have to make sure he's held accountable."

"It's been thirty-five years, Jenn. How are you going to find him? Especially now that you're pregnant."

She put her palms on his chest and her cheek against his shoulder. "I don't know yet. But I can't bring a baby into this world knowing I didn't give it my best." She looked up at him, leaning the back of her head into his arm. "I'm going to be this baby's mother. I'm going to be a mother." She crumpled and Aaron caught her under her arms just before she hit the ground.

"Babe. Shh. Get back up here."

She looked up at him. "Casey hates me. And you aren't excited about the baby. It's all just not what I expected."

He helped her back to her feet. "I am *very* excited about the baby." The more he said it, the more true it became. "There's just been so much this last week. I got caught up in the moment. I'm very happy we are having a baby together."

A steely look crossed her face. "You didn't stick up for me with Casey."

"I think it's better to talk to her about how she's acting in private. It's not okay with me."

"You lied to me for years."

"I didn't tell you. I never lied."

"You didn't warn me you were inviting people that I wouldn't have wanted at my celebration with you."

Aaron felt the world spinning around him. How had things gone from so good so quickly to so bad? Was it pregnancy hormones? He'd heard they could be awful. His father had always said that the only thing to do with a pregnant woman was help her live through it. "I thought it would be nice. I was wrong. I'm really sorry."

She glared at him. "I don't want to go back in there."

"No one will mind that we took a break. We just had a big surprise. And then Casey wasn't nice. You had a shock about the tattoo. It's okay. It will be fine."

She crossed her arms. "It's my celebration. I want to go home."

Help her live through it. He exhaled, then looked in the window at their friends and family. "Okay. Just give me a minute to let everyone know."

"Text them. Call the restaurant with your card. But take me home."

"That will work." He texted Hank, keeping it short and sweet, then turning his attention back to her. "I'm sorry, Jenn. I wanted you to have a nice evening. I meant everything I said in the car. I promise you, I'll talk to Casey. And I'll do anything you need to help you about the tattooed shooter. If it's not Pootie, we'll find him together."

She put her arms around his neck and drooped into him. "Do you mean it?"

"Every word of it."

"I need you. I need us."

He squeezed her tight. "You've got me. We've got all of this, together."

After a minute of swaying and rocking, he said, "Are you ready?"

"Yes. Thank you." She stepped back. Her eyes were almost normal again. Her breathing was under control.

"Would you like to get some food on the way home?"

"McDonald's. Large fries, a Big Mac, and a chocolate shake."

"Whoa. That's not like my vegetarian wife."

Her mouth twitched. "It's your baby I'm carrying after all. I'll probably be craving a side of beef by tomorrow."

He put his arm around her and threw one last glance back at the table. Casey was staring after them, her mouth in a hard line. For the first time, he really saw what Jenn had been telling him about the young woman. There was hatred pure and feral on her face. He'd have to do something about it before it became a bigger problem.

Tomorrow.

Because right now, he needed to take care of his pregnant wife. Everything would be fine.

He would make sure of it.

***

Be sure you double back and read BIG HORN, Jenn and Aaron's first adventure, if you haven't already, while waiting for their next in RED GRADE, coming 2026.

Looking for more stories like this one? Try the Delaney Pace series of Wyoming crime thrillers next and watch for crossover appearances by characters from Jenn's world!

For Sibley and Willett. Thanks for the laughs, adventures, and leaving a small part of our lives intact.
For Eric. Who puts up with two malamutes and me.

ACKNOWLEDGMENTS

Agent Joe Durepos pitched me a story. "A Houston attorney and her husband—he could be an executive in the oil industry, or you could make it something more interesting, like a veterinarian—move to Wyoming and run a mountain B&B, where they have a menagerie of pets and she solves and writes mysteries."

I said, "Joe, that's Eric and me."

He laughed.

I said, "Joe, that's narcissistic."

He said, "It's the type of escape other people dream of. Can you write it?"

Well, duh, of course, I could. It's my life, after all. Only, after I sat down to write it, it strayed some from the original blueprint. In a good way, I hope.

The murder idea came from the actual log splitter in our actual "Snowheresville" (aka Big Horn Hideaway Lodge) barn. I may or may not have based characters on real people I know ;-) And the setting is a little bit Snowheresville and a little bit make-believe.

Thanks for the idea, Joe. I was able to age up the Patrick Flint characters and draw them into the story and pull across What Doesn't Kill You characters as well. There are already five more books planned for this series if it turns out people like them and want me to keep going.

And yet there are more thanks to give . . .

Thanks to my dad for advice on all things medical. Love and hugs to my favorite kissin' cousin (who is not really my cousin), Dr. Kristine "Rockey" Millikin for helping Aaron sound like a real vet. Thanks to Stu Healy and Ryan Healy for keeping me from screwing up Wyoming law. If I did, that's on me, not you guys.

Thanks to my husband, Eric, for brainstorming with and encouraging me and beta reading BIG HORN and WALKER PRAIRIE with me despite your busy work, travel, and workout schedule. And for taking a chance on Wyoming and me.

Thanks to our five offspring. I love you guys more than anything, and each time I write a parent/child (birth, adopted, foster, or step), I channel you. I am so touched by your support for Poppy, Gigi, Eric, and me.

Editing credits go to Karen Goodwin. You rock. A big thank you as well to my proofreading and advance review team.

The biggest thanks, though, goes to my readers. It never ceases to amaze me that you read my novels, that your support has resulted in this mid-life career change that gives me so much joy. From the bottom of my heart, I offer you my gratitude.

BOOKS BY THE AUTHOR

Fiction from SkipJack Publishing

THE *PATRICK FLINT* SERIES OF WYOMING MYSTERIES:

Switchback (Patrick Flint #1)

Snake Oil (Patrick Flint #2)

Sawbones (Patrick Flint #3)

Scapegoat (Patrick Flint #4)

Snaggle Tooth (Patrick Flint #5)

Stag Party (Patrick Flint #6)

Sitting Duck (Patrick Flint #7)

Skin and Bones (Patrick Flint #8)

Spark (Patrick Flint 1.5): Exclusive to subscribers

THE *JENN HERRINGTON* WYOMING MYSTERIES:

BIG HORN (Jenn Herrington #1)

WALKER PRAIRIE (Jenn Herrington #2)

THE *WHAT DOESN'T KILL YOU* SUPER SERIES:

Wasted in Waco (WDKY Ensemble Prequel Novella): Exclusive to Subscribers

The Essential Guide to the What Doesn't Kill You Series

Katie Connell Caribbean Mysteries:

Saving Grace (Katie Connell #1)

Leaving Annalise (Katie Connell #2)

Finding Harmony (Katie Connell #3)

Seeking Felicity (Katie Connell #4)

Emily Bernal Texas-to-New Mexico Mysteries:

Heaven to Betsy (Emily Bernal #1)

Earth to Emily (Emily Bernal #2)

Hell to Pay (Emily Bernal #3)

Michele Lopez Hanson Texas Mysteries:

Going for Kona (Michele Lopez Hanson #1)

Fighting for Anna (Michele Lopez Hanson #2)

Searching for Dime Box (Michele Lopez Hanson #3)

Maggie Killian Texas-to-Wyoming Mysteries:

Buckle Bunny (Maggie Killian Prequel Novella)

Shock Jock (Maggie Killian Prequel Short Story)

Live Wire (Maggie Killian #1)

Sick Puppy (Maggie Killian #2)

Dead Pile (Maggie Killian #3)

The Ava Butler Caribbean Mysteries Trilogy*: A Sexy Spin-off From *What Doesn't Kill You

Bombshell (Ava Butler #1)

Stunner (Ava Butler #2)

Knockout (Ava Butler #3)

Fiction from Bookouture

Detective Delaney Pace Series:

HER Silent BONES *(Detective Delaney Pace Series Book 1)*

HER Hidden GRAVE *(Detective Delaney Pace Series Book 2)*

HER Last CRY (Detective Delaney Pace Series Book 3)

Juvenile from SkipJack Publishing

Poppy Needs a Puppy (Poppy & Petey #1)

Nonfiction from SkipJack Publishing

The Clark Kent Chronicles

Hot Flashes and Half Ironmans

How to Screw Up Your Kids

How to Screw Up Your Marriage

Puppalicious and Beyond

What Kind of Loser Indie Publishes,

and How Can I Be One, Too?

Audio, e-book, large print, hardcover, and paperback versions of most titles available.

ABOUT THE AUTHOR

Pamela Fagan Hutchins is a *USA Today* best selling author. She writes award-winning mystery/thriller/suspense from way up in the frozen north of Snowheresville, Wyoming, where she lives with her husband in an off-the-grid cabin on the face of the Bighorn Mountains, and Mooselookville, Maine, in a rustic lake cabin. She is passionate about their large brood of kids, step kids, inherited kids, and grandkids, riding their gigantic horses, and about hiking/snow shoeing/cross country skiing/ski-joring/bike-joring/dog sledding with their Alaskan Malamutes.

If you'd like Pamela to speak to your book club, women's club, class, or writers group by streaming video or in person, shoot her an email. She's very likely to say yes.

You can connect with Pamela via her website
(http://pamelafaganhutchins.com)
or email (pamela@pamelafaganhutchins.com).

PRAISE FOR PAMELA FAGAN HUTCHINS

2018 USA Today Best Seller
2017 Silver Falchion Award, Best Mystery
2016 USA Best Book Award, Cross-Genre Fiction
2015 USA Best Book Award, Cross-Genre Fiction
2014 Amazon Breakthrough Novel Award Quarter-finalist,
Romance

The Patrick Flint Mysteries

"Best book I've read in a long time!" — Kiersten Marquet, author of
Reluctant Promises

"*Switchback* transports the reader deep into the mountains of
Wyoming for a thriller that has it all--wild animals, criminals, and one
family willing to do whatever is necessary to protect its own. Pamela
Fagan Hutchins writes with the authority of a woman who knows
this world. She weaves the story with both nail-biting suspense and a
healthy dose of humor. You won't want to miss *Switchback*." -
- Danielle Girard, *Wall Street Journal*-bestselling author of
White Out.

"*Switchback* by Pamela Fagan Hutchins has as many twists and turns
as a high-country trail. Every parent's nightmare is the loss or injury
of a child, and this powerful novel taps into that primal fear." -- Reavis
Z. Wortham, two time winner of The Spur and author of *Hawke's
Prey*

"*Switchback* starts at a gallop and had me holding on with both hands
until the riveting finish. This book is highly atmospheric and nearly
crackling with suspense. Highly recommend!" -- Libby Kirsch, Emmy
awardwinning reporter and author of the *Janet Black Mystery Series*

"A Bob Ross painting with Alfred Hitchcock hidden among the trees."
"Edge-of-your seat nail biter."
"Unexpected twists!"
"Wow! Wow! Highly entertaining!"
"A very exciting book (um... actually a nail-biter), soooo beautifully descriptive, with an underlying story of human connection and family. It's full of action. I was so scared and so mad and so relieved... sometimes all at once!"
"Well drawn characters, great scenery, and a kept-me-on-the-edge-of-my-seat story!"
"Absolutely unputdownable wonder of a story."
"Must read!"
"Gripping story. Looking for book two!"
"Intense!"
"Amazing and well-written read."
"Read it in one fell swoop. I could not put it down."

What Doesn't Kill You: Katie Connell Romantic Mysteries

"An exciting tale . . . twisting investigative and legal subplots . . . a character seeking redemption . . . an exhilarating mystery with a touch of voodoo." — *Midwest Book Review Bookwatch*
"A lively romantic mystery." — *Kirkus Reviews*
"A riveting drama . . . exciting read, highly recommended." — *Small Press Bookwatch*
"Katie is the first character I have absolutely fallen in love with since Stephanie Plum!" — *Stephanie Swindell, Bookstore Owner*
"Engaging storyline . . . taut suspense." — *MBR Bookwatch*

What Doesn't Kill You: Emily Bernal Romantic Mysteries

"Fair warning: clear your calendar before you pick it up because you won't be able to put it down." — *Ken Oder, author of* Old Wounds to the Heart

"Full of heart, humor, vivid characters, and suspense. Hutchins has done it again!" — *Gay Yellen, author of* The Body Business

"Hutchins is a master of tension." — *R.L. Nolen, author of* Deadly Thyme

"Intriguing mystery . . . captivating romance." — *Patricia Flaherty Pagan, author of* Trail Ways Pilgrims

"Everything about it shines: the plot, the characters and the writing. Readers are in for a real treat with this story." — *Marcy McKay, author of* Pennies from Burger Heaven

What Doesn't Kill You: Michele Lopez Hanson Romantic Mysteries

"Immediately hooked." — *Terry Sykes-Bradshaw, author of* Sibling Revelry

"Spellbinding." — *Jo Bryan, Dry Creek Book Club*

"Fast-paced mystery." — *Deb Krenzer, Book Reviewer*

"Can't put it down." — *Cathy Bader, Reader*

What Doesn't Kill You: Ava Butler Romantic Mysteries

"Just when I think I couldn't love another Pamela Fagan Hutchins novel more, along comes Ava." — *Marcy McKay, author of* Stars Among the Dead

"Ava personifies bombshell in every sense of word. — *Tara Scheyer, Grammy-nominated musician, Long-Distance Sisters Book Club*

"Entertaining, complex, and thought-provoking." — *Ginger Copeland, power reader*

What Doesn't Kill You: Maggie Killian Romantic Mysteries

"Maggie's gonna break your heart–one way or another." *Tara Scheyer, Grammy-nominated musician, Long-Distance Sisters Book Club*
"Pamela Fagan Hutchins nails that Wyoming scenery and captures the atmosphere of the people there." — *Ken Oder, author of* Old Wounds to the Heart
"I thought I had it all figured out a time or two, but she kept me wondering right to the end." — *Ginger Copeland, power reader*

BOOKS FROM SKIPJACK PUBLISHING

FICTION:
Marcy McKay

Pennies from Burger Heaven, by Marcy McKay

Stars Among the Dead, by Marcy McKay

The Moon Rises at Dawn, by Marcy McKay

Bones and Lies Between Us, by Marcy McKay

When Life Feels Like a House Fire, by Marcy McKay

R.L. Nolen

Deadly Thyme, by R. L. Nolen

The Dry, by Rebecca Nolen

Ken Oder

The Closing, by Ken Oder

Old Wounds to the Heart, by Ken Oder

The Judas Murders, by Ken Oder

The Princess of Sugar Valley, by Ken Oder

Gay Yellen

The Body Business, by Gay Yellen

The Body Next Door, by Gay Yellen

Pamela Fagan Hutchins

THE PATRICK FLINT SERIES OF WYOMING MYSTERIES:

Switchback (Patrick Flint #1), by Pamela Fagan Hutchins

Snake Oil (Patrick Flint #2), by Pamela Fagan Hutchins

Sawbones (Patrick Flint #3), by Pamela Fagan Hutchins

Scapegoat (Patrick Flint #4), by Pamela Fagan Hutchins

Snaggle Tooth (Patrick Flint #5), by Pamela Fagan Hutchins

Stag Party (Patrick Flint #6), by Pamela Fagan Hutchins

Spark (Patrick Flint 1.5): Exclusive to subscribers, by Pamela Fagan Hutchins

THE *WHAT DOESN'T KILL YOU* SUPER SERIES:

Wasted in Waco (WDKY Ensemble Prequel Novella): Exclusive to Subscribers, by Pamela Fagan Hutchins

The Essential Guide to the What Doesn't Kill You Series, by Pamela Fagan Hutchins

Katie Connell Caribbean Mysteries:

Saving Grace (Katie #1), by Pamela Fagan Hutchins

Leaving Annalise (Katie #2), by Pamela Fagan Hutchins

Finding Harmony (Katie #3), by Pamela Fagan Hutchins

Seeking Felicity (Katie #4), by Pamela Fagan Hutchins

Emily Bernal Texas-to-New Mexico Mysteries:

Heaven to Betsy (Emily #1), by Pamela Fagan Hutchins

Earth to Emily (Emily #2), by Pamela Fagan Hutchins

Hell to Pay (Emily #3), by Pamela Fagan Hutchins

Michele Lopez Hanson Texas Mysteries:

Going for Kona (Michele #1), by Pamela Fagan Hutchins

Fighting for Anna (Michele #2), by Pamela Fagan Hutchins

Searching for Dime Box (Michele #3), by Pamela Fagan Hutchins

Maggie Killian Texas-to-Wyoming Mysteries:

Buckle Bunny (Maggie Prequel Novella), by Pamela Fagan Hutchins

Shock Jock (Maggie Prequel Short Story), by Pamela Fagan Hutchins

Live Wire (Maggie #1), by Pamela Fagan Hutchins

Sick Puppy (Maggie #2), by Pamela Fagan Hutchins

Dead Pile (Maggie #3), by Pamela Fagan Hutchins

The Ava Butler Caribbean Mysteries Trilogy: A Sexy Spin-off From *What Doesn't Kill You*

Bombshell (Ava #1), by Pamela Fagan Hutchins

Stunner (Ava #2), by Pamela Fagan Hutchins

Knockout (Ava #3), by Pamela Fagan Hutchins

Poppy Needs a Puppy (Poppy & Petey #1), by Pamela Fagan Hutchins, illustrated by Laylie Frazier

MULTI-AUTHOR:

Murder, They Wrote: Four SkipJack Mysteries,
by Ken Oder, R.L. Nolen, Marcy McKay, and Gay Yellen

Tides of Possibility, edited by K.J. Russell

Tides of Impossibility, edited by K.J. Russell and C. Stuart Hardwick

NONFICTION:
Helen Colin

My Dream of Freedom: From Holocaust to My Beloved America,
by Helen Colin

Pamela Fagan Hutchins

The Clark Kent Chronicles, by Pamela Fagan Hutchins

Hot Flashes and Half Ironmans, by Pamela Fagan Hutchins

How to Screw Up Your Kids, by Pamela Fagan Hutchins

How to Screw Up Your Marriage, by Pamela Fagan Hutchins

Puppalicious and Beyond, by Pamela Fagan Hutchins

What Kind of Loser Indie Publishes,
and How Can I Be One, Too?, by Pamela Fagan Hutchins

Ken Oder

Keeping the Promise, by Ken Oder

Made in the USA
Monee, IL
11 December 2024

73278271R00198